MYSTERY
IN THE
HIGHLANDS

BOOKS BY LYDIA TRAVERS

MYSTERY
IN THE
HIGHLANDS

LYDIA TRAVERS

bookouture

Published by Bookouture in 2023

An imprint of Storyfire Ltd.
Carmelite House
50 Victoria Embankment
London EC4Y 0DZ

www.bookouture.com

ISBN: 978-1-83790-476-1
eBook ISBN: 978-1-83790-475-4

In memory of my sister Debra
(1961–1993)

ONE

Edinburgh
November, 1911

'There's a letter for you on the mantelpiece!' Maud called to Daisy on Monday morning, as she took the toast in its rack and the dish of butter, and carried them from the kitchen through to the sitting room. Daisy was standing beside the dining table, already in the process of opening the envelope.

Daisy pulled out the folded pages, turning to the first sheet as she slid onto the chair. 'It's from my cousin in Fort William.'

Maud poured two cups of tea and passed one to Daisy, before tucking her blue linen skirt under her and sitting down. Daisy nodded her thanks and continued to read the letter, a frown deepening on her forehead.

'Is your cousin well?' Maud spread butter on her slice of toast, before noticing the change in Daisy's mood.

'Aye, Clara is,' Daisy said slowly, moving on to the next page of the letter, 'but she says two members of her local choir have... died suddenly.'

'I'm sorry to hear that.' Maud paused in the act of adding a layer of marmalade. 'Did your cousin know them well?'

'She's kent John Noble since he and his wife moved to the town some years ago. He was the choir's leading bass. A braw-looking man too, Clara says. Anyway, he was found deid by his wife on Wednesday. But the thing that's got Clara rattled is that one of their sopranos, Emily, was discovered drowned in Loch Linnhe on Sunday afternoon.'

'How sad,' Maud murmured.

Daisy looked up from the letter. 'Clara canna understand what possessed Emily to be by the loch in the first place. She wants us to go and stay with her and investigate the deaths.'

Maud considered this. Daisy had been her lady's maid for the last seven years since Maud had turned eighteen. At that time they had lived on Maud's father's country estate in Midlothian, before they had moved to Edinburgh to open the private detective agency, with Daisy now Maud's assistant.

'My cousin is certain something is afoot in the wee town,' Daisy was saying, impatiently dragging a stray lock of her red hair behind her ear which had come adrift from its low pompadour, 'and is feart as to where it might end.'

'That's rather an outlandish claim, don't you think? And yet...' Maud bit into the toast.

It had been a couple of months since she and Daisy had returned from the village in the north-east Highlands, where they had solved the murders of a retired farmer and an artist. Another investigation successfully concluded for the M. McIntyre Agency. *No Case Too Big or Too Small* was their agency's motto. It was time for another important case, Maud decided.

'I think we should visit your cousin for a few days,' Maud said, 'and see if there's anything to it. There's nothing but paper-work to do in the office, after all, and precious little of that.'

'I dinna ken,' Daisy said doubtfully, as she added milk and

three spoonfuls of sugar to her tea. 'Clara might be wrong about there being anything for us to investigate.'

Maud raised an eyebrow. 'Two choir members dead within four days of each other? How old were they?'

Daisy consulted her letter. 'John Noble was of middle age and Emily Black a young woman.'

'Hmm,' Maud murmured, taking a sip of her tea.

Daisy continued, 'The procurator fiscal is looking into their deaths, Clara says, but the public prosecutor has to do that. It doesna mean they've been the victim of foul play.' She set the letter down on the table and helped herself to a piece of toast from the rack.

'Surely your cousin wouldn't have asked us to go if she didn't have some... suspicion?' Maud was struck by an uncomfortable thought. 'We would need to be paid you know, Daisy.'

'She says she's nae expecting us to work for naething.' Daisy loaded her toast with jam. 'Her man's the laird's factor, so she'd pay us our usual rate.'

Maud was relieved. Factors managed estates for their owners, with knowledge of agriculture, business, accounting and the law, and so she knew they were accordingly well paid.

She regarded Daisy for a moment. They'd opened the agency in the summer and had enjoyed a successful few months. Since solving the murders in Braemar, though, there had been only the run-of-the-mill missing pets and observations of errant spouses. All rewarding in their own way, of course, because a satisfied client is what the M. McIntyre Agency aimed for, but something a little more... intriguing would be welcome.

The matter was decided for them that morning, as there were no new cases waiting for them in the post. Maud let up the blind at the window of their first-floor office and paused to look down into George Street below. It was busy as usual on this Monday morning, with people hurrying along the pavement and horse-drawn carts, cable trams and motor vehicles all jostling for space on the wide road.

She lifted the sash window to let in some fresh air, feeling her fair hair stir in its high chignon. The noises outside tumbled in. Maud wished she were as busy as everyone seemed to be in the street below. She turned away, sat in her chair at the desk and idly turned the pages of the day's *The Scotsman*.

'There's a piece on your cousin's mystery murder,' she said in surprise to Daisy.

Daisy hung her hat and coat on a peg behind the door and took her seat at the side of the desk. 'What does it say?'

'Hmm, nothing much. Only that Emily Black, housemaid at the home of the Captain Charles Farquharson, the Laird of Linnhe, was found floating in the loch on Sunday afternoon.'

Maud slid the newspaper along for Daisy to read more easily.

Daisy bent her red-haired head over the page. 'It says here that her drowning is believed to have been a tragic accident.' She scanned the page of the newspaper. 'Nae mention of Mr Noble's death.'

'Which *possibly* means it was from natural causes,' Maud said doubtfully.

Daisy jumped up, crossed the room and pushed down the sash window. 'That's enough fresh air for today.'

Maud smiled at how quickly Daisy, a country lass, had embraced city life.

Daisy dropped back into her chair. 'So, are we going to investigate these deaths?'

They had no other cases to work on, Maud thought, and there was something suspicious about two deaths occurring so close to each other, especially when both victims sang in the same choir.

When she was very young, Maud used to imagine what it would be like to be the willowy and beautiful dark-haired, dark-eyed singer, Lily Elsie. At five feet seven inches, Maud had grown to almost the same height as Lily Elsie and her figure as slender, but her hair remained a pale colour and the only feature to her credit was a pair of large grey eyes. And despite singing lessons, her voice was nothing more than a pleasant alto. But the idea of joining a choir was an appealing one.

'Yes, we are, Daisy.'

'I've thought about it and I agree. After all, we're partners in crime.'

'Partners in *solving* crime.'

'Aye. That too.'

'Really, Daisy, we have never broken the law.'

Daisy raised an eyebrow, and Maud had the decency to blush a little as she thought about the time they'd attempted to break into the home of an MP – but that was to recover stolen love letters. And the time they had assaulted the art gallery owner – but that was in self-defence, and she was fairly certain it wasn't an offence to impersonate a member of the clergy or a gypsy woman or a nun...

'We'll take the first available train to Fort William tomorrow morning,' Maud said decisively.

'Nae your motor car?'

'It would never get up all those hills, and in winter no less.'

Daisy glanced towards the window. A watery sun shone through the pane. 'It's nae snowing...'

'No, but we're in the south-east of the country. Fort William is in the north-west. The weather will be a lot more unpredictable there. The train will be warmer and more reliable.'

'Mr Alexander drove a motor car to the top of Ben Nevis in May this year.'

'Only with great difficulty, Daisy.' The newspapers had been full of the adventure. The Alexander family ran dance halls in and around Edinburgh and had recently added a Ford agency to their enterprises. Keen to show that the little motor car was up to the toughest test, Henry Alexander had driven it to the summit of Britain's highest mountain.

Daisy was not giving up easily. 'But we're nae going to drive up Ben Nevis!'

'Which is just as well, as it took Mr Alexander five and a half days. We'll travel by train,' Maud repeated firmly. 'That will take a mere five and a half *hours*.'

Daisy sighed.

'And the sooner we arrive,' Maud added, 'the sooner we can get started on the case.'

Daisy smiled.

Dressed in their tweed travelling costumes of long coats and full skirts, Maud and Daisy travelled north-west on the Caledonian Railway from Waverley Station in Edinburgh until they reached the village of Crianlarich. They alighted at the low station and carried their Gladstone bags the few hundred yards up the hill to the high station. There the North British Railway train bound for Fort William was waiting for them to board.

'Let's hope there's nae a dead body in *this* compartment,' Daisy said, as Maud took hold of the brass door handle.

Maud thought of the murdered man who had fallen onto her when she'd opened the train door at the little station of Ballater in the eastern Highlands. She shuddered. 'I think the two bodies waiting for us in Fort William are quite sufficient, Daisy.' She opened the door and saw with relief the compartment was empty.

Maud settled in her seat, smoothing her blue tweed coat and adjusting her pale blue hat. The compartment was comfortably warm, especially around her buttoned boots with the heating pipes under the seats. She gazed out of the window as the train carried them on their journey.

The scenery was spectacular. Moorland sweeping up to majestic snow-covered mountains. Bogs and lochs, rivers, and rocky outcrops, with fewer farm buildings to be seen the deeper the train drew them into the Highlands.

'A bit different from Arthur's Seat,' Maud said, thinking of the highest peak in Edinburgh's Holyrood Park.

'Aye, a wee bit.'

And then they were crossing the wilderness of the Great Moor of Rannoch. 'This part of the line is a feat of engineering, Daisy,' Maud said to her friend, remembering her governess telling her the very same thing. 'The line crosses the moor for twenty-three miles. The builders had to float the tracks on a bedding of tree roots, brushwood and thousands of tons of earth and ashes.'

'Nae matter how remote the place is' – Daisy smiled – 'I canna wait to get started on our next investigation.'

'Without knowing any of the choir members—'

'Apart from Clara.'

Maud inclined her head. 'Apart from Clara. Given that, we could spend this time usefully by considering who the suspects might possibly be. Do you know anything about the choir itself?'

'I ken they're awfa good. They're in the final of a competition to find the best choir in Scotland.' Daisy beamed, as proud as if she herself were a member.

Maud smiled. 'That is impressive. When and where is the final to take place?'

'Mid-December in Edinburgh.'

Less than three weeks away, Maud mused. Was there a connection between the deaths and the competition?

'Do you know where the other competing choirs are from?' Maud went on.

'There's one from Cambus o'May, Clara told me, and the other's from Dingwall.'

The former was to the east of Fort William and over one hundred miles away; the latter some seventy miles further north.

'If Clara is correct and the deaths are suspicious, we might reasonably think that a member of a rival choir is to blame,' Maud said, 'but each of those towns seem too far for one of their choir members to be involved, and they're too far for us to visit.'

'Aye, they are without a motor car,' Daisy muttered.

Maud ignored her comment. 'Let us see what transpires when we reach Fort William.'

The train drew into Corrour. 'This is the highest railway station in the United Kingdom,' Maud murmured, peering out of the window. 'And one of its most remote.'

A flock of migrating grey geese flew high over the moor. A herd of red deer, majestic stags and graceful hinds, who had come down from the hills for food and water, raised their heads at the loud honking of birds overhead.

Maud and Daisy reached Fort William at half past four. The sun had set some thirty minutes ago, but it wouldn't be completely dark for another couple of hours. Daisy's cousin, Clara, and her husband, Alasdair Ross, were waiting to greet them at the station.

'It's braw to see you again, Daisy. It's been eight years or more,' Clara said, grinning. She was an older version of Daisy, just as petite and with the same glorious red hair escaping from its pins in the breeze. She turned to Maud. 'And pleased to meet you, Miss McIntyre.'

Maud smiled, instantly sure she'd enjoy Clara's company. 'Please, call me Maud.'

Introductions were made to Alasdair and they all piled into his Model T motor car.

'Hold tight, ladies!' Alasdair drove smoothly away from the

station, and within minutes they passed through the small town and were on the road to the Ross's house on the laird's estate.

Clara chatted merrily over her shoulder to Daisy in the back seat beside Maud, and Maud contented herself with admiring the passing scenery.

'Daisy, Maud,' Clara said suddenly, pointing out of the window towards a stretch of water, 'that there's Loch Linnhe, where poor Emily Black drowned.'

Maud and Daisy turned to look at the expanse of grey water, grim in the fading light.

'It's a sea loch,' went on Clara. 'In local folklore the loch was said to be the home of an *each-uisge*, a water horse. Do you remember, Daisy? Grandma used to say it offered bairns rides on its back. But once they were on, their hands became stuck to the beast, and it would gallop off into the loch to drown and then eat them.'

Daisy shivered. 'Water horse or not, I'd be feart to go in there.'

'Is it possible Miss Black slipped on a muddy bank and fell in?' asked Maud.

Clara turned and fixed her eyes on Daisy and Maud. 'I suppose it's *possible*, but I'd say nae likely.'

'And why is that?'

'Because it was a dreich, wet afternoon, so she wouldna have gone out for a walk and especially not there.' Clara shook her head. 'She couldna even swim, poor lass.'

'Do you think she went to meet someone?' put in Daisy. 'A lad, maybe?'

Clara sighed heavily. 'If she had met a laddie, she didna tell me.'

'Do you know who found her body?' Maud asked.

'Captain Farquharson, the laird. He was walking his dog and saw her floating close to the bank. She was chubby but nae tall and he managed to drag her out, but it was too late, I'm sorry to say.'

A sombre silence descended on the occupants of the motor car. After a short while, Daisy coaxed Clara back into a more lively conversation.

Maud leaned forward in her seat to speak to Alasdair. 'Is the mountain I can see Ben Nevis?'

'Aye,' he said over his shoulder. 'Though Ben Nevis is an English translation from the Gaelic name, *Beinn Nibheis*.'

'And what does that mean?'

'*Beinn* is mountain.'

'And *Nibheis*?'

'It's usually translated as malicious.'

'Oh...'

'You don't need to worry – unless you're planning on climbing it?'

Maud laughed. 'Certainly not.' Although that would be quite an achievement, she thought, and the view from the summit must be splendid. 'Why malicious?'

'Possibly because of the snowstorms that envelop the summit. In November, the temperature up there is usually about thirty-four degrees. But in December, it drops some five degrees to well below freezing.'

Alasdair turned off the road and through a pair of tall pillars marking the beginning of a long driveway. 'This leads to Linnhe Castle, where the laird stays,' he said.

Maud tried to catch a glimpse of the laird's house, but the avenue curved away into trees in the distance. The laird had found Emily Black's body, so he would have to be interviewed, Maud decided.

'And this track,' added Alasdair, 'takes us home. *Taigh Bàil-lidh* – the house of the factor.'

He turned the vehicle into an avenue on the left-hand side and drew the motor car to a halt in front of a large stone house.

Maud also saw outbuildings and a gate in the wall at the side of the garden leading into woods, which she supposed was a shortcut to Linnhe Castle.

'Come in,' Clara said, climbing out of the motor car without waiting for her husband to open her door. 'Donald, our son, is away at university in Aberdeen, Maud, but Susan is here and will be sure to have the tea ready for us.'

The sound of the motor engine must have alerted Susan, for a girl flung open the door. A golden Labrador came running out of the house after her, its tail wagging furiously.

Clara turned to the girl, whose red hair was pinned into side swirls. 'This is my lass, Susan.'

Susan – whom Maud knew from Daisy was almost fourteen years of age – smiled prettily and dropped a small curtsy. '*Feasgar math.*'

'*Feasgar math.* Good afternoon, Susan.'

Clara professed herself delighted by Maud's pronunciation of the greeting in Gaelic.

'It's braw to see you again, Daisy.' Susan's smile widened.

'And this,' Clara went on, indicating the Labrador gambolling around them, 'is Ellie.'

'*Feasgar math*, Ellie,' said Maud, bending down to tug gently at the dog's ear.

Maud and Daisy were each shown to their rooms. Maud stood at her window and gazed at the snow-topped Ben Nevis looming in the distance. The malicious mountain, overshadowing the little town, she thought with a small shiver. Would it play a part in their investigation?

Chiding herself for such a ridiculous fancy, she hastily unpacked and washed. When all was tidied away, she smoothed her pale blue blouse with its square white collar, and went downstairs. In the sitting room she found Clara, Daisy and Susan already there, with Clara presiding over a large silver teapot which caught the firelight.

'Do you have everything you need in your room, Maud?' asked Clara with a smile.

'Yes, thank you.' Maud took a seat on the sofa. 'I must apologise for being late down, but I was enchanted by the view from my window.'

Clara's smile broadened. 'Aye, that view is bonnie, isn't it?'

Maud longed to discover what Clara knew of the two deaths, but with young Susan in the room she took the lead from the girl's mother.

Ellie had wasted no time in padding quietly out of her basket in the corner of the room and now sat by Maud's side, her chin firmly pressed down on Maud's knee. As Maud rubbed behind Ellie's ear, the large dog attempted to climb onto Maud's lap.

'Ellie, go to your basket!' ordered Clara.

The dog flung herself on her back and lay with her paws in the air. Her mistress prodded her with her foot. Ellie gave a broad smile, flopped onto her side and began to snore loudly with one eye half-open to see if she was being watched.

Maud laughed. 'I miss having my own dogs, but Daisy and I have little time to give to one such as this.' She bent over and rubbed the Labrador's warm pink belly.

'Alasdair has gone to the estate office to catch up on some work – or so he says,' said Clara, 'but I ken fine he feels trachled by women's blether.'

Maud was sorry he found women's conversation exhausting. But perhaps if men listened more to women, they might learn something, she thought, as Clara picked up the teapot.

'Tea?' Clara asked.

'Thank you, yes.' Maud replied, watching the golden liquid pour from the silver pot.

As soon as the tea and the slices of delicious Dundee cake had been consumed, Susan was sent to complete her schoolwork and the three women were at last able to talk freely.

'The choir practises twice a week in the village hall, on Tuesday evenings and Saturday afternoons,' Clara said. 'If you're nae too tired after your long journey, I'll take you this evening to meet the other members.'

'Those that are left,' Daisy said, shooting Maud a dark look.

'The post-mortem's been done on John Noble and he died of natural causes,' continued Clara, with a small frown.

Maud's heart fell. Had the trip been for nothing? 'How did he die?'

'A heart attack, it seems.'

'That's a pity.' Daisy sounded disappointed. 'I was looking forward to another real case.'

'Really, Daisy,' Maud said, a note of reproof in her voice. 'We mustn't wish for people to be *murdered*.'

'Nae.' Daisy didn't look convinced. 'I suppose not...'

'And Emily Black?' Maud went on. 'What of her death?'

Clara shook her head. 'The procurator fiscal says it was a tragic accident, so nae further enquiries are needed. It looks like I may have been too hasty in asking for your help.'

'Hmm,' Maud said. 'We'll see about that.' These deaths in the choir shortly before the competition final were grounds for some suspicion.

'You dinna agree with the procurator fiscal's finding?' asked Clara.

'Nae, we dinna,' said Daisy.

'What Daisy means,' said Maud, 'is that we at the McIntyre Agency are reluctant to believe in coincidence when it comes to death.'

That evening Maud and Daisy followed Clara into the wooden village hall. A black cylindrical Perfection oil heater stood in the centre, giving off warmth and a welcome glow through its window. There were a number of people – perhaps a dozen,

Maud thought – standing about and chatting in small, solemn groups.

A short wiry-looking woman Maud took to be in her early forties came forward to meet them. She wore a black dress of crêpe, signifying she had been recently widowed. Below her little black coif, her grey hair hung over one shoulder, twisted into a long plait.

Her small, inquisitive face smiled up at them. 'Clara, you've brought two new members. Delightful!'

'This is my cousin, Daisy Cameron,' said Clara, 'and her friend, Maud McIntyre, who are visiting me from Edinburgh.'

'From *Edinburgh*? My goodness!'

Clara turned to Maud and Daisy. 'And this is Mrs Noble, the choir mistress.'

'Beatrice,' said the older woman with a smile. 'We don't stand on ceremony here.'

'I'm very sorry for your loss,' Maud told her.

Tears sprang to Beatrice Noble's eyes. 'Thank you. It was so sudden and tragic.'

'And Emily Black.' Maud shook her head sympathetically. 'Another sad death.'

A shadow passed across the choir leader's face. 'Yes, very sad. I understand Police Constable Beggs has informed the procurator fiscal that the poor girl must have slipped and fallen into the water.' Beatrice sighed. 'It was foolish of her to walk by the side of the loch late in the afternoon at this time of year, especially as she couldn't swim.'

Maud said nothing.

Beatrice's bottom lip trembled and she gave a small sniff. 'The deaths of my husband and of Emily have come just as we are preparing for a major competition, you know...'

'Clara has informed us.'

'Did she also inform you that the winners are to dine at

Holyrood Palace and be presented with a trophy by His Majesty, King George V?'

'She did.'

'Maud has met the King, you ken,' Daisy put in.

'Really?' Beatrice stared at Maud in fascination, waiting for more information.

'It was purely by chance,' Maud admitted. 'I was walking in the hills near Balmoral and His Majesty was there, taking his luncheon with a small shooting party.'

'The King shared his smoked salmon with her,' went on Daisy with a conspiratorial wink.

Beatrice's eyes grew wider. 'Perhaps you will meet him again,' she said, after staring for a moment at Maud, 'if we win the competition, that is. Will you be staying with Clara for long?'

As long as it takes, Maud thought. 'Daisy and I expect to be here for at least a fortnight.' That was how long it took to solve the Braemar case, and so it seemed a reasonable assumption.

'And you both hope to be part of the choir?'

'If that is possible.' Maud had earlier asked Clara not to mention that she and Daisy were private detectives. Being in the choir would certainly help with their investigation and enable them to observe the members while keeping a low profile. 'I have had singing lessons,' Maud added, referring to a time when she still lived at home with her father.

Beatrice Noble nodded, now turning her attention to Daisy. 'What do you sing?'

Daisy smiled. 'I like "Daisy Bell" and "Ask a Policeman"—'

'My friend sings soprano,' Maud put in quickly, having heard Daisy singing on occasion around the flat, and before her friend could deliberately misunderstand and list any more comic music-hall songs. 'And I'm a passable alto.'

'Clara will show you both where to put your coats. Then, Miss McIntyre, if you would like to face me with the other altos.

Miss Cameron, please stand over there on my left between your cousin and Mrs Ivy Fraser, who has the voice of an angel, by the way.' Beatrice smiled at a plump woman, probably in her thirties, with dark glossy hair and dressed in a burgundy skirt with matching hat. 'The gentlemen will be on my right as usual.'

Having hung up their coats, Maud and Daisy joined the others.

Beatrice clapped her hands for everyone to take their positions in the hall. When they had all settled, she said brightly, 'Ladies and gentlemen, we have two new members. From Edinburgh, no less. Miss Maud McIntyre and Miss Daisy Cameron.' Beatrice indicated each in turn, to a general murmuring and interested gazes. 'We are back to our full complement of fifteen singers, which means we can produce some delightful three-part harmonies. The ladies will be here only temporarily, visiting Clara, but I trust long enough to assist us in winning the competition.'

And be on hand in case any other unnatural deaths happen to take place between now and then, thought Maud.

TWO

The following morning Maud performed a few *pliés*, *elevés* and *relevés* and a couple of twirls of her Indian clubs in her room before going down to the dining room. She and Daisy were eating a late breakfast when the door opened and Clara came in.

'The postie has just brought this for you,' she said, crossing to the table and handing Maud a small square envelope.

On it was written in heavy black ink *Miss McIntyre*, care of Clara's address. 'I asked the General Post Office to forward our business correspondence while we were away. I hope that was not too presumptuous of me.'

'Nae at all.' Clara made no move to leave.

'Open it, then, Maud,' said Daisy.

Maud hesitated, unwilling to reveal any new case to a third party. Clara, sensing this, said, 'I have to go to the market shortly, so would you mind if I left you both for a wee while?'

'Of course not, Clara,' Maud told her. 'Please don't think you need to take us hither and yon, visiting places. We're not tourists, after all, but here to work on an investigation.'

Clara smiled. 'That reminds me. As you have nae way of

getting about, you can borrow Susan's and my bicycles for the time you're here, if you wish.'

'Bicycles?' said Maud nervously. 'I'm afraid we don't know how to ride them.'

'You do ken, Maud.' Daisy grinned. 'You rode on Rabbie Geddes's bicycle.'

'That doesn't count.' Maud shot Daisy a warning look.

'It'll all come back to you as soon as you're on one.' A wicked grin lit Daisy's face. 'She was seated on his handlebars and dressed as a nun at the time, Clara, but she still didna fall off.'

'You sound as eccentric as the laird, Maud!' Clara laughed. 'And it seems like you have a good sense of balance, so I'm sure you'll get the hang of it in a trice.'

'We shall see,' said Maud doubtfully, not wishing to appear too eager. In truth, she was keen to learn.

'Anyway,' went on Clara, as she nodded at the white envelope in Maud's hands. 'I'll leave you to your letter and I'll be back for luncheon at one o'clock.'

When Clara had left the room, Maud picked up a clean knife and slit the envelope open. She pulled out the single sheet of white paper. 'Good heavens.'

'What is it?' Daisy asked eagerly.

Maud frowned. 'It's some sort of a rhyme.' She scanned the page. The words were handwritten in the same heavy black ink as had been used on the envelope.

'*Some* sort of a rhyme? Either it's a rhyme or it isna.'

'Well then, yes, it *is* a rhyme.'

'Read it out then,' Daisy urged.

Maud set down the knife, cleared her throat and began.

> *Are they dancing to the beat?*
> *Is that the place where we shall meet?*
> *Out in the open countryside*

> *Where there's nae a place to hide*
> *At this scene they must beware*
> *The danger may be in the air.*

There was a pause.

'That's it? Naething else?'

'At the bottom it says...' Maud paused.

'Aye?' said Daisy, prompting her.

'*See if you can stop me*. And it's signed with an X.'

Daisy frowned. Maud slid the sheet of paper along the table for Daisy to read. 'It sounds like the note is from the killer, Maud. He's daring us to catch him.'

Maud nodded grimly. 'But why send it to us? We've told no one that we are private detectives, apart from Clara and Alasdair.'

'We can trust them to say naething,' put in Daisy.

'And why send such a clue, exposing himself – and his next murder – in this way?' Maud felt a little frisson of excitement that they were now indeed working on a real case.

'He must be off his heid.'

'He's certainly got a nerve,' said Maud.

'He could just bump off the singers without warning anyone.'

'Exactly.'

'He wants to *show* how clever he is, I suppose.'

'It proves your cousin was right about Emily being murdered at least.'

Daisy read the note again. Her frown deepened. 'I've nae idea what the wee rhyme means.'

'Neither have I, but it must mean something, or why bother sending it? It is surely a clue to where the next murder will take place. But *when*?' Maud thought for a moment. 'We know there were four days between the deaths of John Noble and Emily Black.' She shot a significant look at Daisy.

'Michty me.' Daisy jumped up from the chair. 'Tomorrow is the fourth day after Emily's murder.'

'Which might mean the next victim will die tomorrow.' Maud's stomach gave a lurch. They'd been sent a clue, possibly taunting them about a murder that would take place the very next day, and the rhyme made no sense.

'Maybe the whole thing is a hoax,' Daisy said, sitting back down.

'It's possible, and I'd like nothing better than for that to be true,' said Maud, 'but why would anyone make up such a thing?'

'Just someone having a bit of fun at our expense, maybe?'

'It has to be a person who knows we're here to investigate the murders.'

'Who kens that? Clara and Alasdair. Nae Susan, as Clara doesna want her to ken that's why we've come.'

'I know you said we can trust your cousin and her husband, but someone must know. Perhaps the choir members?'

'Aye,' said Daisy slowly, staring at Maud. 'The clue is written as a poem and we ken they can rhyme.'

Maud was reminded of the previous night's session with the choir, which had begun, as usual they were told, with a voice warm-up exercise. Each member sang a little poem about what they had been doing since they last met. Maud flushed as she remembered her own embarrassing attempt.

Daisy laughed, instantly identifying the source of Maud's discomfort. '*Maud is my name, so glad I came,*' she said with a grin. 'Nae that mine was much better: *My name is Daisy, I'm not lazy.*'

They both laughed.

'Do we believe this message is genuine?' Maud asked, when they'd settled down again. 'I think it is.'

'So do I.'

'We have one, possibly two, murders to investigate. If we

can prevent another taking place, so much the better. Right,' said Maud, 'we need pencils, paper and a map of the local area.'

'I'm sure Clara will have everything in yon desk. She willna mind if I have a look.'

Daisy crossed to the bureau in the corner of the dining room and rummaged about. Maud took up the envelope again and examined the postmark. It had been posted the previous evening in Fort William. That information was not much help. She read through the clue again, but frustratingly nothing jumped to the front of her mind. Daisy returned to the table with the necessary items and Maud poured out a fresh cup of tea for them both. They made themselves comfortable and bent their heads over the page.

'It's nae easy, is it?' Daisy said after a few moments.

'Let's try and break it down a bit. We need to find out who last saw Emily Black alive and where,' Maud went on. 'What we do know is her body was found on Sunday shortly after sunset...'

'Which is nae long after four o'clock.' Daisy began to scribble on the notepad.

'On that basis, I think the next murder will also take place in the afternoon.'

'Tomorrow afternoon,' Daisy confirmed.

'Yes. If we look at the first line – *Are they dancing to the beat* – it sounds as though we're being directed to a dance. A tea dance, perhaps.' These had grown out of the afternoon tea tradition and were held on summer and autumn afternoons, lasting until the early evening.

'Aye, maybe. A band with ices, champagne and cakes sound good to me.' Daisy smiled. 'They're popular in garrison towns.'

'You do know that the fort was built by the so-called Lord Protector, Oliver Cromwell, after his invasion, specifically to suppress the local clans, especially the rebellious Camerons?' Maud sent an amused glance at her friend.

Daisy laughed. 'We Camerons have always been trouble.'

'That fits in with what I know.' Maud chuckled. 'But, of course, Fort William no longer has troops permanently stationed in the town.'

'As we ken from our last case, there are barracks on the outskirts of Inverness.'

Maud shook her head. 'It's over sixty miles between the two towns. I doubt many young men, no matter how hot-blooded, would travel down from Inverness for a tea dance. No, my guess is that it would need to be somewhere closer to Fort William.'

'I'll ask Clara if she's heard of one being held around here tomorrow afternoon.'

'Good idea. Now, the next line.'

'*Is that the place where we shall meet?* That tells us naething.'

'What about the third line? *Out in the open countryside.*'

'It looks like the dance is being held outside the town.'

'*Where there's nae a place to hide?* I suppose that means it's a fairly secluded spot.'

'Aye, but most places round here could fit that description.'

Daisy was right, thought Maud. This part of the country was wild and mountainous, with isolated glens and lochs.

'And why would anyone want to hide at a tea dance?' Daisy went on.

'I agree. It doesn't seem likely. If we take the last two lines together. *At this scene they must beware, the danger may be in the air.*'

Daisy snorted. 'In the air, what does that mean?'

'Well, we never thought it would be easy being a detective, Daisy.'

'I ken.' Daisy propped her chin in her hand. 'We only have today, before the next murder.'

'Without any other leads, the rhyme is the only thing we have to go on.'

Daisy let out a huge sigh and sat up. 'Best get on with it then.'

Half an hour later, Maud slid her pencil into her cottage loaf pompadour, pushed away the map, sighed and sat back in her chair. 'We're getting nowhere.'

'I wouldna say that. We've ruled out Inverness Castle, the Glenfinnan Viaduct...'

Maud smiled. 'We should arrive at a solution eventually, if it's only by a process of elimination.'

'Perhaps it *is* a hoax,' Daisy said, frowning.

'I don't think it is, Daisy. Mr X is giving us a chance to catch him.'

'Nae much of a chance, with a clue like this,' Daisy muttered. 'So, what have we got?'

'The place has to be some distance from other people and where a tea dance is to be held.'

'What about *beware*?' Daisy asked. 'And *danger in the air*?'

'The gathering has to be in the open air.'

'It canna be a tea dance, nae in November.'

'Could the danger come from a hot air balloon or one of those new aeroplanes?'

She and Daisy looked at each other and laughed.

'You're right, we can probably rule out the balloon and aeroplane,' Maud said.

'More than probably, but Mr X does talk about air.'

'Neither of us believes that Mr X might be planning to murder his next victim by dropping something from the sky at a tea dance. That sounds a strange thing to do...'

'So does wanting to murder someone in the first place,' Daisy pointed out.

'Well,' Maud said, straightening in her chair, 'we need to involve the police. It's our duty to give this note to the constable and he can take it from there.'

Daisy held out her hand and waggled her fingers. 'I'll make a copy of it before we do.'

Maud handed Daisy the missive. 'Naturally.'

'Are we going to tell the constable why we're here?'

'I don't see how we can avoid it. Mr X knowing we're private detectives is the only logical reason he would send me the note in the first place.'

Clara's house had a telephone and Maud asked the operator to put her through to the police.

'Fort William Police Office,' came the voice. 'Constable Beggs speaking.'

Maud gave her name, explained the situation and the suspicious death of Emily Black, but just as she did so, she was interrupted.

'There was nothing suspicious about Miss Black's drowning, miss,' the constable interjected sharply.

'And yet my friend and I have received a clue in the form of a rhyme, giving the location of the next murder.'

The constable gave a short laugh. 'And who was the note from?' he asked.

'He simply signed himself X.'

'It's someone playing a practical joke.'

Maud bristled. 'Haven't you read *A Study in Scarlet*?'

'I'm afraid not. My wife's the one who reads all the nonsense novels in our household. I'm a bit tied up with investigating *real* crimes.'

'Sir Arthur Conan Doyle should be compulsory reading for all police officers, in my opinion,' Maud said stiffly.

She didn't know why she had chosen that novel, other than it was the first Sherlock Holmes story. He talked about a scarlet thread of murder running through life and of the duty to unravel it.

'I recommend you change your reading habits and settle

down this evening with a nice love story, Miss McIntyre,' Constable Beggs said in a soothing tone.

'Good day, officer.' Maud felt herself flush and hung up the telephone piece firmly.

'What did he say?' asked Daisy, standing at Maud's elbow.

'He told me to read a romance.' Maud's flush deepened. The *nerve* of the man!

Daisy snorted. 'You mean he didna believe us? We canna ignore the clue...'

'We can't and we won't, Daisy. We will continue to investigate this case ourselves.'

The hall clock struck one o'clock and shortly afterwards Maud and Daisy sat down to luncheon with Clara, Susan and Alasdair.

'By the way, I've heard that a friend of yours has arrived to stay with the laird,' Alasdair said to Maud, as they were finishing the chicken timbales in mushroom sauce.

'Oh?' she replied. 'I can't imagine who that could be.'

'A gentleman by the name of Lord Hamish Urquhart.'

Of course, thought Maud, as she placed her cutlery neatly on the empty plate. Who else? Their paths had crossed many times since Lord Urquhart came to her agency only days after it opened for business. He would have been her first client had he not decided a woman was incapable of the task of detecting. She'd soon proved him wrong, of course, in the Duddingston case, but it still rankled Maud. Lord Urquhart was far too full of himself for her liking. Yet he was definitely Maud's type: very tall, aristocratically handsome and appeared to have some intelligence. They had last met on the Braemar case, when that night he had placed his jacket, warm from his body heat, around her shoulders... Her heart picked up speed...

'Clara,' Daisy was saying, 'are there any tea dances tomorrow afternoon?'

Clara laughed. 'Dinna tell me you're bored already?'

'Nae, we just wondered.' Daisy directed a significant glance at Susan, preoccupied now with talking to her father.

'Oh.' Understanding dawned on Clara. 'I dinna think so. I've not heard of any. Have you, Alasdair?'

He glanced up. 'Sorry, my dear, I didn't catch what you said.'

'I asked if you ken of any tea dances tomorrow afternoon.'

Alasdair looked perplexed and shook his head. 'No.'

Maud's pulse had gradually returned to its normal speed, and they all chatted amiably for a while. As Susan rushed out to return to school, Alasdair dropped his napkin onto the table.

'I must get back to the estate. There is still a lot to do, helping Gillespie. Jamie Gillespie's the head gamekeeper and ghillie. A ghillie is the guide on a shoot,' he added to Maud and Daisy.

Daisy rolled her eyes. 'We ken what a ghillie is.'

'Aye, well, we're up to our eyes getting ready for the shoot tomorrow.'

A shoot – and tomorrow! Maud and Daisy exchanged a significant glance. *The danger may be in the air...*

'That must be interesting,' Maud said casually. She'd been brought up on her father's estate, but thankfully he didn't countenance shooting for sport. No, she was interested in the laird's shoot for a very different reason.

Seeing her interest, Alasdair added, 'The laird rears about five hundred birds and holds four shoots a year, with six guns and twelve beaters at each shoot.'

'Are any of the choir members going?' Maud asked.

Alasdair frowned as he considered her question. 'Mrs Rankin will be one of the guns as usual, and I think a couple of other singers are beaters. Are you interested in shooting?' He got to his feet.

'Even if Maud were, dear, all the places are taken,' Clara said. 'Now off you go and dinna be late for dinner.'

As soon as he'd left the room, Maud turned to Clara. 'Can we join the beaters?' Beaters were employed to flush out the birds towards the guns and so would give Maud and Daisy an excellent view of proceedings.

Clara dabbed her mouth with her linen napkin and placed it by the side of her plate. 'Why ever would you want to do that?'

'That note we received this morning told us that another choir member is going to be murdered tomorrow,' said Daisy, getting straight to the point.

'Nae!' Clara put her hand to her chest.

'I'm afraid so, Clara,' went on Maud. 'And we need to warn those who will be there, at the shoot.'

'Oh dear... Well... as Alasdair said, Jane Rankin will be there. She's a long-standing member of the choir, one of the altos. And I'm sure the two McDougall brothers will be acting as beaters.'

'Then we need to go as beaters too,' said Daisy.

Clara frowned. 'But it's only men who do that job.'

Daisy's eyes were alight with the thought of a disguise. 'We didna have space in our luggage to bring any undercover costumes. Can we borrow some of Donald's clothes?'

Clara looked from Daisy to Maud. 'Surely you're nae proposing to dress as... as *men*?'

'We're rather practised at it,' said Maud, smiling inwardly on seeing Clara's jaw drop.

'Do you have any clothes or not, Clara?' Daisy demanded.

'I suppose if you're really determined to go,' said Clara, a note of doubt in her voice, 'you could try some of Donald's things. He's done some beating for the laird. His bedroom is opposite yours, Daisy. Have a look, both of you. His clothing might fit, but I doubt any of his footwear will. You'll find some nicky-tams in there as well.'

Maud knew nicky-tams were strings that tied around the

legs and were useful in preventing mice from running up the inside of the trousers. She thanked Clara, and made a note of the respective addresses of Mrs Rankin and the McDougall brothers.

There was something else Maud had to ask their hostess. 'Clara, I hope you will excuse my question as I do not wish to offend, but might you have inadvertently let any of the choir members know Daisy and I are here to investigate the recent deaths?'

Clara shook her head. 'Nae.'

'We were sure you hadna, but we had to ask.' Daisy gave her cousin a reassuring smile. 'They'll have to ken soon enough, anyway.'

'At least *the danger may be in the air* part of the clue now makes sense,' said Maud, as she and Daisy climbed the stairs to Donald's room.

'What about the first line, though – how does that fit in?'

Maud tried to remember the exact words. '*Are they dancing to the beat.*'

'Aye, they beat sticks on trees and the ground, which is why it's called beating, but it's the dancing bit I dinna get.'

'I suppose some might see the action of the gun aiming and firing, handing it back to the loader, taking the newly filled shotgun from him and shooting again, as a fluid movement, like some sort of a dance.'

'Och, well, I hope we're right about this,' Daisy said, as they reached the landing, 'or we're going to look awfa glaikit.'

'It makes more sense to me than a tea dance. And we're not going to look foolish because I've no intention of telling the police.' Maud's voice was firm. 'Whether we're right or not, there's one way to find out.'

. . .

Jane Rankin was a strapping woman, with a weather-beaten face and brown hair cut short. Her house, by contrast, was pleasant: the furniture old-fashioned and comfortable-looking, most of the wall space filled with bookcases. A window at the far end looked onto the garden, where a magnificent sunset of red and purple had set the sky ablaze. Mrs Rankin didn't bother to hide her annoyance when the footman showed Maud and Daisy into her drawing room.

'Yes?' she said, standing in front of the fire roaring in the grate, the back vent of her coat parted, the better to warm her wide tweed-skirted backside.

Mrs Rankin might be an alto, thought Maud, but her voice was deep enough to sing contralto.

Without being invited, Maud took a seat, admiring a splendid Chinese vase lamp on a side table as she did so, and Daisy followed suit. Jane Rankin dropped heavily into an armchair and glared at them.

'We have come, Mrs Rankin,' Maud began, 'with some worrying news.'

'Then get on with it.'

Maud ignored the incivility. 'I am the proprietor of the M. McIntyre detective agency and Miss Cameron is my assistant. We have reason to believe that an attempt will be made on the life of another choir member at the shoot tomorrow and—'

Jane Rankin let out a great guffaw. '*Private detectives*? I knew you'd waste my time. It's well known that Emily Black drowned. There was no *murder*, Miss Maud, as you and your assistant seem to think. The constable has found no evidence to support such an outrageous suspicion.' She stood up and rang for the footman. 'There's something about the lower orders that if left unchecked, they get themselves into *trouble*. And the Black girl was as much a magnet for it as any of her class.'

Daisy glared at Jane Rankin. 'We're aye Jock Tamson's bairns.'

Maud hid a smile at Daisy's use of the saying that meant no one person was innately better than another.

The door opened. 'Andrews' – Jane Rankin spat the footman's name – 'show these two out.'

Odious woman, thought Maud, as they had no choice but to follow the footman out.

'We're all Jock Tamson's bairns?' she said, as they descended the stone steps to the road. 'I thought you were a royalist, Daisy.'

'I am.' Daisy's face was still pink from Jane Rankin's comments. 'We *are* all his bairns, apart from the royal family.'

'I see,' Maud continued, her voice thoughtful. 'Jane Rankin's reluctance to discuss the case might mean that she's involved in some way.'

'That wouldna surprise me.'

'Did you notice the emphasis she put on *trouble?'* Maud went on, as they made their way along the lane.

'Aye,' said Daisy. 'It made me wonder if the poor girl was in the pudding club.'

'Daisy! That is a crude expression.'

'Sorry. In the family way then.'

Maud supposed that term was a little better. 'That was undoubtedly what Jane Rankin wanted us to think. Of course, it might account for Emily drowning herself. A young woman, unmarried, the father of the child unable or unwilling to marry her... Poor Emily.' She shook her head sadly.

'But we don't ken that she did drown herself, Maud. And if she did, it wouldna have been because of that. I'm sure Clara would have noticed if Emily had been in the family way. That Rankin besom's our most likely suspect.'

'Perhaps, but what motive could she have?'

She and Daisy arrived at George and Thomas McDougall's cottage on the laird's estate. It was after four o'clock and the sun had set, so they were certain the two brothers would have finished work for the day. They were right, and Maud and Daisy were shown into the brothers' modest sitting room. Two worn armchairs faced the empty hearth, and rough matting covered the stone flags. A small table was laid for their evening meal with two spoons and the remains of a brown loaf on a wooden board.

The men looked to be somewhere in their thirties and spoke in soft voices. Both were dark-haired with thick eyebrows; Thomas, the younger one, had a head of curls and full lips. Could he have been Emily Black's young man? Maud briefly wondered. He was certainly attractive. The older brother, George, politely gestured for Maud and Daisy to take a seat.

'Thank you,' said Maud, 'but no.' The smell of soup drifted into the room, presumably from their kitchen next door. 'We will not keep you from your dinner.'

The brothers listened respectfully as Maud and Daisy explained they believed there would be an attempted murder at the shoot, and Thomas thanked them for coming.

'I don't think they really believed what we told them,' Maud said, as they made their way back to Clara's house.

'Nae one else has,' pointed out Daisy, 'so why should they?'

'We are not strangers to such a reaction in our investigations, Daisy. But we will, regardless of the odds, solve the case.'

The following afternoon Maud and Daisy dressed in Donald's outgrown shirts, jackets and trousers, both legs tied below the knee with nicky-tams.

'Now the whiskers,' Maud said, opening the top drawer of her dressing table.

She pulled out the selection of whiskers she'd brought with her from Edinburgh. Pushing aside her hairbrushes and pins, she spread the facial disguises on the top of the dressing table. 'Which would you prefer?'

'It's like choosing between boiled sweeties,' Daisy said with glee. 'A moustache' – she plucked a large reddish-brown one from the collection – 'and side whiskers.'

Maud took a neat, fair moustache for herself. She spread a little dab of theatrical glue above her upper lip and pressed the Van Dyke whiskers into position. Daisy took the glue and did the same with her more flamboyant bushy moustache and its matching side whiskers.

Maud next put on one of the two tweed caps lying on the bed and pulled it low, covering her tightly-pinned hair. She stood in front of the long looking glass, placed her hands on her hips and stood with her legs apart.

Daisy followed suit and laughed. 'Two muckle laddies. Dinna forget to walk with a swagger,' she added.

They let themselves out of the front door and strode along the track towards the wooded area of the park where the shoot was to start. One of Daisy's nicky-tams came loose and she stopped to re-tie it.

'I feel a right teuchter,' she said.

'Peasant or not, remember our role is to keep an eye out for a potential *murderer*,' Maud admonished, as they set off again.

They reached the coppice of mixed Scots pine and decid-uous trees, which provided good cover for a variety of birds, whatever unfortunate feathered creature it was they were shooting today. Twenty or more beaters waited. She noted that the two McDougall brothers were there, but before she was able to consider the other men, Jamie Gillespie called that the shooting party had arrived.

The six shooters stood on the outskirts of the wood, all wearing Norfolk jackets, knickerbockers and fedora hats, chat-ting while their loaders prepared their guns. Lord Urquhart stood head and shoulders above the group. Perhaps, thought Maud, that was what made him so... impressive... A strong figure, despite the knickerbockers.

'There's Lord Urquhart,' Daisy hissed to Maud, 'and I suppose that lump in a man's tweed must be Jane Rankin. I wonder who the others are.'

The guns had begun to take their places. 'I imagine the tall thin gentleman at the other end to Lord Urquhart is the laird, but I don't know about the three guns in between.'

Jamie Gillespie, wearing a bowler hat as befitted a head gamekeeper, distributed sticks to those that didn't have any and called to the beaters to start driving the birds towards the guns. Maud spotted Alasdair talking to Jamie, before she and Daisy set off with the others, walking slowly through the coppice in a line, tapping the tree trunks and beating the thickets with their sticks as they went, whooping and whistling.

Hundreds of birds flew up, high and fast, over the guns. Jamie Gillespie moved with them, his spaniel at his heels, glancing along the length of the line to make sure that all the beaters were keeping to the same pace.

They reached the edge of the wood, close to the line of guns.

The guns were firing in rapid succession, the air thick with the scent of gunshot, and bird after bird came thudding to the ground, when through the air there came the chilling sound of a man's scream.

THREE

There was silence. Everyone stood stock-still.

It's Lord Urquhart, Maud thought wildly. He's been shot.

And then a shout passed along the line of beaters. 'One of the guns has been shot! It's Mrs Rankin!'

Maud's heart skipped a beat. Not Lord Urquhart, but the deep-voiced Jane Rankin.

Maud and Daisy dropped their sticks and ran through the last stretch of trees towards the crumpled woman. Jamie Gillespie broke into a run and reached her before they did. The laird had already detached himself from the other guns and was kneeling over the unmoving woman lying on her back on the grass. Jane Rankin's fedora lay where it had fallen behind her. Lord Urquhart stood with his hand on the laird's bowed shoulder.

Alasdair sprinted across the grass and joined them.

'Alasdair,' said the laird, removing his hat and revealing closely clipped greying hair. He looked up. 'Tell them to keep back.'

'Keep everyone back, Jamie!' Alasdair instructed the gamekeeper, his voice stern.

Jamie nodded and held out an arm against the beaters as they too emerged from the wood. 'Stay back.'

'What happened?' asked Maud, out of breath.

Lord Urquhart removed his hat and faced Maud and Daisy. 'It's Mrs Rankin.' His tone was sober.

'Is she...?' said Daisy.

The laird stood up and turned towards them. His face with its neat moustache was very white and the hand not clutching his fedora was covered in blood. 'Yes, I'm afraid so.'

Maud looked down at the body. The scattering of lead shot had caught Jane Rankin in the forehead and eye, and blood pulsed out from the wounds. Maud's stomach turned at the sight.

Lord Urquhart took off his jacket and spread it carefully over Mrs Rankin's face. Daisy dropped to her knees and put her ear to the woman's chest. A moment later, she rose and shook her head at Maud. Maud was not surprised, given the dreadful wounds, but they needed to be sure.

The laird called in a shaky voice across to the beaters standing together. 'One of you go and get the doctor.'

Maud turned to look at the beaters. George McDougall was amongst them, and his younger brother Thomas, both looking shocked. No one had moved.

'Both of you go,' said Maud, looking at the brothers. 'The constable will want to be here before Mrs Rankin's body is removed.'

'I'll get the doctor,' Thomas McDougall said, coming to his senses. He took to his heels and ran across the fields, followed quickly by his brother.

The laird gazed after him, as if he was unsure what to do next.

'Captain Farquharson, where had Mrs Rankin been standing in the line?' asked Maud.

Her cap had fallen off in the dash to the scene and now, her fair hair escaping from its bun, the laird seemed to notice her for the first time.

He frowned, looking her up and down in confusion. 'Who are you, Miss...?

'McIntyre. Private detective. And my assistant, Miss Cameron.' She indicated Daisy, who removed her own cap to reveal she was also indeed a female. The laird stood looking from one to the other, as if unable to take in what he was seeing.

Alasdair stepped in. 'These ladies are staying with me and my family, Captain.'

'With your family, eh? But why?' The laird narrowed his eyes at Maud.

'I can vouch for their being private detectives.' Lord Urquhart stepped in. 'And I can assure you that they are *very* good at their job.' He turned to Maud, his eyes widening as he gazed at her moustache. 'Though how they come to be here dressed like this, I'm at a loss to say.'

Captain Farquharson glanced from Lord Urquhart to Maud and stared hard at her for a moment more before he spoke.

'In answer to your question, Miss er...'

'McIntyre.'

The laird nodded. 'Mrs Rankin was standing next to me, and I was at the end of the line of guns.'

Maud looked towards the remaining three guns. They stood in a small group, looking uncomfortable, hands in their pockets. The few dogs all stayed quietly by their owners' sides. Maud briefly examined each man's face; none of them betrayed anything other than shock.

The laird put his hat back on. 'Tell the men what's happened, will you, Alasdair, and ask them to go home. Then tell everyone else to do the same. It's too cold to stand about, and there's no point in their waiting here.' Everyone, including

Lord Urquhart, turned to leave. 'No, Hamish, I'd like you to stay,' he added.

'I'll also organise something on which to carry Mrs Rankin, when the doctor and police have been,' Alasdair said and hastened off.

The laird stared out over the field, awaiting the doctor.

The groups of men began to move slowly away in twos and threes: the beaters across the field in the direction of the village; Jamie Gillespie and the loaders carrying the guns, the cartridge bags strapped across their chests and the dogs at their heels, heading for the path towards the back of the laird's house; the three remaining members of the shooting party striding towards the main door of the castle.

Maud watched them go. Their quiet steps over the grass in the gathering dusk added to the unreality of the scene.

A dog barked, was hushed quickly, and the reality of the scene came back to Maud. Mr X had been present today and had killed Jane Rankin. Who he was, and why he'd done so, Maud had no idea. Could one of the beaters have concealed a shotgun under his jacket and fired the fatal shot? Maud was certain that was not possible. She or Daisy would have noticed such a bulky object, surely, even under a loose-fitting garment. And in order for a shotgun to kill, the person has to be only a few yards away. True, there was a lot of noise, with the beating of their sticks and the shouting to frighten the birds from their cover, but still...

Could Mr X have been hiding in the woods, using all the noise and activity as his cover? It wasn't possible. Was it one of the guns?

'What a terrible accident, and to an experienced gun.' The laird's voice broke into Maud's thoughts.

'Not an accident, but a crime,' she said.

Captain Farquharson paled. He turned to Lord Urquhart for support.

'Take it from me, Charles, if Miss McIntyre and Miss Cameron are here, then there is mischief afoot.' Lord Urquhart turned to Maud. 'Can I be of assistance to you?'

Maud forced herself to think. It was hard not to be distracted when Lord Urquhart fixed his dark eyes on her like that. She was glad she had a job to do, something productive to think about.

'Thank you, but no,' she replied. 'The police constable will be here soon and I expect we will get some details from him after he has conducted a thorough investigation,' she said, drawing their attention away from Daisy, who was furtively lifting the jacket covering Jane Rankin. 'I think, Captain Farquharson, that the constable will want a list of everyone who was here today as soon as you can supply one.'

'Everyone?'

'In the meantime,' Maud continued, 'can you tell me the position of the other guns?'

The captain said nothing, gazing absentmindedly across the fields.

Maud looked enquiringly at Lord Urquhart.

He considered for a moment. 'I was at one end of the line, Sir Robert Smith was next to me and Mr Marcus Taylor next to him. Harry Affleck must have been between Taylor and Mrs Rankin, because Captain Farquharson was definitely furthest away from myself.'

Maud ran the names quickly through her head to memorise the order. She glanced at Daisy, who gave her a brief nod to indicate she had finished her inspection of the wound.

'How could this have happened?' The laird returned his attention to the conversation. 'Who could have done such a thing?'

'Who indeed?' Maud murmured. 'You saw nothing to indicate how this... incident could have occurred?'

The laird turned his gaze on her. 'I know I was standing

next to poor Jane, but I saw nothing until after she screamed and fell.' He shook his head. 'It's inconceivable.'

Inconceivable, perhaps, thought Maud, that a murder could take place in front of so many and the culprit not be obvious. Yet Jane Rankin had been murdered, of that she was sure.

The afternoon's pale sun had been succeeded by a soft pink-grey of early dusk. Most of the birds had gone.

The laird groaned. 'Oh, where is that doctor?'

'He'll be on his way, Charles,' said Lord Urquhart, his voice soft.

And at that moment, the doctor came into sight, hurrying over the grass towards them, bag in hand. A solid-looking policeman followed behind. He must be the infuriating Constable Beggs, Maud thought.

'Ah, Dr Robertson.' Relief was evident in the laird's voice, as the two men reached the little group.

'Captain Farquharson.' The doctor, a grave man with a thin tight-lipped face, nodded a greeting and knelt to examine the body. He removed Lord Urquhart's jacket and peered into Jane Rankin's face, felt for a pulse in her neck and turned his head to address the laird.

'She's quite dead, I'm afraid.' He replaced the garment over Jane's face.

The laird bowed his head for a moment. 'Such an appalling thing to have happened.'

'I'll have to notify the procurator fiscal as it's a sudden death,' said the doctor, rising, 'but I'm certain he'll decide that no crime has been committed. It's clear from the wounds that the shot was fired from a reasonably short distance, but not as a direct hit. I'm sure the fiscal will come to the same conclusion.'

'So you don't think that Jane was murdered?' asked the laird, hope in his voice.

'At this juncture I see no reason to suspect that Mrs Rankin's death was anything other than a terrible accident.'

Maud bit her tongue. If the man wanted to think that, so be it. But she had learned her job at Sherlock Holmes's knee…

Constable Beggs stepped forward, clearly unhappy that the doctor had stolen his lines. 'Aye, that's right, Captain Farquharson, I will inform the procurator fiscal as soon as I return to the police office.' He removed his pocketbook. 'In the meantime, in order to determine whether or not a crime has been committed, I'll need to gather some evidence.'

'You won't need me here any more, Charles,' said the doctor. 'And as Mrs Oliphant in the town is in the early stages of labour, I need to visit her now.' He gave a last glance at Jane's body, her head covered in Lord Urquhart's jacket and her muscular knickerbocker-covered legs. 'A woman with a forceful personality, Mrs Rankin, but such a tragic way to go.'

'Alasdair is organising a way of getting her… well, that is the body… to the mortuary,' the laird said.

'Good.' Dr Robertson turned to the constable. 'Beggs, you know where to find me to take my statement.' He nodded to the little gathering and strode away.

Pulling out a pencil and opening his notebook, Constable Beggs looked around at those remaining. 'Did anyone see what happened?'

'I was standing the closest to Mrs Rankin,' the laird began. The soft gentle nickering and the footfall of horses took his attention.

They watched Alasdair and another man, presumably one of the laird's estate workers, arrive with the shooting brake drawn by two black horses. Alasdair brought the cart to a halt a few feet from Jane's body and both men dismounted. While the other man held the horses' heads – Maud knew that the smell of blood and death made these animals nervous – Alasdair laid a blanket on the ground next to her.

The constable stepped forward and helped Alasdair to roll

Jane Rankin's body onto the blanket. They lifted it onto the cart and set it between the two benches facing each other.

'Take the body to the dead house, my man,' instructed the constable.

Alasdair looked towards the laird for confirmation, but the older man was staring off into the distance.

'You were saying, Captain?' said Constable Beggs, brushing the soil from the knees of his uniform.

'Was I?' The laird looked about as if for help to remember. 'Ah, yes. Did I see what happened? The beaters had been coming out of the wood, laying about the thickets with their sticks and putting up the birds nicely. The guns were firing, bringing them down.'

The laird stopped speaking again as Alasdair climbed into the brake and took a seat to accompany the body, while the other man took the driver's seat. They all watched as the horses took the strain and the cart began to move slowly off across the field, towards the avenue leading into town. Drawn by the two black horses, it looked suitably funereal.

Maud turned back towards the laird. 'You were saying that the guns were firing at the birds?' she prompted him.

Constable Beggs jumped at the sound of her voice. He turned, gazed at her, a puzzled look on his face, and seemed to notice the two female beaters for the first time.

The laird pulled the constable's attention back. 'That's about it, I'm afraid. I ran to Jane, but I was too late, she was already dead.'

'And you knew this because...?'

'Good God, man, the fact that her face was pulped was a pretty good indicator.'

'Hmm.' Constable Beggs made a few notes in his pocket-book and looked up again. 'Did anyone else see anything?'

Maud spoke up. 'Miss Cameron and I were amongst the beaters—'

'Miss Cameron?' He glanced at Daisy. 'That's a good local name,' he said approvingly, before turning to Maud. 'And what is your name, miss?'

Maud drew herself up to her full five feet seven inches. 'I am Miss McIntyre, private—'

The constable frowned. 'Miss McIntyre... I know that name. Aren't you the female who telephoned my office yesterday to report a murder about to happen?'

'I did indeed, Constable.'

'And now I find you here,' he said severely, 'and in some sort of disguise. What am I to conclude from that?'

Goodness, did the man really think she had telephoned the police to report a forthcoming murder and then committed it and waited calmly for the officer to arrive?

'You could conclude that Miss Cameron and I were correct and that a murder *has* been committed,' Maud said firmly.

Lord Urquhart drew a sharp breath. 'We don't know for certain there's been a murder here,' he said. 'Unfortunately, accidents do sometimes happen at a shoot.'

'And who are you, if you don't mind me asking?' The constable turned his attention to Lord Urquhart.

'His name is Lord Hamish Urquhart and—'

The constable cut Maud off mid-sentence. 'And what, may I ask, are you doing here, Lord Urquhart?'

'He is one of the guns on my shoot.' The laird was clearly offended on behalf of his guest.

The constable flushed.

'Constable Beggs,' Maud said, unable to hide her impatience, 'what is your opinion about this incident?'

He shook his head. 'With what I've learned so far, I'd say it was a very sad accident.'

'Despite the telephone call I made to you yesterday?'

'Despite your supernatural powers, yes, miss.'

'I see. So you do not intend to find out who fired the fatal shot?'

The constable stiffened. 'This isn't the first time someone's been killed on a shoot, and I doubt it will be the last. It's not for us to judge these things. I will be guided by the procurator fiscal, but it seems that it was most likely an unfortunate shot.'

'Are the guns hit often?'

Constable Beggs frowned. 'It's not unknown for a beater to be hit. Of course, it is not usually the case that one of the *guns* is shot, and in the face too. Mrs Rankin was unlucky.'

'Unlucky?' muttered Daisy. 'You could say that...'

The group turned as one at the rumbling of the game cart. They watched for a moment as two men alighted from the seat, nodded their greeting to the laird and began quietly to load it with the dead birds.

'We should all return to our homes,' said the laird. 'It is getting dark.'

The gloaming was indeed deepening. The constable replaced his notebook and pencil in his uniform pocket. He touched his helmet, bid them good evening and turned to go.

'Dinna you want the address we're staying at, Constable?' Daisy called after him.

He turned round. 'Why ever would I want that, miss? The laird's account of this sad occasion is good enough for me. If I need to know where you are staying, I'm sure any one of the beaters could furnish me with that snippet of information.' He set off across the field.

'Watch your manner, man.' Lord Urquhart took a step towards the constable.

'Time to go, Hamish,' said the laird, a restraining hand on his arm. He looked over at Maud and Daisy. 'Ladies.'

Maud recognised it for what it was: an order to leave.

'Is there a Mr Rankin?' she asked, reluctant to go until at least this question had been answered. 'He needs to be told.'

The laird stared blankly at her, his face still pale.

'I'm sure the police constable will inform the poor woman's husband,' Lord Urquhart said quietly, 'but don't worry, I'll go there as soon as I've seen Charles home.'

The game cart, drawn by an old carthorse, began slowly to pull away, pairs of birds swinging from the iron structure.

'You had best go back to the house of Mr and Mrs Ross,' Lord Urquhart went on.

Maud sent him a look to show she was not satisfied with the constable's questioning.

'Please take care, Miss McIntyre,' Lord Urquhart murmured. 'If your suspicions are correct, there are dangerous people around.'

'Only one, Lord Urquhart,' she replied, 'and I intend to find him.'

She and Maud set off towards the copse, beyond which lay Clara's house. Maud glanced back once, briefly, and in the dusk saw the two shadowy figures following the game cart, walking across the field towards the castle as a faint mist rose from the ground.

Everything about this case might be equally hazy, Maud thought, but she would clear a way through, prove everyone wrong, and find the murderer.

'Constable Beggs might be satisfied it was an accident, but we know it wasn't.' Maud's heart was heavy as she and Daisy walked through the dusky woods. 'Oh Daisy, I wish we could have prevented it.'

'We couldna have,' said Daisy.

'We knew it was going to be someone at the shoot...'

'Aye, but we didna ken the actual person who was going to be killed. And we tried to warn the woman that her life was in danger, but she just looked right scunnered and all but threw us out.'

It was true that Jane Rankin had been irritated by their advice to take care, but nonetheless... They had not solved the clue in time. A wave of quilt washed over her.

'We solved the clue, Daisy, but didn't manage to prevent the crime.'

'Then we'll have to try harder next time, won't we?'

'Next time? Do you believe there will be a next time?'

'There's bound to be. Mr X has got away with two, maybe even three, murders.' Daisy's voice was grim as she took Maud's arm in hers. 'Neither the doctor nor the constable thinks Mrs Rankin was murdered. I canna see the monster giving up until either he's caught or he's done away with all the people he has a grudge against.'

They walked the rest of the way in silence and reached the gate to Clara's house. A lamp glowed softly through the curtained window into the darkness of the November day. It was a welcoming sight.

But Maud barely noticed it. Her thoughts were taken with one thing. Who had fired the shot that killed Jane Rankin, and how had they managed to do so without being seen?

FOUR

The sitting room of Clara's house was bathed in a warm red glow from the banked-up fire. Maud and Daisy stood in their stockinged feet in front of the hearth, holding out their hands to the flames. Maud hadn't realised until then how cold she'd become.

'Oh, my dears!' cried Clara, entering from the kitchen and carrying a tray of tea things. 'I heard you come in and knew you'd be in urgent need of a cup of tea.' She set the tray down on a low table. 'Would you be more comfortable if you, er, removed your facial hair and changed your clothes first?'

'Of course, Clara.' Maud dropped her hands and glanced down at the jacket and trousers with their nicky-tams. 'I'm sorry, I should have thought – we must be dirty.'

'I didna mean that,' said Clara. 'I'm used to more than a few twigs of heather from Donald. I was just thinking of your comfort.'

'In that case.' Daisy dropped into an armchair. She ripped off her red-brown moustache and side whiskers, winced and rubbed her face. 'Tea would be braw.' She eyed the plate on the tray. 'And some of that Victoria sponge cake. All that fresh air gives you an appetite.'

Maud brushed down the back of her trousers with the palms of her hands before taking an armchair and carefully peeling off her fair moustache. 'Have you heard what has happened to Jane Rankin, Clara?'

'Alasdair sent over one of the stable lads to let me know. Jane wasna a very pleasant person, it's true, but it's a shocking thing to have happened. He said not to hold dinner for him; he'll get something from the cook at the castle.'

Maud was glad. She had no wish to explain their beaters' role to Alasdair so soon, and it would be easier to discuss the afternoon's events without him.

Clara sat down and poured out the tea. 'Did either of you see anything?' She passed the first steaming cup to Maud.

Maud accepted it with thanks. 'I'm afraid we don't have the whole story.'

'Oh.' Clara looked disappointed. She placed a cup of tea on the low table next to Daisy. 'Help yourselves to a slice of cake. And then perhaps you can tell me if you think it was an accident.' She poured a cup of tea for herself. 'The stable boy was sure that Alasdair and Constable Beggs think so.'

Clara settled back in her deep armchair, awaiting more information.

Maud hesitated. She and Daisy had a duty of discretion, but Clara was their client. The question was how much to tell her? Daisy caught Maud's eye, reading the same dilemma there.

'We canna say much at this stage of our investigation, Clara,' Daisy said. 'We'd hate to say we thought so-and-so was the guilty person, only to find later that couldna be the case. All these people' – Daisy waved her hand vaguely – 'are your friends and neighbours, after all.'

'We wouldn't want to make things awkward for you,' Maud said.

'The letter that came for you yesterday,' Clara said slowly. 'Should you nae have told the constable?'

'I did.'

'Then why—'

'He didna believe her,' Daisy said.

There was silence in the room for a moment.

'He should have,' went on Maud, 'but I don't expect the police in Fort William get many people telling them that a murder is about to take place. This means that Daisy and I must focus our energy on the case. And that we need to keep to ourselves the fact that we received a clue.'

Clara bit her lip. 'Of course. I understand. Dinna worry. No one will hear a word of it from me. Let's just enjoy our tea and you can tell me more when you...'

'Ken more?'

'Aye.'

They sipped the hot tea in silence, then Clara blurted out, 'Shouldna I be worried for my own safety? I'm a member of the choir.'

Maud and Daisy exchanged a concerned glance. 'Aye,' said Daisy, 'it might be best if you have someone with you at all times.'

But who to trust? Maud thought.

'Alasdair has to go to work and Susan to school.' Clara sent a dubious look at the dog, who was basking in front of the crackling log fire. 'Ellie goes to the office with Alasdair when it's possible, but when she's here she's nae use as a bodyguard.'

The dog didn't move, but she thumped her tail hard on the rug to indicate she knew they were talking about her.

'There's Netta, of course,' Clara went on, a little more cheerfully. 'I willna take any risks, so dinna worry about me.'

'If we receive a clue that we think might refer to you in any way,' Maud said, 'we'll tell you immediately and help you arrange extra precautions.'

Clara looked relieved. 'But who could be doing all this? It doesna make sense.'

'We did wonder if it mightna be someone from another choir, one of those which didna make it to the final, maybe as some kind of revenge?' Daisy told her.

Clara flushed. 'Some of the choir stayed over in Edinburgh after the semi-finals to see the show of the famous illusionist, the Great Lafayette. It was his last show, as that night the Empire Theatre burned down.'

'I remember,' Maud said, wondering why Clara was telling them this.

'I was glad I didna go, even though all the audience got out safely. Well, Walter Stevenson has the deepest voice of the basses, because he smokes heavily – his pipe, you ken – and at first we all thought he'd set the theatre on fire.' Her flush deepened. 'He'd had a front row seat,' she added. 'Of course, then we heard that a lantern had fallen onto the stage, so the blaze had been a terrible accident.'

'But you think it shows it's possible that someone – not to point a finger at Mr Stevenson – might go to great lengths to get revenge?' Maud asked.

Clara nodded unhappily. Then she brightened, seemingly struck by a thought. 'I'll write straight away to the other two choirs still in the competition, to see if there's been any funny business. I ken a member in each of them,' she said, pleased to be able to do something. She shot Daisy a smile. 'We Camerons get everywhere.'

Daisy smiled back at her cousin. 'Aye, a great clan, as I was telling Maud earlier.'

Maud blinked. 'You mean when you told me the Camerons have always caused trouble?'

'Same thing,' Daisy responded.

'I'll let you know when I hear back,' Clara said.

'And if all is well with them,' said Maud, 'we'll know to focus on the Fort William choir.'

Maud and Daisy excused themselves and made their way upstairs.

'Come to my room when you've had your bath,' Maud said to her friend at the top of the staircase. 'We need to discuss the case in private.'

Maud soaked herself in the bath, enjoying the hot, scented water on her chilled skin. She wrapped herself in a large towel and dashed back to her bedroom to find a fire had been lit. She dressed herself in her purple linen dress with its three-quarter length sleeves, high belt and white collar and cuffs embroidered in purple. As Maud fastened on tiny pearl earrings while seated at the dressing table, she finally felt herself again.

She rose and moved over to an armchair. Taking a fresh notebook from her bag, Maud opened it, uncapped her pen and began to make notes. By the time Daisy joined her half an hour later, Maud had asked Netta to bring hot drinks for them and she had filled the first few pages.

'You've been busy,' Daisy said, glancing at the notes in the open book on Maud's lap.

'I've written down all we know so far, plus some ideas. Take a seat and we can work through this together.'

Netta appeared with a hot toddy for Maud and the cup of tea Maud knew Daisy preferred. They thanked the maid and Daisy settled herself eagerly in an easy chair. 'I've had my own thoughts too. There's naething like a hot bath to get the ideas flowing. So, what do you have so far?'

Maud took a warming sip of her hot whisky, lemon and honey and read the notes aloud.

'One. The death of John Noble, suspected heart attack.

Two. The murder of Emily Black, suspected drowning. Three. The murder of Jane Rankin, shooting.' Maud paused.

'That's it?' asked Daisy, putting down her cup of tea.

'Only regarding the victims,' Maud said. 'Next are my tentative theories.'

Daisy nodded for her to continue.

'One. Mr Noble. Could it be that he had been so frightened by something that his heart stopped beating?'

This is what had happened in the Sherlock Holmes's story *The Sign of the Four*. Major Sholto was about to reveal to his two sons where he had hidden the treasure he had secretly brought back from India, when a bearded man appeared at the window and the Major died of sheer fright.

'You mean that the killer kent that John Noble was feart of... say, spiders and made sure he saw a muckle one?'

Maud suddenly saw this was possible. 'I had been thinking of an accidental frightening to death, but you could be right, Daisy, that the killer knew and it was done on purpose.'

Daisy gave a pleased smile. 'What is number two?'

'Miss Black. Was she drowned because she was with child? That is, did the killer lure her to the remote loch, perhaps with the promise of a future together, and then pushed her into the water, knowing she couldn't swim?'

'Who kent she couldna swim?'

'Now *that* is what we need to find out.' Maud made the appropriate note in her book.

'And,' continued Daisy, 'do we actually ken she was in the family way?'

Maud sighed. 'No, we don't know that for certain. I wonder if a post-mortem was carried out on her body?'

'Nae doubt it wasna, since she died by accidental drowning. And for that matter, we also dinna ken if she threw herself into the loch to end her life.'

Maud nodded her agreement. 'The fiscal recorded death by drowning. He would never put suicide on the death certificate.'

'What have you got next in your notebook?'

'Three. Mrs Rankin. She could have been shot by accident and the culprit was too afraid to admit it.'

'So that's three *possible* murders, rather than *actual* murders?'

Hmm, that was certainly what it looked like from Maud's notes. 'Despite what I've just mentioned, I think we can say for certain that the last one was a deliberate killing because of the clue we were sent.'

Daisy shook her head. 'But I canna see a pattern.'

Maud finished her hot toddy and set down the glass. 'Supposing we are correct that all these incidents are related, who are our suspects? The list is huge.'

'If we start with the definite murder of Jane Rankin, there's...' Daisy nodded at Maud's notebook. 'Dinna forget to start a new page in your wee book and call it prime suspects.'

She waited while Maud did so.

'So, our suspects are...' Daisy paused, thought for a moment, then reeled them off. 'One of the guns by accident, one of the guns on purpose, a beater on purpose, a poacher by accident, or a person nae part of the shoot but lurking in the woods waiting for the chance to shoot her.' She drew a breath.

Maud hastily added them all to her new list. 'Let's try and narrow it down.' Her fountain pen poised, she looked up at Daisy. 'If it was one of the guns, then Jane Rankin would have had to turn her head towards that person, given that the lead pellets hit her in the face. We should make a note of the men and their positions at the stand.'

'Left to right,' Daisy began, 'there was Lord Urquhart...'

Lord Urquhart, thought Maud. Why was he always at the scene of a crime? Well, not always, unless he had frightened Mr Noble to death and pushed Emily into the water. He was staying with the laird, she reminded herself, because he was part of that set: the parties, visits to country houses, hunting, shooting. It didn't mean there was anything sinister about his whereabouts. On the other hand, it didn't mean there *wasn't*. But what possible motive could he have?

'Maud?' Daisy was looking at her. 'You havena written down Lord Urquhart's name. You nae gone sweet on his lordship, have you?'

'Lord Urquhart,' Maud said firmly, writing his name with such force that her pen nib almost tore through the paper. 'Then Sir Robert Smith, if I remember correctly.'

'Aye. And Mr Marcus Taylor, and...' Daisy wrinkled her brow. 'Who was the next one?'

'Harry somebody. Yes, Harry Affleck. Next came Jane Rankin.'

'And Captain Farquharson at the end,' finished Daisy. 'He seems the most likely suspect for our Mr X since he was the only person on the shoot that kent the other two victims.'

'He would have been taking a huge risk, as he might have been seen by any one of the beaters.'

'I'm nae so sure. We were walking towards them, right enough, but we were also watching where we put our feet so as not to go ars—'

'That's true, Daisy,' Maud said quickly. 'The ground was riddled with rabbit holes and tree roots, and no one wanted a broken ankle.'

Daisy hit the palm of a hand to her forehead. 'Michty me, we've forgotten the loaders!'

Maud's heart sank. 'That means another three possible suspects.'

'Three? How do you make that out? There were six loaders, one for each gun.'

'Only three loaders would have been close enough to kill Jane,' Maud said, suddenly realising this narrowed down their investigation. 'The further away the shooter, the larger the circle of shot. That means we're looking at those standing closest to Jane. Her own loader and the two working for the guns on either side, which were Harry Affleck and the laird.'

Loaders stood to the side of their shooter and a little way back, Maud remembered. Had one of the three taken a further step back so as not to be seen, caught Jane Rankin's attention and then peppered her in the face with shot? She was an experienced shooter, it seemed, and would be practised in handing her gun to the loader without turning to look at him. If it had been a loader who killed her, they would have had to be quick. The other loaders would not have seen it happen as their focus would have been entirely on their job of accepting each empty gun, loading it with shot, handing it back to their shooter and repeating the process in quick succession. Add to this the noise and activity of all the guns firing, who would have noticed?

'So we now have as potential suspects two guns – those standing on either side of Jane – and three loaders. We can discount a beater, a poacher or a skulking Mr X, as they would have been too far away to inflict the injuries.'

'My money's still on the laird,' Daisy said. 'He was the first to reach her after she'd been shot. What if she hadna been killed outright by the pellets and he got there quickly to finish her off? After all, she screamed, so she didna die straight away, did she? And he had blood on his hand.'

Maud nodded. 'As if he'd put his hand to her face? Or to her mouth, perhaps, to stop her breathing.'

'It's nae looking good for the laird, is it? Or do you think Mr X might have disguised himself as a beater, same as we did, and been able to get close enough to take that shot?'

'Not unless he stole away from the group, and I think Jamie Gillespie would have spotted that. He was watching us all to ensure we kept moving forward at the right pace and in line. Realistically, then, that leaves us with the laird or Harry Affleck, or one of the three loaders.' Maud looked at her list. 'That takes us further forward.'

'What's the thing that connects the victims?'

'Singing.' Maud drew up another heading: Further Theories. 'You know, Daisy, the forthcoming competition has to be relevant to this case. The choir members are being murdered one by one, with less than three weeks until the final.'

'Aye. Else why them and why now? Put as number one under further theories a member of one of the two remaining choirs,' suggested Daisy.

'Clara's information may help us there.'

'Number two. A member of one of the losing choirs.'

'Have we not dismissed that idea?'

'Nae matter. I thought you liked to be methodical?'

'I do.' Maud duly wrote down number two.

'Right,' went on Daisy. 'Three, a member of the Fort William choir.'

Maud nodded and added this to her list. 'There's still the problem, though, of why a choir member would want to ruin their chances of winning the competition by killing off their own members, isn't there?'

'Number four,' Daisy went on blithely. 'Jane Rankin didna like what she called the lower orders, so she might have wanted to do away with Emily.'

Maud frowned. 'That's a bit weak, not least because Mrs Rankin herself is now dead.'

'Och, never mind. Put it down anyway.' Daisy smiled. 'It looks braw to have pages filled in your wee book.'

Maud returned her friend's smile. They needed as much encouragement as possible, even if it was simply a few more completed pages in her notebook.

'I have another theory,' Maud went on. 'Mrs Rankin was dressed the same as the men and, in those clothes and given her bulky build, she could have looked like one of them. Perhaps she was shot by accident.'

'You mean Mr X mistakenly thought she was the mannie who was his intended victim? Aye, maybe.'

Maud turned back to a page she had written before Daisy joined her. 'And now what about Mr X himself? What do we know about him?' She paraphrased her notes. 'He likes to rhyme, is aware of John Noble's phobia – that is, *if* Mr Noble had one – is persuasive enough to lure a young woman to the loch side on a late November afternoon, and has access to a gun and is a good shot.'

'And could get close enough to be sure the shot had a chance of killing Jane Rankin.'

'Next,' said Maud, still writing, 'plan of action. We need to find out if Mr Noble had a deep-seated fear of anything, if Emily Black had a beau and if so whether she'd told anyone of an appointment with him on Sunday afternoon. And then we need to make some enquiries about Harry Affleck and the three loaders.'

'But even if Emily did have an appointment with a laddie, it might nae have been him who shoved her in the loch. It might have been someone who ken she was meeting her beau and got there first.'

'Or after.' Maud nodded, making notes. 'Or even someone who'd seen her by chance at the loch and took the opportunity to push her into the water.' She pushed a stray lock of hair behind an ear. 'Although why a passing stranger would want to drown Miss Black, I cannot imagine.' She sighed. 'I don't think we can make much progress until we've interviewed the laird. After all, he was the one who pulled Emily Black's body out of the water and he was standing next to Jane Rankin when she was shot.'

'Aye, and if that interview comes to naething, we'd better

hope the next clue will point us in the right direction,' Daisy said.

They sat in silence for a while. Another clue meant another murder was due to take place. Maud knew that she and Daisy would need to try harder to prevent another soul falling victim to the elusive Mr X...

FIVE

'Daisy and I would like to take up your offer to borrow the bicycles,' Maud said to Clara over breakfast on Friday morning.

Lacking the divided skirts recommended for female cyclists by the Rational Dress Movement, Maud had dressed for the occasion in a smart thick cream jumper with a rolled neck, balloon sleeves and decorative buttons on the shoulders, and her voluminous blue tweed walking skirt which allowed for unrestricted motion. On her feet were her chestnut brown lace-up ankle boots with a small heel.

Maud was aware that a number of men, and indeed some women, had denounced cycling as unladylike and unchristian, and had stated that the bicycle was the devil's agent both morally and physically. But Queen Victoria had owned two Salvo Sociables. Admittedly, these were huge tricycles, but the principle was not dissimilar. Maud smoothed down her skirts and picked up her teacup, pleased with her purposeful yet elegant appearance.

Clara smiled with approval. 'You need to be able to get around on your investigations and bicycles will allow you to do that. We could wait until Susan or Alasdair arrive back for luncheon, or I could show you how to ride the machines now?'

'Nae time like the present.' Daisy ate a forkful of scrambled egg. 'We canna be asking Alasdair for a hurl every five minutes.'

'He doesna mind taking you in his car to where you need to go,' Clara said.

'I ken. But it might not always be handy for him. And it'll be braw to be able to get around on our own two... wheels.' Daisy grinned.

Clara nodded and cut into her rasher of bacon. 'By the way, Maud, I met your friend at Mr Rankin's house yesterday.'

'A friend of mine at Mr Rankin's?' Whoever could she mean? Maud wondered.

'I thought I should visit Jane's husband to express my condolences and to see if there was anything the poor man needed. And who should be there but...'

'Lord Urquhart.' Maud suddenly remembered. He had said yesterday he would break the news to Jane's husband, if Captain Farquharson wished him to.

'That's right.' Clara beamed. 'He spoke highly of you, and of our Daisy of course.'

Maud longed to ask what he'd had to say about them, but that would not have been appropriate.

Daisy swallowed a mouthful of egg. 'What did his lordship say?'

'Daisy!' admonished Maud. 'A lady doesn't ask that question.'

'Aye, but I'm nae lady – so what did he say, Clara?'

Clara sent Maud an amused glance. 'I dinna think I should say. But you can be certain it was a compliment.'

'And why shouldna it be?' Daisy took a gulp of her tea. 'We're good at our job.'

'I thought he was a very pleasant young man.'

'He can turn on the charm right enough when he wants to,' Daisy said dismissively.

'And it was good of him to call on Mr Rankin,' Clara continued.

She shot a glance at Maud, but Maud only gave a brief nod of agreement and continued to eat her breakfast. Lord Urquhart, a man she'd originally decided was a womanising buffoon, had only slightly redeemed himself in her eyes since they had first met in the summer. He might be tall, dark and blessed with a classically handsome face, but...

'When Lord Urquhart showed an interest in the choir,' Clara was saying, 'I suggested he came along to the next practice. He seemed to like the idea and said he would be delighted to meet you both again.'

Maud felt herself flush. Insufferable fellow. Everywhere she went, he seemed to be. But she would not let him insinuate himself into her investigation.

Their breakfast finished, Maud and Daisy followed Clara outside into the courtyard, taking with them the flat caps they had worn at the shoot the previous day.

Two black bicycles leaned against the side of the steading. Both were decidedly severe-looking, despite the smart little wicker baskets attached to the front.

'To start with, you should bicycle for only a few miles on a flat stretch of ground,' Clara said, pulling one of the machines away from the stone wall.

'Oh... good.' Maud's resolve was beginning to weaken.

'There's nae wind today,' went on Clara, 'and that will help. Susan and I keep the tyres inflated, so you will have a nice, smooth ride.'

Maud stared at the bicycles in disbelief. They looked so... unbelievably unstable. How could it be possible to balance on two such thin wheels? She knew it was because she had seen others do so and had experienced it herself during the handlebar adventure, but she hadn't been in charge of the contraption then, and at no point had it felt natural.

Clara laughed. 'Dinna worry. If Susan and I can do it, then so can you, Maud. It isna that difficult as long as you keep your skirts well out of the way.'

A detective must be fearless at all times, Maud thought. She wondered whether Holmes had ever had to learn to ride a bicycle? Maud couldn't immediately remember reading a story in which the great detective jumps on a bicycle and pedals away. Or Miss Gladden, or Lady Molly of Scotland Yard, or M. Dupin...

'Who wants to go first?' said Clara.

Maud and Daisy looked at each other. Maud raised her eyebrows. Daisy raised hers higher.

'I will,' said Maud. She would show those fictional detectives a thing or two.

Clara looked her over. 'You'd best have Susan's bicycle, as she's almost the same height as you.'

Maud gazed at the larger of the two machines: its metal frame and small leather seat, the shield over the chain and part of the back wheel. She swallowed.

With one hand, Clara took hold of the handlebars and moved it a little away from the barn wall.

'Step over this,' she said, pointing to the low curved part of the frame, 'and sit on the saddle.' With her free hand, Clara took hold of the back of the seat. 'When you push off, mind not to get your skirts caught in the pedal.'

Maud lifted one boot over the low bar and stood with her legs either side of the frame. She took a deep breath and did a little jump up into the saddle. Clara let out a small scream as the bicycle toppled over, and it and Maud fell against the wall of the barn. Her cap landed on the ground.

'You were supposed to keep your feet on the ground,'

gasped Clara, struggling to stop the machine and its passenger from falling any further.

'You didna say that!' Daisy cried, helping Maud untangle herself and her skirts from the bicycle. 'Are you all right, Maud?'

'Perfectly, Daisy, thank you.' Maud affected a breeziness she did not feel. She picked up the tweed cap, brushed it down and replaced it on her head. 'Shall we try again, Clara?'

'Perhaps we should wait until Susan is home? Or Alasdair? He's stronger...' Clara sounded doubtful.

'Certainly not,' Maud said. It would be too humiliating to have such an audience. 'I'm sure I can master this.'

'Well, then, I'll hold the bicycle again and you sit on the saddle, but keep your feet on the ground. Usually it's toes only, but you're a wee bit taller than Susan, so it should be easier for you.'

Maud did as instructed and Daisy watched with apprehension.

'I'm all right, Daisy. This is quite comfortable, after all.'

Clara gave her instructions on keeping the pedals turning, how to squeeze the brakes to bring the bicycle to a halt, and then she continued, 'Now I'm going to let go, but I'll run alongside you until you've got the hang of it.'

Maud nodded and pushed off.

'Pedal!' cried Clara. 'You must keep pedalling!'

For a few brief seconds, Maud struggled to retain her balance. Then she tumbled sideways with a cry and landed in a heap in the courtyard.

'Don't move!' Clara cried. 'Have you broken anything?'

Maud tested herself gently. 'I can move all my limbs.' Clara moved the bicycle off her and Maud sat up and gave a rueful smile. 'And I thought I was doing so well.'

'You were,' Clara said. 'Practice makes perfect, after all.'

Goodness, Maud thought, how she disliked that expression.

Once again, she mounted the bicycle and this time pedalled off.

She felt as light as air as the bicycle wheels turned beneath her. For a moment, she was sure she could not breathe. But then her breath came in a great gasp, and she shrieked with fear and excitement. A thrill flooded the pit of her stomach as she flew across the courtyard. She was bicycling!

The small barn loomed up, suddenly very close.

'Turn the handlebars!' called Clara.

Maud wrenched them round, the bicycle wobbled and once again she fell sprawling on the ground. This was not unlike learning to ride her first pony, she thought. 'You must get back on immediately,' her father had said, 'before you lose your confidence,' and he had been right. She got to her feet, rubbing her shoulder, and waved to Clara and Daisy, hovering like anxious parents at the far end of the courtyard.

Maud straightened her skirts and climbed back on the bicycle. This time she managed to cycle in a large circle, once, twice, three times, without mishap. A horse stared in surprise out of a stable door as she swept past.

She ought to stop now, Maud thought, and give Daisy a turn. What had Clara said about bringing the bicycle to a halt? Stop pedalling, squeeze both brakes equally, slide off the seat and put one foot on the ground.

Gripping the handlebars and applying the brakes, Maud came to an abrupt halt where Daisy and Clara stood. She jumped from the saddle before the bicycle could fall sideways again.

'Well done, Maud!' Daisy said with a smile.

Maud laughed. 'That was fun – although I think I need to work on my stopping technique.'

Clara turned to her cousin. 'Now it's your turn, Daisy.'

After a series of shrieks of alarm and bursts of laughter, Daisy completed a few rounds of the courtyard on Clara's bicycle and her cousin pronounced them ready to travel on the road.

'If we're nae back by dinner time,' Daisy said, with one foot on a pedal as she prepared to push off, 'send out a search party as we'll likely be lying in a ditch.'

Despite Daisy's comment, Maud felt confident as they bicycled sedately along the deserted country road. She thought of Conan Doyle's story, *The Adventure of the Solitary Cyclist*. When Miss Violet Smith cycled along a lonely stretch of road, to and from the railway station for her weekend visits to her mother, she was always followed by a strange man on his bicycle. Each time he kept his distance behind her and then disappeared without a trace, never letting Miss Smith get near him.

Involuntarily, Maud glanced behind, her bicycle wobbling a little as she did so. But there was no one there.

'Careful, Maud!' Daisy cried. 'You nearly collided with me.'

'Sorry!'

'When do you think the next clue will come?' Daisy asked, as they pedalled side by side.

'The first one came the day before Mrs Rankin's murder. If Mr X follows the same pattern, that means he has the next death planned for Monday with the clue arriving on Sunday. That means two days yet.'

'Clara said that two of the choir's sopranos, Maggie and Helen, work in the laird's house,' Daisy went on. 'We can talk to them at choir practice tomorrow afternoon and find out what they kent about Emily's private life.'

Once again, the laird's name comes up, thought Maud.

They passed a fingerpost sign. *Inverlochy Castle, 4 miles.* 'We could cycle there one day,' Maud said.

'Isna it just a pile of old stones?'

'It's a ruined thirteenth-century castle,' Maud corrected her. 'A medieval stronghold built by the Comyns. When Robert the Bruce became king, he captured and burned it.' She spoke absentmindedly, her thoughts back again with the laird. 'Daisy, I think we should visit Captain Charles Farquharson this morning.'

'What, now?'

'Yes. We have a number of questions for him.'

'Then we need to turn around.' Daisy swivelled her handlebars and immediately the bicycle swerved, and she was tipped into the hedgerow. She struggled to her feet and brushed the leaves of copper birch from her thick green cardigan jacket.

Maud stopped pedalling and removed a twig from her friend's cap. 'Remember we're still novices at this bicycling lark, Daisy.'

'But we're nae new to *detecting*. Now, let's go and see what we can find out from the laird.'

As they cycled up the driveway flanked by Scots pines, a four-storey stone castle with a central tower came into view. Maud took in the different styles of the building, its battlements and roofs of various heights, which suggested it had been constructed over various centuries.

She and Daisy leaned their machines against the wall and crunched over the gravel to the heavy front door, which was framed by a pointed arch. Daisy lifted the massive knocker in the shape of a lion's head and let it drop. It fell with a resounding thud, to her obvious satisfaction.

After a few minutes, the door swung open and an elderly butler stood catching his breath. Maud decided to answer his as yet unasked question.

'Miss Maud McIntyre and Miss Daisy Cameron, at present staying with Mr Alasdair Ross.' She handed the man her card. 'We are here to see Captain Farquharson.'

The butler glanced down at the card in his hand. 'If you

would care to wait in the hall,' he said with a slight pant, and stood aside for them to enter.

Inside, the castle was no less intriguing. Numerous doors led off the dark hall, panelled with oak and hung with stuffed stag heads. A huge fireplace, the dog irons empty, was inset in one wall, and against another stood a grandfather clock with a loud tick.

'I will ascertain if the laird is at home to visitors.' The butler bowed and set off towards the back of the house.

Maud turned to Daisy, who was darting a slightly nervous look about the hall.

'Daisy,' Maud said, 'remember we are here as private detectives, not as maids.'

Daisy gave a wan smile.

'Back straight and make sure you look the captain in the eye.' Maud straightened her own shoulders and gave a reassuring smile to her friend.

The sound of a door opening somewhere in the distance and the scampering of paws on the stone floor heralded the arrival of two black Labradors. They bounded over towards Maud and Daisy with purpose in their gleaming eyes.

Maud took one look at the dogs' filthy legs and feet, held up her hand and said in a firm voice. 'Stop. Sit.'

The dogs immediately did as bid. They sat panting and staring at Maud, waiting for further instructions, their wet tongues lolling and their tails thumping on the flagstones. Maud's passing thought that she and Daisy might not be suitably dressed for the visit immediately evaporated.

'Oh, well done, madam! There are not many who can get the pair to do as they are told.' The laird marched down the hall towards them, wearing a worn tweed jacket, a kilt of faded blue and green tartan and a pair of muddy gumboots. 'We are just back from a bracing walk, as you can see.' He beamed.

The butler was trailing along behind him. 'Your boots, sir,' he began, his anxious eyes on the offending items.

'Good point, Crichton. Best not wear them upstairs, eh?' The laird toed off his boots and left them in an untidy pile on the floor. He dropped the dogs' leashes after them. The butler produced a pair of soft leather slippers and the laird slid his feet into them.

'Well, ladies, so good of you to call, but I'm not altogether certain if we have met.'

Maud held out her hand. 'We met briefly yesterday, Captain.'

'Did we?' He frowned a little, took her hand and shook it.

He shook Daisy's hand and looked at them both. Then, clearly realising something more than shaking hands was required, he said, 'Well, would you like to come into the morning room?'

'Thank you.' Maud glanced at the dogs. Were they to be invited into the room with them?

Captain Farquharson's gaze followed hers. 'Tessie and Bessie, to your baskets.'

The dogs rose, sent Maud a sorrowful look and dashed back down the hall, disappearing through an open door. The butler's stays creaked as he bent to pick up the leashes and the gumboots.

'Shall I have tea sent up, sir?'

The laird appeared not to hear his butler.

'Very good, sir,' said the elderly servant and hobbled after the dogs.

'This way, ladies,' the laird said.

Maud and Daisy followed him up a spiral staircase, the low heels of their boots tapping on the stone treads.

'You will observe that the stairs curve upwards in a widdershins direction,' he told them over his shoulder as they climbed. 'This was to protect the occupants from invaders. It gives the defender the benefit of being able to make a right-handed swing of his sword arm.' He turned and demonstrated with a swish of his right arm before again proceeding up the stairs. 'Whoever thought of that was a veritable genius. The enemy mounting the stairs would find their right hand confined and would not be able to wield their weapon.'

'I hope none of the lairds were left-handed,' Daisy murmured.

The staircase continued to rise, but they turned off and walked along a dark, twisting passage. He opened a small, rounded door and led them into a modest-sized, comfortable-looking room with a low ceiling and a single window facing south to catch the rays from the winter sun. Framed landscapes decorated the walls, a bearskin lay on the floor and a fire blazed merrily in the hearth.

'I find this room best in the winter. In the drawing room a man could freeze to death before anyone noticed.' He gave a hearty laugh.

He gestured for them to take a seat on the sofa, as he settled himself in an ancient armchair. 'Now, to what do I owe the honour of this visit?'

'Captain Farquharson,' Maud said, 'we were at the shoot yesterday—'

He shook his head. 'That can't be right. There were six guns and I'm sure I would have noticed if two of us were young ladies. Three, of course, including Mrs Rankin.'

Jane Rankin was hardly young, thought Maud.

'We were with the beaters,' put in Daisy.

The laird frowned. 'Good Lord. You're the two females who were dressed as boys.'

'We are private detectives, Captain, and were at the shoot disguised as beaters to keep an eye on the proceedings. To make sure no one was killed,' she added. Except that they didn't manage to do that.

'Well, you failed on that account. Just talked about murder, if I remember aright.'

Maud hastened on. 'Can you tell us what you saw at the... um... incident?'

He frowned. 'A terrible accident. We – the guns, that is – were firing and bringing down the birds, when suddenly I heard Jane Rankin cry out and fall to the ground.'

Maud waited for him to continue. When he didn't, she asked him another question. 'I remember your saying almost those very same words yesterday. Tell me, have you had any other recollections of the incident since?'

'That's it, I'm afraid.'

'You have no idea from where the shot came?'

He sent her a puzzled look.

'That is, the direction from where the shot came?' she amended.

'From the front, it had to have been.'

Maud and Daisy exchanged a glance and waited for the laird to make further comment. None came. A log fell in the hearth, sending sparks up the chimney.

'How do you think that might have happened?' Maud pursued.

'I didn't see anyone come up to her and let off their shotgun in her face, if that's what you mean.' He sighed. 'Poor Jane. She was a spirited filly.'

'Aye, poor Mrs Rankin, as you say,' Daisy said, 'and so soon after the death of Miss Black.'

The laird shook his head sadly. 'Two members of our small community gone, just like that.'

'How did Emily Black seem to you on the day she died?' Daisy asked.

'I couldn't say. You would need to speak to my housekeeper, Mrs Wilson.'

That was Helen Wilson, Maud thought, one of the sopranos.

From the depths of the hall there came the unmistakable skirl of bagpipes playing. Daisy glanced at Maud and pulled a face.

The laird's face lit up. 'If you ladies will excuse me, luncheon calls.' He stood.

'Did you see anything at all out of the ordinary?' Maud pushed him again for an answer as she and Daisy got to their feet.

'On which day?'

'Either.'

'No, neither.'

Maud suppressed a click of her tongue. It wouldn't do to show her annoyance.

'Is that tune "Scotland Forever"?' she asked politely, as he escorted them back down the curved stone staircase.

'Stirring stuff,' he said, pride in his voice. 'When the pipes are played by brave Scottish regiments, famed throughout the world for their military prowess, there's nothing like it. The pipes instil fear in the enemies of the British Empire and raise the morale of those they are coming to relieve. Aye, the warrior traditions of the Scots run deep.'

They reached the bottom of the stairs. The sound of the bagpipes, now louder, came from a room off the hall, which Maud supposed was the dining room. The laird politely but firmly ushered her and Daisy out of the house and shut the door behind them.

'It's a wonder it's nae the piper who's been murdered,' Daisy said, as they stood on the steps.

Maud laughed. 'I quite like them. But never mind about the pipes, Daisy,' she said, serious again. 'Think what we have learned from the laird.'

'Oh aye, that he thinks Jane Rankin "a spirited filly".'

'I think we need to interview Helen Wilson. We won't do it now as she'll be too busy to give us her full attention, but we can speak to her tomorrow afternoon at choir practice.'

They mounted their bicycles and arrived home in good time for luncheon. Hardly had the maid closed the front door behind them than an excited Clara came bustling out of the sitting room. She met them in the hall.

'There's a gentleman here to see you.'

'It's nae Lord Urquhart, is it?' said Daisy, sending Maud a cheeky grin.

'Nae, it's another gentleman,' Clara told them, her voice low as she ushered them towards the sitting room. 'You've got another case!'

SIX

A well-dressed country gentleman with a steel-rimmed pince-nez on his nose got to his feet as they entered the room.

'This is Mr Austin,' said Clara. 'Mr Austin, Miss McIntyre and my cousin Miss Cameron. The private detectives from Edinburgh,' she added with pride.

'Ladies.' He gave a sober bow of his head and shook each of their hands in turn.

'There now, introductions over, and I will leave you to speak in private.' Clara withdrew, closing the door behind her. They all sat down.

'I believe you are in need of the services of the M. McIntyre Agency.' Maud arranged her tweed skirts, to give him time to arrange his thoughts.

He gave a little cough, glanced down and turned his hat in his hands. 'It is a delicate matter.'

'It always is, Mr Austin.' Maud gave her most efficient smile. 'You can be sure we are most discreet. But first, sir, how did you hear of our services?' She thought it likely to have been through Clara, but felt she should ask. 'Our office is in Edinburgh, after all, and not Fort William.'

'It was Mrs Noble who informed me,' he said. 'She happened to mention when she was arranging the Advent greenery and candles in the kirk that Miss McIntyre and Miss Cameron, who were staying with Alasdair Ross, were private detectives. Mrs Noble has been a little under the weather since her dear husband departed this earth, and sadly there are no children to console her.'

Maud couldn't hide her surprise. 'Mrs Noble mentioned us?'

'Yes, she's an ardent member of the congregation and a great help to the minister and his elders.'

So Beatrice Noble had not said the reason for their being in the Highlands. Maud supposed Beatrice found it difficult to talk about what was happening to the choir members, given the death of her husband.

'That was kind of Mrs Noble, to recommend us,' she said.

'Indeed, she spoke very highly of you.'

Why was that? Maud wondered. True there wasn't a detective agency in the town, so there was no other business Mr Austin could have approached, but Beatrice Noble had specifically praised them, it seemed. Yet she and Daisy hadn't solved any crimes since they had arrived in Fort William.

'I would like you to... observe my son,' Mr Austin went on.

'Your son? May I ask why you wish us to do this?'

He met her eyes. 'I am sure he is secretly involved with an unsuitable woman.'

'Unsuitable?' Maud was immediately reminded of their Braemar case involving art forgeries. She thought of the painting by Picasso, *Les Demoiselles d'Avignon*, not on public display but rumoured to depict the interior of a Barcelona brothel. She frowned. Was there a bordello in Fort William? Were she and Daisy being asked to pass themselves off as women of the night to observe this man's wayward son? She glanced at Daisy. Her assistant took great pleasure in adopting a disguise, but...

'What do you mean by unsuitable, Mr Austin?' Daisy was asking.

'The young woman in question is...' He was having difficulty bringing himself to utter whatever it was. He removed his pince-nez, polished the lenses with a clean white handkerchief and replaced the spectacles on his nose. '*Working-class.*'

Maud blinked. Was that a euphemism for prostitute? Apparently not, for he went on, 'I am very much afraid that she will seduce my son—'

'Lucky son,' Daisy murmured.

Maud shot her a warning look, but fortunately the gentleman had not heard, for he continued unabashed, 'and induce him to promise matrimony, and when he does not marry her, she will threaten to bring a case for breach of promise. My son is an elder of the kirk and I would not like to see such a stain on his character.'

Dear me, thought Maud, looking at Mr Austin's troubled expression. A man's promise to marry a woman was considered a legally binding contract, and if he changed his mind, he would be liable to pay damages. Few middle- and upper-class women brought such cases, because of the public scrutiny of intimate matters it necessarily involved. Most cases were between a working-class woman and a middle-class man. Typically, the man would promise to make her his wife, then desert her. Maud sighed. Would that ever change?

'You can imagine how a breach of promise case against my son would have not just legal and social repercussions, but also spiritual,' Mr Austin added. 'As you will know if you are a member of the Presbyterian kirk, each church is led by its minister and elders.'

'Yes, I am aware of that, Mr Austin,' Maud said.

'Then you will also be aware that elders are elected. And

that after being ordained by the minister, they are appointed for life and are responsible for pastoral matters within the parish.'

'A breach of promise case against an elder would indeed be shocking,' she murmured.

'This type of blackmail is becoming more common, if one is to believe what one hears,' Mr Austin continued.

'One doesna,' Daisy muttered.

'Forgive me, Mr Austin,' said Maud, a little louder than she would normally speak, in order to suppress any further such mutterings from her friend, 'but I wouldn't have thought an elder would have enough money to be of interest to a blackmailer.'

'You are quite right, Miss McIntyre. I would have to pay off the young woman from my own income.'

So to the legal, social and spiritual concerns, one must add financial, Maud thought. There was something else to consider, too, but she had no intention of pointing it out to Mr Austin. If a woman could successfully claim that she and the man were married by cohabitation by habit and repute, under Scots law she would have the same rights as a woman married in church. For this type of marriage, the woman would have to persuade the court that they lived as husband and wife and that her friends and relatives believed the couple to be married.

'Will you accept the case, Miss McIntyre?' He scanned her face anxiously.

Daisy had already pulled a notebook from her bag. 'If you could give me your son's details, I'll let you have a wee note of our terms. Then we'll get to work on the investigation straight away.'

As soon as the necessary information had been exchanged and Netta had shown Mr Austin out, Maud turned to Daisy.

'Mr Austin doesn't know the young lady's name or where she works. We should therefore start by keeping the son's lodgings under observation.' Maud smiled at the eager expression on

Daisy's face. 'Would you like to do that? It'll give you another opportunity to wear a disguise.'

Daisy's eyes widened. 'Are you sure you dinna want to?'

'No, you keep an eye on the enamoured elder, Daisy.' Maud knew how much her assistant liked to wear a disguise and, in truth, being shorter she was more adept at fitting in on a busy street. 'In our Braemar case, I obtained the killer's confession when I was dressed as a nun. Now it's your turn.'

'To dress as a nun?' Daisy grinned.

Maud laughed. 'It's up to you what you wear, although I'm not sure that would be the most appropriate disguise in this present case.'

'Och, well, I'll dress as...' Daisy thought for a moment. 'It has to be something I can get hold of easily, since we havena brought any disguises with us apart from the whiskers. Ah! I have the perfect idea.'

'Yes?'

'A quine selling matches. Clara may have some old clothes I can borrow. I'll ask her at luncheon.'

'Daisy,' Maud said thoughtfully, 'why do you think Beatrice Noble spoke so highly of us?'

Her friend frowned. 'I did wonder that myself. Could it be that she wanted to send another case our way?'

'But to what purpose?'

'Because she wants to give us more work...?' Daisy spoke slowly as the thought came to her. She stared at Maud.

'You are thinking what I'm thinking?' Maud said. 'That perhaps she wishes to distract us from spending time investigating the murders?'

'That doesna seem likely. One of the deid was her husband. More like she's one of those do-gooders. You see them in every kirk.'

'In every part of life, I imagine. Well, we won't spoil her faith in our abilities or let him down by not discovering the intentions of the young woman – and of the young man, for that matter.'

As Maud was lying on her bed reading after luncheon, Daisy burst into Maud's bedroom clutching a bundle of clothes.

'From Clara.' She dropped the garments on the end of the bed and grinned.

Maud put down her book, *The Half-Hearted*, a story of manners and romance in upper-class Scotland and an action tale of adventure and duty in India. The novel by John Buchan had been thoughtfully placed in her room by her hostess.

'I'm glad that Clara approves of our activities,' she said, 'as it is obvious that Alasdair doesn't.'

Daisy pulled a face. 'Aye, that was a wee bit difficult earlier, with his, "What on earth were you doing on the shoot? You could have been killed," and, "Are those Donald's clothes?"' She brightened. 'But I'm nae going to greet over it."

The idea of Daisy weeping over such a triviality was impossible to imagine. 'As you say, your cousin is happy to help us.' Maud sat up and plumped the pillows behind her back. 'Show me what Clara lent you.'

From the small pile, Daisy lifted a hat – a confection in dark grey velvet, collapsed on one side. 'What do you think?' Daisy went on. 'It's nae bad, is it?'

Unlike Maud's preferred hat, which was a pale blue with a darker blue feather to complement her fair hair, the orange of Daisy's current favourite hat screamed against her red hair. The dark grey velvet she now held in her hand could only be an improvement. 'It's perfect.'

Next, Daisy held up a brown woollen coat that had seen better days. 'It's going to the kirk's jumble sale next month, but I can borrow it until then.'

Maud smiled. 'I hope you won't have to observe the young gentleman every day until then.'

'So do I. The weather's getting colder every day. I bet it's a lot warmer down in Edinburgh.'

'Put on the hat and coat,' Maud said, 'and let's see what you look like.'

Daisy took the velvet bonnet over to Maud's dressing table, sat on the stool and placed the hat on her head. She turned her head this way and that in front of the looking glass. Satisfied, she rose, pulled on the coat and twirled.

'It's perfect,' Maud said. 'With a plain scarf tied at your neck, you will look the part of a matchgirl.' She paused. 'Although...'

'Aye, I havena the swollen face that comes with phossy jaw.' Daisy automatically put a hand to her jawbone. 'Those poor women and girls.'

Exposed to phosphorus vapour during the manufacture of matches, most of the workers – many of whom were females – slowly died a dreadful death. It started with toothache, then the swelling of the gums, moving on to tooth loss and abscesses, and within six months the jawbone would be entirely dead.

'Thank goodness the use of white phosphorus is now prohibited,' Maud said. 'It's just a pity it took the government twenty years after the matchgirls' strike.' The action had been taken at the Bryant & May factory in London, but Bryant & May also had a factory in Glasgow.

'Things need to improve, Maud,' Daisy said with a sigh. 'The country can't go on treating the poor like this. I'd like to see things change for the better in my lifetime.'

So many issues that needed to be dealt with, including votes for women, but with the likelihood of a great war looming, what were the chances? Maud sighed and turned her attention back to Daisy's appearance.

'There are no fresh dates at this time of year, but you can

put half an apple inside one cheek instead. That'll give the impression of a swollen face.'

Daisy glanced at the little clock on the mantel. 'It's three o'clock. I'll leave this hat and coat in my bedroom and see you downstairs for an early cup of tea.'

Maud watched Daisy go, then putting aside her novel to return to later, she changed into her cream blouse with high collar and pearl seed buttons and the rose-pink linen skirt before making her way downstairs. As she did so, she saw the maid stoop to pick up an envelope from the doormat. Could it be the next clue? No, Maud told herself, surely it wasn't due until Sunday, the day before the next murder. She continued to descend the stairs.

Netta straightened and examined the name on the envelope, then turned, holding it out as Maud reached the hall.

'Letter for you, Miss McIntyre.'

'Thank you, Netta.'

With a mixture of excitement and trepidation, Maud took the small square envelope. The name and address were written in heavy black ink and there was that distinctive curl at the bottom of the letter *y* in *Miss McIntyre*. The handwriting was clearly identical to that on the first envelope.

The second clue had arrived.

SEVEN

As Netta moved towards the kitchen, Daisy trotted down the stairs, dressed in her green cardigan over an ivory V-neck blouse and a brown skirt.

'Has something happened, Maud?' she said. 'You look peely-wally.'

'If I'm looking pale,' Maud said in a low voice, 'it's because of another communication from Mr X.' She held up the envelope.

'The next clue?' Daisy whispered. 'So soon?'

'I think so. Quick, come into the sitting room.'

Daisy followed her into the room and they each took an armchair by the fire. Maud began to open the envelope.

'If it is the clue, it's come early,' Daisy said. 'We didna expect it until the day before the next—'

Daisy stopped as Maud hushed her. The door opened and Netta popped her head round.

'Would you ladies like your tea now? The kettle is on the stove and the water won't take long to boil.'

'That would be most welcome, Netta. Thank you.'

As soon as the maid had departed, Maud tore open the

envelope. 'It *is* the next clue,' she confirmed, glancing at the single sheet of paper.

'I hope it's nae as cryptic as the last one.'

'Once again it's all we've got to go on. We *have* to find the culprit before he claims his next victim.'

'Nae a completely impossible task then?'

'We have three murders to investigate, and if Mr X would leave us alone to get on with solving them, we would be able to do so within the week.' Perhaps that was a little boastful, for they had arrived in Fort William on Tuesday and today was Friday, and they were not even close to concluding the case.

Daisy nodded at the note. 'What does it say?'

Maud read it aloud.

> *TNT or dynamite?*
> *It will give them quite a fright*
> *Where will this event occur?*
> *It will surely cause a stir*
> *Can you guess where we will be*
> *Or will you just be drinking tea?*
> *X.*

'It's Mr X all right,' Daisy said, 'but what's TNT?'

'It's a kind of explosive.' Maud frowned. 'I don't know what the initials stand for, but I've heard that the German armed forces are using TNT in their artillery shells. They explode once they've penetrated the other ship, unlike the British shells, which are filled with lyddite and explode when striking the outside of enemy warships. TNT does a lot more damage.'

'How do you know all this, Maud?'

'My father told me, when we discussed the possibility of war with Germany.'

Daisy shook her head. 'We dinna want to go to war with them, then.'

'Indeed not.'

Germany had eventually backed down over their threat to go to war with France, and at the beginning of November the two countries signed a peace treaty. And yet the fear of aggression rumbled on. In the United Kingdom government, there were opposing views. Some argued that whenever a conciliatory approach had been used with Germany, she had abused it; while others were against provoking a powerful, and increasingly isolated, country. It seemed, thought Maud, as they approached the end of 1911, all sides were expecting a European war sooner or later. It was a sobering notion.

She turned her attention back to a more immediate problem and looked at the letter in her hand. *'TNT or dynamite?* Dynamite is mainly used in mining and quarrying...'

'I wonder if there's a quarry round about.'

Netta entered carrying the tray of tea things.

'Perfect timing, Netta,' Maud said. 'We have a question which I hope you can answer.'

'I'll do my best, miss.' Netta said, setting down the tray.

'Do you know if there is a quarry in the area?'

The slight frown on her face disappeared. 'Oh yes, miss, there is. It's only a few miles north of the town. It employs a number of the local men, including my Albert.' A blush appeared on her pleasant face.

'You are betrothed, Netta?'

'Yes, miss.' She smiled shyly.

'My very best wishes to you both.'

'Thank you, miss.' Netta made a little curtsy before leaving the room.

As soon as the girl had gone, Daisy got to her feet. 'The quarry must be where the next murder is to take place.'

'Wait, Daisy,' said Maud. 'We don't know if Mr X will strike tomorrow, the day after the rhyme was delivered, which is what happened with the first clue, or if the murder will take place on

Monday, following the pattern of four days after the previous death.'

Daisy sat down again.

'Perhaps Mr X wants to give us more of a chance to solve the clue,' Maud went on.

'Aye, last time we'd barely arrived in Fort William when we were sent the first note. I'd say he's keeping to one murder every four days.'

'Let's hope so, Daisy.' Maud poured two cups of tea.

'Otherwise, we have nae chance.' Daisy picked up her cup and saucer. 'One thing we can be sure of is that the killer will strike in the late afternoon again, judging by the last line of the wee verse: *Or will you just be drinking tea?*'

'I agree. But,' Maud continued, 'we should consider the rest of the clue.'

'Read it again.'

Maud did so, while Daisy drank her tea.

Daisy wrinkled her brow. '*It will give them quite a fright,*' she repeated. 'Is that part of the clue, do you think: *them?*'

'You mean there might be more than one victim this time? Perhaps. Or it might be a way of not revealing the sex of the victim.' Maud tutted. 'Although it's grammatically incorrect to use the word as a singular pronoun, of course.'

'Of course,' murmured Daisy. 'What about the *quite a fright* bit?' she went on. 'An explosion is bound to give a fright to whoever is there. That doesna add anything.'

'Unless it's a person – or *persons* – who wouldn't normally be at the quarry. An explosion would give *them* a fright. But surely a warning hooter must be used to alert everyone on the site that the dynamite is about to be set off.'

'Maud,' said Daisy slowly, 'I've had another thought. The second line from the end: *Can you guess where we will be.* Do you think the killer has an accomplice?'

Maud's heart sank. Two Mr X's? 'We must hope not.

Finding one is proving challenging.' She straightened her back and spoke firmly. 'No, I don't think so. The word *we* is most likely referring to the victim and Mr X. We are fairly certain of the venue and the date. What about the victim – who is that likely to be? Who could possibly be lured to a quarry?'

'If it's another member of the choir' – Daisy paused as she thought – 'it has to be a mannie because a woman at the quarry would stand out a mile.'

'Not if she were in disguise.'

Daisy looked crestfallen. 'Aye, there is that, I suppose.'

They both gazed into the fire for a while. Maud hoped the explosion was to be at the quarry and not another place where an inferno might result. No, that couldn't be the case, as Mr X didn't want indiscriminate killings, but the death of specific choir members. Yet which ones? Not to mention *why*?

'Let's work on the assumption that we're not looking for a woman in disguise,' she said to Daisy. 'It's possible that a degree of strength would be required in the process of bringing about an explosion. That confirms we're looking for a male murderer as well as a male victim.'

'In the bass section, there's George and Thomas McDougall...'

'The McDougall brothers again,' Maud murmured.

Daisy nodded. 'They were also at the shoot. Beaters, like us, but did we nae decide Mr X couldna have been a beater?'

'We did.' Maud sighed. 'We don't want to go round in circles. On the other hand...'

'We must keep an open mind?'

'Yes.' Maud smiled. 'Who else is there in the bass section? Joseph Watson and Walter Stevenson.'

'That's all; just the four of them.'

'We need to find out where they are employed.'

'We can do that at choir practice tomorrow evening.'

'What puzzles me most, Daisy,' Maud said, 'is why Mr X is

killing off members of the choir. I keep coming back to the competition, but that doesn't explain exactly why he doesn't want them to win.'

'Or even to take part, at this rate. There willna be enough folk left to make up a choir.' Daisy poured herself a second cup of tea. 'Dinna forget yours.' She nodded at Maud's cup. 'It must be getting cauld.'

Maud drank her tea absentmindedly. 'He's a murderer, carefully planning his deadly crimes, a criminal of the worse type in my opinion. And he's sending us these light, amusing verses, which makes him monstrous to boot.'

'Where's it all leading to? He canna be meaning to murder the whole choir, surely?'

'Let us hope not.' Maud put down her empty cup.

'Och, well, if one of the four basses works at the quarry, then he can get his hands on explosives which means he'll be the murderer—'

'Or the next victim,' added Maud, frowning as she leaned back in her chair. 'I've been thinking. On the very small chance that the murder is to take place tomorrow afternoon, I'll visit the quarry—'

Daisy spluttered into her teacup. She wiped her mouth hastily with the back of her hand. Maud glanced at Daisy's clean white linen napkin still folded on the tray, but said nothing.

'Nae without me, you won't. If you're going to put yourself in danger, then I'm coming too.'

Maud smiled at Daisy's unfailing loyalty. 'I was going to say I'll visit the quarry in the morning, when I'm sure we can have no fear of an explosion then, and when you are out on the case of the love-struck elder.'

Daisy wrinkled her nose, and Maud could tell she was torn between accompanying Maud to the quarry, even though the possibility of the murderer striking early was slim, and donning a disguise. The disguise won.

'All right.'

'See if you can borrow a small wooden tray from the cook. You can buy matches in the High Street. Then take up a place in Victoria Road to keep an eye on the young man's lodgings there. The brown coat and the hat you tried on yesterday looked warm enough for a few hours' observation. For my part, I'll speak to the manager at the quarry, tell him of our concerns and ask him to keep an especially watchful eye on things. With any luck, I'll also discover that one of our four bass singers works there.'

Daisy nodded. 'And with any luck, *I'll* spot my fellow with the lassie on his arm. And then I'll put to him his faither's belief that they're indulging in sculdudrie.'

'Daisy, your choice of phrasing leaves something to be desired.'

'Aye, but you have to admit it fits perfectly.'

Maud had to admit that it did. It sounded more earthy... more fun... than the word *fornication*. 'Be tactful,' she warned.

'As ayeways.' Daisy smiled.

Daisy left early the next morning to make sure she had time to collect some boxes of matches and to be in place for when the young clergyman left his lodgings.

Maud was relieved to find that Susan did not wish to use her bicycle on Saturday morning, as she had taken the liberty of dressing in her blue tweed skirts and cream blouse with high-necked lace collar under her blue tweed coat. Her blue hat with its dyed feather and a pair of small amethyst and pearl earrings completed her appearance. Maud was the proprietor of the M.

McIntyre Agency and she needed to look smart, even if she was bicycling to a quarry.

She smiled at her reflection in the mirror on the oak hall stand. Professional but still feminine was her motto. The ensemble she was wearing would do nicely.

In the courtyard there was a nip in the air and overhead the sky was a chilly faint blue. Her coat and the exercise would ensure she stayed warm. She mounted Susan's bicycle and pedalled off.

Keeping to the quiet country lanes, Maud travelled north, passing drystone walls overgrown with moss and ivy. Bicycling up the gentle incline in the road was harder than she had imagined, but she resolved not to complain. Poor Daisy would have to stand on the pavement for a couple of hours, getting colder by the minute, to keep watch on the lodgings of Mr Austin's son.

After a while the landscape changed. She spotted a sign saying *To Neptune's Staircase* and made a mental note to explore that one day, if they had time. Before long she could see the quarry faces cut into the hill, and nearby a spoil heap from the largest of the quarries. She pedalled uphill past a row of identical cottages, presumably built for the quarry workers. When she finally entered the site through a pair of open gates and came to a wooden building which had the look of an office, she felt her legs might not support her. Her calves ached and her heart thumped madly in her chest from the exertion. She dismounted and stood by the bicycle for a few minutes, looking around at the quarry, catching her breath and waiting for her leg muscles to stop quivering. Men in overalls and caps were moving about nearby and one or two curious faces turned towards her. Somewhere in the distance a steam shovel hissed and clanked.

Maud turned her attention to the hut and saw the words *Mr Burrell, Manager* on a sign on the door. She leaned her bicycle against the wall, mounted the two wooden steps and rapped with her knuckles.

The door was flung open.

'Aye?' the fellow barked.

Maud saw a man who looked in his late sixties, with a purple face, a big nose and fierce eyes. Taken aback by the sight of a young lady standing there, his harsh voice softened a little.

'Aye?' he asked again.

'Mr Burrell?'

'Aye.'

'My name is Miss McIntyre.'

'Aye?'

Goodness, did the fellow have any other words in his vocabulary? She had to raise her voice against the din of machinery. 'I have been engaged to look into a small number of suspicious deaths in Fort William and I have reason to believe another such death will take place here on Monday.' Maud was inclined to believe in Daisy's assessment of four days between each murder.

Mr Burrell frowned. 'I have no idea what you are talking about.'

'May I come in?' she asked, raising her voice. 'It would be more comfortable to talk inside than to shout outside!'

He nodded and stood back for Maud to pass.

It was quieter inside, but hardly any more comfortable than standing on the steps at the front door. The manager's office contained only a desk covered to overflowing with papers, a chair drawn up with the stuffing hanging out and an oak filing cabinet. A lamp hung from the ceiling and what Maud supposed was the man's overcoat lay in a heap on the floor.

'Would you like a seat?' He pointed to a disreputable-looking chair.

She smoothed down the skirt of her tweed coat. 'No, thank you.'

He took a pipe from his jacket pocket and a pouch of tobacco. While she waited, he filled the pipe and put a match to it. She drew in a sharp breath as he shook the match roughly and threw it into the wastepaper basket at the side of his desk.

'Don't worry, Miss McIntyre, no explosives are kept in the office.'

'Thank goodness.' She managed a thin smile.

'What were you saying about a death here tomorrow? We keep to the tightest of procedures on this site, I'll have you know.'

She inclined her head. 'I don't mean to cast aspersions on your safety practices, Mr Burrell, only to warn you that it's possible.' Probable, more like, she thought.

Mr Burrell scowled.

'I should have explained myself better.' Maud stuck out her hand. 'I'm the proprietor of the M. McIntyre Agency and I'm here on business. I am a private detective who is presently engaged on a case...'

'A lassie?' He stared at her outstretched hand but made no move to take it.

'Yes, a lassie. And,' she continued, as she dropped her hand and smoothed down her coat once more, 'I've been sent a warning that there is to be an explosion at the quarry in two days' time.'

The manager let out a great guffaw. 'An explosion at a quarry? Well, there's a novelty.'

Maud felt her cheeks flame. 'More than that, Mr Burrell. The explosion will be a deliberate act calculated to cause a death.'

He fixed her with a harsh look. 'And what are the police doing about it?'

'Nothing.' Maud realised the constabulary's lack of interest in the deaths didn't help her argument. 'It has fallen to the M. McIntyre Agency to investigate.'

'A lassie.'

'Yes.'

Mr Burrell shook his head and motioned her over to the window. 'Follow me.'

When Maud came to stand beside him, he gestured through the dirty glass. 'Over there you see the gunpowder magazine,' he pointed beyond the hive of activity to a stone, windowless building set some distance away. 'That's where the explosives are stored. At the local railway station there's a special siding where the gunpowder arrives in steel wagons. From there the sealed wooden crates are loaded onto our carts to be brought here. I'm satisfied the transport and storage of our explosives are as safe as can be. Some forty men are employed in the quarry and I take great care to ensure they are all trustworthy.'

He turned back to Maud. 'So you see, Miss McIntyre, there can be no carelessness with the sticks of dynamite, and there will be no death here on Monday, suspicious or otherwise.'

But could he really vouch for forty men? Although it was really only four she was interested in.

'Mr Burrell, can you tell me if you employ any men by the names of—'

'Not only will I not tell you who works here, lassie, I will also not give you any more of my time. Private detective, indeed. A woman's place is in the home.'

'A man's place is in the way,' she retorted.

He laughed and opened the door. 'Good day, miss.'

'But—'

'Good day to you.'

'And to you,' Maud said, summoning her most haughty tone.

She strode out of the door and down the steps. Retrieving her bicycle, she climbed on and pushed off. The heel of her boot caught in the hem of her skirt, there was a ripping sound and the bicycle wobbled. 'Bother,' she muttered. She would have to repair that before she wore the skirt again.

The man's loud laughter rang in her ears as she pedalled away.

By the time Maud arrived back at Clara's house her cheeks were still flushed, but now it was from the cold air that had bit at her face as she bicycled down the hill.

She had washed off the dust from the road and changed into a soothing lilac cashmere jumper and grey linen skirt with pleats at the bottom when Daisy knocked and entered her room. One look at Daisy's face showed Maud that her friend's morning had been as unsuccessful as hers.

'You didn't spot the elder in a compromising clinch?' she asked.

Daisy shook her head.

'Never mind, you can't expect to solve a case so quickly.'

'I ken, but that doesna mean I'm nae disappointed. There was no sign of the fellow. Either he was indoors the whole time or he was out.'

Maud smiled. 'It has to be one or the other.'

Daisy dropped onto the stool and considered her face in the mirror. 'It was too cauld to stand there any longer. Look at me. I have a red nose.' She caught sight of Maud's reflection in the looking glass. 'And dinna say it matches my hair.' She sighed.

'I was warmer, but from cycling and righteous indignation.'

Daisy sat up. 'Why? What happened at the quarry?'

'The manager informed me in no uncertain terms that a death there was impossible because he took the greatest care with safety and when choosing his workers.'

'Fair enough, I suppose,' Daisy said a little dubiously. 'Did you find out if any of our four basses work there?'

Maud shook her head. 'He wouldn't tell me.'

'I'll ask Clara. So he didna believe in the warning we've been sent?'

'Not only that, he didn't believe that a woman was capable of investigating a crime. He was amused by the thought, to be specific.'

Daisy leaped off the stool. 'I hope there is an explosion on Monday and that *someone* is killed! That would serve him right.'

'Daisy! We mustn't wish for that.'

Daisy sank down onto the dressing table stool again. 'Nae, of course not, Maud. It's just that...'

Maud knew what she meant. Their very first client had also found the idea entertaining. No doubt the quarry manager wouldn't be the last man to think the same.

'Oh well, as the American poet Longfellow said, *Excelsior!*'

'Sorry?'

'A loose translation is *onward and upward*, although it was an unfortunate motto for the young man in the poem, as he eventually perished in the snow.'

'He sounds right glaikit to me.'

'I must agree, given that he ignored all warnings.'

Maud thought of the warning rhymes she and Daisy were receiving from the killer. The murderer was taunting them. Did that mean they, too, were in danger? A detective must have backbone when investigating a crime, she reminded herself, and straightened her posture.

'Better luck tomorrow,' she told Daisy. 'It's Sunday and our client's son will be going to church. Are you happy to try again, or would you like me to take over the watch?'

Daisy's eye gleamed. 'I'm going to solve this particular case myself, even if I freeze in the process.' She pulled off the velvet hat. 'I hope dinner's ready. I'm starving. All I've had to eat is that half an apple I'd wedged in my cheek.' She glanced down at her matchgirl costume. 'I'll get out of these things and see you downstairs. Oh, and I'm looking forward to choir practice this afternoon,' she called over her shoulder as she went out the door.

Daisy left the room, singing "The Bonnie Banks o' Loch Lomond". The rising strains of '*Loch Loooo...*' reached Maud's ears through the closed door and descended again, '*...mond.*'

Maud mulled over the evocative song for a moment, about a Jacobite soldier captured after Culloden, imprisoned in gaol in Carlisle and awaiting execution. He addresses another soldier, who is about to be released and who will have to walk the long 'high road' home over the mountains. The condemned man tells the other that his own soul, according to Celtic legend, will fly by the 'low road' back to the bonnie lands of Scotland.

Maud was about to practise her alto part of the song when a realisation suddenly came to her. A pattern to the deaths. John Noble, bass. Emily Black, soprano. Jane Rankin, alto. The next victim had to be a man and not just because the clue suggested the murder would take place in the quarry.

If the pattern she saw was correct, the next person to die would surely be another bass – but which one?

EIGHT

'Ladies and gentlemen!' Beatrice Noble clapped her hands for attention. 'Everyone into their places, if you please.'

Maud bristled with annoyance that there had been no opportunity to speak to the other choir members, or to watch for any of them acting strangely. She didn't know how the killer had discovered, in time to send the first clue, the reason she and Daisy had come to Fort William, but everyone in the choir must be considered a suspect.

'See what you can learn during the break,' she whispered to Daisy, before hurrying to join the other altos in the centre of the hall.

Mrs Noble smiled at them all. 'We will begin, as usual, with each of us singing a line or two about ourselves.'

Maud struggled to think of something suitable. *Who is the killer in the choir? Something something something dire? Higher? Fire?* No, that wouldn't do. It would cause panic amongst the members. By the time it was her turn, she managed to sing, '*Even in this chilly weather, 'tis good to walk amongst the heather.*'

When everyone had completed their warm-up exercise,

Beatrice announced, 'On Wednesday evening we practised "I Love a Lassie" and "The Bonnie Banks o' Loch Lomond". This afternoon we will concentrate on the other two of our chosen pieces for the final of the competition. These are another traditional favourite: Robbie Burns's "A Red, Red Rose", and the old Gaelic nonsense song, which we hope will amuse as well as delight the judges: "Brochan Lom".'

"Brochan Lom" was the song Maud had heard the children sing in Braemar school when she and Daisy were investigating the case in that little village. A nonsense song with a cheerful tune. Maud smiled – she was looking forward to learning it.

'It is one of those pieces known as mouth music,' Beatrice continued, 'as it was used to create music for dancing in the absence of instruments. For those who have recently joined us' – she gestured towards Maud and Daisy – 'the words are very simple and easy to learn. *Brochan tana, tana, tana, brochan lom na sùghain.*' She smiled. 'Repeat twice, with a slight variation on the fourth line.'

'Excuse me, Beatrice,' Daisy asked, 'but what does it actually mean?'

'It translates as *meagre and thin porridge, thin, thin, meagre porridge.*'

Her eyes widened. 'That's it?'

'That is, as you say, it. The rest of the choir will sing and you two new ladies join in when you feel able.' Beatrice gave Maud and Daisy a tight smile.

She counted in the different parts of the choir, and they began to sing. The meaning of the words might be a trifle banal, Maud thought, but sung in Gaelic the song was enchanting. She caught Daisy's eye and they smiled at one another. Within minutes, they were singing along with the rest of them.

Suddenly, the hall door was flung open. All eyes turned towards it. There stood Lord Urquhart, looking far too handsome in his dark three-piece suit, white shirt and a moss-green cravat.

'Am I late?' Removing his hat, he smiled. 'I'm terribly sorry if I am.'

He neither looked nor sounded it, Maud thought.

'Ah, Lord Urquhart, I presume?' Beatrice said stiffly. 'I was informed by Mrs Ross that you wished to join us. You are a little late, but as it is your first session you will be forgiven.'

Lord Urquhart gave a slight bow and walked towards the centre of the room. The other altos parted as if by common consent, and the eyes of all the females, both altos and sopranos, gazed at him.

Yes, he is attractive, Maud wanted to tell them, but he is also conceited and somewhat dim-witted.

As if to prove the last point, he enquired, 'Shall I stand with the other gentlemen?'

'Unless you wish to sing alto? Or perhaps soprano?' Maud muttered.

He turned towards her. 'Miss McIntyre. I heard you had joined the choir.'

She had forgotten – *almost* forgotten – how dark and sparkling his eyes were. She remembered him leaning towards her in the darkness of his car one rainy evening in Braemar, and now she found herself wondering how it would feel to test the softness of those lips...

'If you would, Lord Urquhart.'

Maud blinked. Had she spoken her thoughts aloud? No, of course she hadn't. That was a ridiculous notion. It had been Beatrice Noble replying to his question as to where he should stand. He smiled at Maud as if he had read her thoughts and strolled across the hall to stand in the bass section.

'We will return to singing "Brochan Lom",' Beatrice said.

'Are you nae going to ask his lordship to sing a rhyme first?' called out Daisy.

Beatrice simpered. Really, there could be no other word for it. 'I don't think that's necessary. Lord Urquhart comes with the recommendation of Captain Farquharson.'

'Aye, but have you heard his lordship sing?' Daisy muttered.

Lord Urquhart sent a cheerful smile towards Daisy. He assumed a manly square-shouldered attitude and on cue joined in with the singing. He *was* able to hold a tune, Maud was forced to admit to herself.

Beatrice was also correct in that "Brochan Lom" was easy to learn. While she sang, Maud did her best to avert her attention from Lord Urquhart. The problem was that it was necessary to be *aware* of what each section was singing and that meant she was also aware of *him*.

Berating herself for such shallow thoughts, Maud turned her attention to the little group of sopranos standing to her right. Besides Daisy and Clara, there was the buxom Mrs Ivy Fraser and two women of middle years who both worked at the castle.

Maud next discreetly considered the other altos. Jane Rankin was no longer with them, of course. That left a slender young woman who Clara had told them worked as a housemaid in the town, and three elderly sisters named Faith, Hope and Charity, who had worn black silk since the death of their parents many years earlier. The sisters, together or separately, seemed their least likely suspect, Maud thought.

Her attention now went to the basses: the two McDougall brothers, a stocky fellow, a lanky young man... and Lord Urquhart. Maud's gaze stayed on him a little too long, and she dragged it away. She was in danger of being distracted by him, and that must not happen.

Maud made herself examine the situation logically. Lord Urquhart was merely a Scots man of above average height, she reminded herself. She was aware of him because (one) his features were more classically noble than any other gentleman she had ever met, (two) his physique was more muscular than any other gentleman she had met and (three) he turned up with exasperating frequency. Those points hardly justified her wasting her time thinking of him.

Her mind calm and rational once more, she focused on the song.

Too late, Maud realised everyone had stopped singing and that Beatrice was glaring at her.

'I'm afraid your attention appears to be elsewhere, Maud. The last line of the chorus begins not *Brochan tana* but *Brochan lom.*'

'My apologies, Beatrice. It won't happen again,' Maud said firmly, keeping her gaze on the choir leader.

Beatrice nodded. 'We will start again from the beginning.'

After some thirty minutes, a short break was called for those who wished for a glass of water from the little scullery off the rear of the hall. Daisy immediately dashed over to the basses. Daisy on her own could not engage all of them at once, Maud thought, and yet they must be spoken to. Maud turned – and collided with something large, hard and warm. She staggered.

A firm hand caught her arm and steadied her. 'What a hurry you are always in,' Lord Urquhart said with a smile.

A delightful but subtle scent of lime, lemon and lavender wafted to her nostrils, and she had to fight the ridiculous desire to close her eyes and inhale the mixture.

'Blenheim Bouquet by Penhaligon's,' he said and released her arm.

Maud took a step back. 'I wanted to have a word with one of the basses,' she said, her tone stiff to hide her embarrassment at his sudden closeness.

'And here I am,' he said with a grin. 'One of the basses.'

'Indeed,' Maud managed, trying not to breathe in his scent again. 'But not, I fear, the right one.'

She saw Daisy in conversation with the stocky man. That

must be Mr Stevenson, the fellow Clara had told them she was sure worked at the quarry.

'Please, excuse me,' Maud said to Lord Urquhart, and started towards the other men who stood around in a small group, making awkward conversation as men do when talking to each other, Maud had often observed.

Barely had she reached them than Beatrice called everyone back to order. As Daisy passed Maud, she winked at her. Well done, Daisy, Maud thought. Her friend had the information they sought, but Maud would have to wait until the end of the session before she could find out more.

The remainder of the hour went quickly. Beatrice briefly halted their practice to rebuke Joseph for hitting a wrong note, 'not for the first time,' she added, but otherwise Maud was reminded that singing never failed to lift one's spirits.

At the end of the session, Beatrice called for everyone's attention before they left.

'I am going away on Tuesday for a couple of days to the west coast, so I'm afraid we must postpone the next practice until Thursday.'

There were some murmurings amongst the choir members.

'I'm sorry I have to ask you to make this change, but we are so close to the competition that we cannot afford to miss a session. I'm sure you understand.'

'Can you nae change your wee holiday?' asked Daisy.

Beatrice Noble flushed. 'No, Miss Cameron, I cannot. I will be visiting my sister.'

'Whereabouts on the west coast?' said Maggie, one of the sopranos.

The slightest hint of a shadow crossed Beatrice's face. 'Arisaig.'

'A pretty place,' commented Maggie.

Beatrice gave a tight smile and turned to address the choir.

'I will see you all again at the usual time on Thursday evening. *Chi mi thu ma bhios sinn beo.*'

'What does that mean?' Maud murmured to the young woman wearing a jaunty blue hat who stood next to her.

'See you if I am spared.'

Maud frowned. 'What an extraordinary thing to say.'

Anne Ritchie smiled. 'Not for Beatrice. She says it at the end of every session.'

As the singers broke into small groups in the hall, the women to chat and the men to take their goodbyes, Beatrice drew Maud aside.

'Perhaps you will be good enough to keep me informed of the progress on this case, Maud?' she asked.

'Of course.'

'The well-being of this choir affects me deeply, as you can imagine. My husband,' she gave a pinched, watery smile, 'and then the deaths of the others, has been very disturbing for me.'

To say the least, Maud thought.

'If we can win in the final, it will have all been worthwhile.'

Maud frowned. 'I'm sorry?'

'I mean, those members of the choir who have been gathered will be able to look down from heaven and see that we have won this prestigious competition.'

'That would be a comfort indeed,' Maud managed to murmur.

Beatrice moved away to gather up her music sheets and Maud looked around for Daisy. Her friend was making her way towards her.

'Yes?' she whispered urgently to Daisy.

'I've spoken to Walter,' Daisy said, her own voice low. 'Walter Stevenson. He definitely works at the quarry.'

Maud glanced across the room at the man with his square, stolid face and red whiskers. She remembered there was something Clara had mentioned about Walter Stevenson one morning over breakfast. Something about the semi-finals of the choir competition being held in the very same theatre the day before the inferno that killed the Great Lafayette...

'Daisy,' she murmured, 'do you remember Clara told us that some of the choir had stayed over in Edinburgh after the semi-finals to see the famous illusionist's show?'

'Aye, and that she said she was glad she hadna, even though all the audience got out safely.'

'Mr Stevenson has the deepest voice of the basses, Clara said, because he smokes heavily—'

'And that at first they all thought he was the one who'd set the Empire Theatre on fire,' Daisy put in eagerly.

'She went on to say that then they heard about the lantern falling onto the stage, so the blaze had been a terrible accident.'

'But you wonder if Walter Stevenson is capable of doing such a thing?'

'It has crossed my mind...'

Could he possess the destructive qualities that Clara and others had, albeit briefly, attributed to him?

'It's possible, Maud. And the more I think about it, the more possible it seems.'

'I'm not so sure... Clara must have meant it in jest.'

'Well, I think it's worth investigating nonetheless,' Daisy said firmly.

Maud frowned. 'We need to warn him that his life might be in danger.'

'But he might be the one *causing* the danger,' Daisy pointed out.

'We need to warn all the men, but discreetly,' Maud added, 'as we don't want to create alarm.'

'Or let the murderer know we're on to him?'

'If we speak to each man separately, we should be able to gauge from his response whether or not he is the killer.'

'We'll take two basses each.' Daisy saw Maud hesitate.

'Och, there are now five of them. Do you also want to do his lordship?'

'I should think he's safe from the killer's clutches, as he has only just joined the choir. You speak to Walter again and to Joseph Watson, and I'll take George and Thomas McDougall. Quickly now, before the group disperses.'

Daisy snatched up her hat, gloves and bag and hurried off. Maud gathered her own belongings and approached the McDougall brothers, who were making their way towards the door. The two men looked at her in surprise.

'I wonder if I might have a word with you, gentlemen?'

'Aye,' said George with a frown.

'Perhaps outside the hall, where it is quieter?'

They nodded and followed her through the door and out onto the pavement. The hedgerows were dark shapes in the fading afternoon light and there was a chill in the air.

'You know of course that Miss Cameron and I are private detectives,' she began.

Men of few words, the brothers nodded.

'There is no easy way to say this,' she went on, 'but we believe the life of one of the basses in this choir might be in danger."

'Nae.' It was George, the older of the two.

'I'm afraid so.'

'Why?' His younger brother now spoke.

'That's a good question and I wish I knew the answer,' she admitted. 'But John Noble is dead—'

'Of a heart attack.' George gave a firm nod. 'We all ken that.'

'And Emily Black—'

'The poor lassie took her own life.' Thomas again.

'As well as Jane Rankin—' Maud persevered.

'One of them shooting accidents.' George shook his head.

Maud sucked in a breath between her clenched teeth. 'And now I've received information that there's to be another death, this time in an explosion. Do either of you gentlemen ever visit the quarry?'

They looked at each other, puzzled.

'Nae,' said Thomas. 'We work for the laird; George at Home Farm and me in the stables.'

'That's right,' went on George. 'Walter Stevenson is employed at yon quarry, nae us.'

'And you never go there?'

'Nae,' said Thomas. 'We have nae need to.'

Seeing she was going to get no further with the two reticent brothers, Maud thanked them and went off in search of her assistant. She found Daisy standing on the little patch of grass, in the process of bidding goodbye to her two bass singers. Maud then noticed Lord Urquhart and Clara exiting the hall together.

'Come, Daisy,' Maud said, taking hold of Daisy's arm and drawing her round the shadowy corner of the village hall.

'Are we hiding from his lordship?' Daisy asked with a smirk.

'Hiding? Certainly not,' Maud said. 'That would be undignified.'

She waited until she heard the deep voice of Lord Urquhart take his leave of Clara, before peering round the edge of the building.

Clara spotted Maud and her eyes grew large. 'Maud! What on earth are you doing there?'

Did Lord Urquhart pause in his step? He didn't look round, so it might have been a figment of Maud's imagination. Whether he had heard Clara's exclamation or not, Maud wasn't going to give him the satisfaction of thinking she had been hiding from him. Because of course she hadn't been.

'Merely sheltering from the wind,' Maud said, stepping onto the path, Daisy behind her.

Clara laughed. 'What a pair you are.'

'A pair of *detectives*,' put in Daisy, coming to Maud's rescue. 'We need to keep an eye on our suspects, you ken.'

Clara assumed a serious expression, but Maud suspected she was as quick-witted as her younger cousin.

'Goodness, look!' Maud said, her hand to her hat in the non-existent wind. 'There's Helen Wilson.' She nodded towards the older woman leaving the building. 'I'd like to have a word with her, Clara. We can follow behind you and Daisy.'

The two cousins set off along the darkening road. Maud hurried over to where the laird's housekeeper was beginning her walk in the same direction.

'Mrs Wilson, could we walk together?'

The woman shot Maud a surprised glance, but she seemed happy to agree. 'Certainly, lass.'

Mrs Wilson was small, with an upturned nose that gave her a superior look, which Maud supposed was useful in keeping order amongst housemaids. Had Emily Black confided in Helen Wilson? It seemed more likely that she would confide in someone her own age, but perhaps Emily had wanted the counsel of an older woman.

'How are you liking life in Fort William?' Helen asked in her soft Highland accent. 'Perhaps a wee bit quiet after Edinburgh?'

'Not so quiet with the recent deaths,' Maud said.

'Aye.' Helen Wilson shook her head sadly.

'That's what I would like to talk to you about, Mrs Wilson, if you don't mind.'

Helen Wilson came to an abrupt halt on the road and stared at Maud. Her face was still just visible in the gloaming. 'Me, lass? Whatever do you think I'll be knowing about the deaths?'

'I didn't mean it quite like that,' Maud hastened to reassure her. 'Shall we carry on walking and I'll explain?'

The other woman gave a nod and they set off again.

'I wanted to ask you about Emily Black. I believe she worked as a housemaid at Captain Farquharson's house?'

'Aye...'

'And I wondered if she said anything to you about going out that afternoon, on the day she drowned?'

Helen Wilson was silent for a moment. She does know something, thought Maud. Daisy and Clara were some distance ahead now and the only sound was Maud and Helen's boots on the road.

Eventually, the housekeeper spoke again. 'I don't like to break confidences, you understand?'

'Of course,' Maud said in a sympathetic tone.

'But...'

Helen Wilson fell silent again. Goodness, Maud thought, if she doesn't tell me soon, we will be back at the factor's house. She had to say something.

'Was Emily meeting someone by the side of the loch?'

'Aye, I think she was.'

Maud's heart leaped. Was she about to solve one part of the mystery?

'Do you know who it was?' she asked gently.

'Och, no.'

Maud's heart sank. 'Emily didn't confide in you?'

'She was hardly likely to do that, Miss McIntyre, given our respective positions.'

Maud wasn't really surprised by the housekeeper's response, although she was disappointed. 'But she did have a friend – a *special* friend, perhaps?'

Mrs Wilson nodded. 'It was a man; that much I do know. She was walking out with him. On those afternoons she wore her prettiest blouse.'

'Then it was usual for her to meet him by the loch on a Sunday afternoon?'

'It was. Sunday afternoon was her time off. Emily always let me know when she was about to go out, as I like to know where my girls are.'

'How did she seem to you when she left that afternoon?'

'Happy, as she always was when she went to meet her young man.'

'So she had been seeing him for some time?'

'For the last few months, I would say. Definitely since the summer.'

Maud thought for a moment. 'It would have been light then until late at night.'

'As I've already told you, she kept to the same time.'

Whoever the man was that Emily met, he must have been able to get away only at that time of day. But get away from what?

'What time was it that she went out, Mrs Wilson?'

'She was already wearing her coat and hat when she came to tell me she was off, and that was not long after the servants had their midday meal. It would have been about half past two, I reckon.'

Half past two. 'How long does it take to walk from the castle to the loch?'

'It's not far. About thirty minutes, I would say.'

So Emily must have reached the water side by three o'clock. 'And what time did she usually arrive back?'

'In time to help with the afternoon tea at half past four.'

That would give Emily one hour with her man friend. More than long enough for there to have been an argument, for the housemaid to be pushed into the dark waters – and for her assailant to have left the isolated scene before the other servants at the laird's house noticed she was missing.

But who was it Emily had gone to meet?

NINE

'When Emily didn't return by tea time, what happened?'

'What do you mean, what happened?' Mrs Wilson looked in astonishment at Maud. 'We could hardly send out a search party, with so much to do at the castle.' She softened her tone. 'Of course I was concerned about her, Miss McIntyre, but I simply thought the foolish girl had lost track of time. The butler, Mr Crichton, would have informed the captain if Emily hadn't appeared by the time dinner preparations began, but of course then she was found...' The housekeeper's voice faltered.

Found by the laird.

'I'm sorry, Mrs Wilson,' Maud said. 'This must be very upsetting for you.'

Mrs Wilson wiped away her tears with a plain cotton hand-kerchief. 'Emily was a wee sonsie thing and a good lass. She didn't deserve to die.'

Deserve to die? Did Mrs Wilson suspect foul play? 'Do you think it wasn't an accident, Mrs Wilson?'

The housekeeper pulled herself together. 'It *was* an accident,' she said firmly. 'The procurator fiscal said so.'

'Yes, of course.'

They walked in silence for a while. The twilight had deepened further and Maud was finding it increasingly difficult to make out Mrs Wilson's features. Now she could just discern ahead the entrance to the avenue leading to Linnhe Castle. Quickly she asked another question she needed an answer to.

'Did everyone in the laird's household know that Miss Black couldn't swim?'

Mrs Wilson wrinkled her brow. 'I don't know about everyone, but certainly all of us below stairs knew.'

'What made her comment on such a thing?'

Mrs Wilson gave a rueful smile. 'Emily told us over supper one evening. John, the young footman, had been teasing her about her going off every Sunday afternoon to the loch.'

'So it was common knowledge?'

'It wasn't as if her not being able to swim was something to be kept secret.'

They reached the laird's long driveway, turned down it and walked on.

'I'm sorry I can't think of anything else to tell you,' said Mrs Wilson, as they paused at the track leading to Clara's house.

'Thank you for talking to me,' Maud said. 'I will see you at choir practice on Thursday and I'll try not to bother you with questions on the way home afterwards.'

'If it helps find who's doing this, Miss McIntyre, feel free to bother away.'

When Maud entered the house, Daisy was loitering in the hall, clearly bursting with information to share. Maud gave her friend a warning look as she removed her gloves, hat and coat, and handed them to the maid.

'Has Mrs Ross asked for tea in the sitting room?' she asked Netta.

'Yes, miss. That is, she asked me to bring a tea tray for you and Miss Cameron, and to say that she will join you in a little while.'

How very considerate of Clara, Maud thought, to let her and Daisy have time together to discuss the case, when Clara must be longing to ask questions herself.

'Thank you, Netta.'

'Well!' said Daisy, as they moved into the sitting room and she took a chair by the fire. 'You go first. What did you learn?'

Maud took the chair opposite Daisy. 'Mrs Wilson said that Emily had a man friend and that she'd been meeting him every Sunday afternoon by the loch, going out at half past two and returning by half past four.'

Daisy leaned forward eagerly. 'Did she say who he was?'

'She doesn't know.'

Daisy sank back into her chair. 'Another dead end.'

'Not quite. Mrs Wilson said the relationship has been going on since the summer—'

'That long?' Daisy rolled her eyes. 'The poor lass must have been in love.'

'Or at her wits' end. If she was with child, on this occasion she might have met the man to tell him of her situation...'

'In the hope that he'd marry her?' Daisy shook her head.

'But if Emily had thought her lover would marry her, that suggests he's not already married.'

'Or that she *thought* he wasna already married, or that he'd *said* he would divorce his wife and marry her.'

'Hmm.' The Court of Session could grant a divorce, but the court had to be satisfied there had been adultery, desertion or cruelty. As these grounds could be difficult to prove and legal action was expensive, separation was the usual remedy. 'At least we now know a little more about Emily's circumstances and very nearly the exact time she left the house, as well as when she was found in the water.'

'If we can believe Helen Wilson and the laird,' Daisy muttered.

'Really, Daisy, are you suggesting the two of them are

working together and that *they* should be at the top of our suspect list?'

'Nae, of course not. But I do think that out of all the choir members, only Clara shouldna be on that list.'

'I confess to thinking the same myself.'

A tap on the door heralded Netta with the laden tea tray. Daisy's eyes lit up and she sat forward. Maud waited until Netta had left the room before she spoke again.

'Tell me what you learned from Walter Stevenson and Joseph Watson.'

'Och, nae so much from Mr Stevenson,' Daisy said, pouring tea for the two of them. 'But Joseph Watson – he's a forestry worker on the estate – told me some funny wee stories about Captain Farquharson.'

'Such as?'

'He told me about the day the laird took it into his heid to cut down a tree which he said was too close to the castle and making one of the rooms dark, but he sawed into the wrong side of the trunk and the whole thing crashed through the window. What a daftie!'

'That would certainly have made the room lighter and more airy,' Maud commented.

'The glass went fleein all over the place, according to Joseph Watson. He said it was lucky that none of the maids were near the window at the time.'

Maud frowned. 'They were fortunate.'

'Aye, but wait,' Daisy went on eagerly. 'There was another time when he was up a step ladder in the gun room, and his waistcoat caught on the handle of a cupboard storing the cartridges. The ladder went over and he was left dangling there for a wee while, until the cupboard came away from the wall – he landed with a terrible crash and brought the cupboard and all the cartridges tumbling down on top of him. His heid took a right dunt!'

Maud nodded. Was there a point to this story?

'And—'

'I think those two are probably enough examples for the time being, Daisy. Tell me what you discovered in relation to our investigation.'

Daisy took a sip of her tea and helped herself to a sandwich. Before she could speak, or take a bite, the door opened once more and in breezed Clara.

'I hope you've finished your private blether because I'm starving,' she said, sounding very much like her younger cousin. She closed the door behind her, hurried across the room and dropped onto the sofa. Daisy passed her a cup of tea.

'Imagine going to stay in Arisaig,' Daisy said, as smoothly as if it had been exactly what she and Maud had just been discussing. 'It may be pretty, but there's naething there.'

'It depends on what you mean by nothing,' Clara put in. 'Beatrice told me it has a beautiful beach with pure white sand—'

'But nae a bonnie place to be in the winter,' Daisy said, the egg sandwich halfway to her mouth.

'Aye, maybe you're right,' Clara conceded.

'The area has an interesting history,' Maud added. 'It used to belong to Norway—'

'Did it?' Daisy snorted. 'I dinna see why they should have a bit of Scotland.'

'The Vikings took it in the eighth century in one of their raids, so it was a while ago.'

'Same difference.' Daisy took a large bite of her sandwich.

'I didna ken that, Maud,' said Clara, interested. 'Do go on. I'd like to hear a bit more about the place. Alasdair's great grandfather came from over that way and Alasdair's often said we should visit one day.'

'Can your husband get the time off? He seems to be indispensable to the laird.'

'You may be right. Then if I canna see the area for myself, at least I can hear about it.'

'As long as you are interested. I'm afraid I tend to get a bit carried away by the history of a place, as I'm sure Daisy will tell you. Where was I?'

'The Vikings,' said Daisy, taking another egg sandwich from the plate.

'Thank you, Daisy, the Vikings. After them, the area became part of the Kingdom of the Isles,' went on Maud. 'But it's been part of Scotland since the thirteenth century, although with the lairdship passing between various men and with the usual battles and bloodshed.'

'Men.' Daisy tutted. 'Will they never learn?'

'It would seem not,' Maud had to admit.

'Beatrice said she might also pay her respects to the place where Bonnie Prince Charlie left for France, after the collapse of the Jacobite Rising, you ken.' Clara smiled. 'She's quite keen on history too. I'm sure you'd have got on well together if you'd met at a better time in her life.'

Maud wasn't convinced about that.

'It's also known as the Road to the Isles,' added Clara, 'because from Arisaig a person can get a boat to the islands of Eigg, Muck and Rum.'

Maud had heard the train journey further west was breathtaking too. Travelling on the North British Railway across the curved Glenfinnan Viaduct with its twenty-one spans, and alongside shimmering lochs and herds of red deer crossing this wild part of Scotland would be a delight indeed.

'Perhaps Beatrice just likes peace and quiet.' Maud said.

'This area not quiet enough for her then?' Daisy retorted.

Clara raised her eyebrows. 'Apart from the murders, you mean?'

'Arisaig's a long way to go for a few days' holiday,' Daisy muttered.

'The journey there by train isna much more than an hour,' her cousin told her. 'Anyway, I expect after being so suddenly widowed, Beatrice wants to spend time with her sister.'

Maud could understand that. She herself had often longed for a sister. She loved her three older brothers, of course, but it wasn't the same as a sister. Maud smiled at Daisy, who was the closest she had to such a companion.

When tea was finished, the pair made their way upstairs. Maud shepherded Daisy into her room. 'Now, Daisy, finish telling me exactly what Walter Stevenson and Joseph Watson had to say.'

That night, Maud pondered the situation as she prepared for bed. She had earlier unpinned her hair, washed it using a solution of two raw eggs and two tablespoons of water, and dried it in front of the fire in her bedroom. Dressed now in her white flannel nightgown with ribbon at the neck, she sat at the dressing table and began to braid her long, pale hair.

Daisy had told her that Walter was employed at the quarry and he'd had nothing to say to Daisy other than he never made a mistake with explosives. They could hardly accuse him of being Mr X just because he worked with such materials. Although not making a mistake could also be interpreted as he knew exactly what he was doing when he placed the sticks of dynamite just so.

Maud paused in the braiding of her hair. Unlike the thickset Walter Stevenson, Joseph Watson looked as far removed from a killer as was possible. He was tall, thin and stooped, clean-shaven but with straggly sandy hair tucked behind his ears. Maud cautioned herself as she resumed folding her hair into a plait. Sherlock Holmes's physical description of his archenemy Professor Moriarty in *The Final Problem* was not dissimilar. And Joseph Watson was a forestry worker, so there must be strength in that frame. But what could this man have to gain in killing three people – a fourth on Monday if he could get away with it – and whose only connection with each other was membership of the choir?

She sighed and smoothed a fine layer of cold cream over her face, neck and décolletage. There was so much about Mr X that was perplexing.

As she slipped beneath the sheets, Maud told herself firmly that tomorrow would bring them a day closer to solving the case.

Maud felt equally positive the following morning. She performed some *pliés* to stretch every muscle in her legs before moving on to a few *tendus*, slowly brushing her foot outwards and back. The Indian club swipe completed her exercises: swinging the club behind her, then forward passing her ear, taking care not to hit her head, and repeating, taking equal care not to smack herself in the back.

Then she dressed in her grey pleated skirt and white blouse with blue collar and cuffs, and went downstairs to breakfast.

'Good morning, Daisy,' she said to her friend, who was already seated at the table.

'Morning, Maud,' said Daisy, lifting the teapot in its cheerful knitted cosy and pouring out two cups. To her own she added plenty of sugar. 'It's chilly out there, so I'm preparing myself for another freezing day as a matchgirl. I'll take up position on the other side of the street to the elder's house and watch his comings and goings.'

'It's Sunday,' put in Maud, 'so at least you'll know where he'll be going today.'

'Aye. I'll start off in Victoria Road, wait for him to leave his lodgings and follow him to kirk,' Daisy declared. 'I'll be the last one in and the first one out, so I'll leave my tray of matches in the kirk porch when I slip into the service. No one in Fort William kens me well enough to wonder what I'm up to, apart from the other choir members, and I can pull my bonnet right down so they willna recognise me.'

Maud hesitated. 'If you're sure that's what you want to do?'

'It's the best chance I have of getting a keek of him at his front door, without hanging around for hours again in the cauld.'

Maud agreed. 'It's unlikely he'd want to be seen with the woman on his arm on the Sabbath.'

Daisy grinned. 'Fresh from sculdudrie?'

Annoyingly Maud's thoughts went immediately to Lord Urquhart. 'Very well, Daisy.' She spoke briskly, the colour in her cheeks rising as a result of the image that had appeared in her head. She tried to remember the plan Daisy had outlined.

'If I dinna get a chance to speak to the elder, or his lassie, beforehand, then I'll nip out as soon as the service is finished and wait again outside his lodgings. It's nae far from the kirk to Victoria Road.' Daisy finished her tea and got to her feet. She looked at the cup longingly. 'I hope he doesna stay behind after the service to blether with the old wifies over a cup of tea.'

Maud had recovered her senses and was once again her business-like self. 'I'll let Clara know what you're doing, and she'll think of some excuse to explain to Alasdair and Susan why you won't be walking to church with us. Oh, and Daisy,' Maud called, as her friend opened the door of the dining room. 'Remember not to come into church with the piece of apple in your cheek!'

'Och, it'll give me something to chew on,' Daisy threw over her shoulder, 'if the service goes on too long, that is.'

A little breathless, Daisy slipped into the pew beside Maud. She nodded over at her cousin and family seated further along, before whispering to Maud. 'He has a woman, right enough. She came with him to the front door of the building and they kissed goodbye on the doorstep.'

'Goodness, that was brazen of him,' Maud murmured. 'Did you—'

The organist began to play and the minister entered by the transept door. The congregation rose as one.

As they sang, Maud focused her attention on the evergreen arrangement near the altar with its five candles. Four blue candles in a circle and one purple in the centre. Only one of the blue was lit today, the first Sunday in Advent, to symbolise hope. What had Beatrice Noble been thinking of and hoping for, Maud wondered, when she arranged the wreath?

Under cover of the service, Maud glanced around at the congregation. Was the murderer present? What a pity, she thought wryly, that Lombroso's theory of the 'criminal type' was largely discounted. The Italian army doctor had believed that criminals could be identified by physical traits such as protruding jaws, bushy eyebrows, excessively long arms... Maud allowed herself a small inner smile. Such a distinctive appearance would certainly be of great help to the detective.

After the fifth lesson had been read, a strong tenor voice caught Maud's ear. She glanced across the aisle to see it was Mrs Noble. Maud had heard the older woman sing each of the three parts when teaching them a new song, but she was surprised that Beatrice Noble preferred the lower range usually sung by men.

'*Dispel the long night's lingering gloom,*' Beatrice sang with feeling.

How sad for her, Maud thought, to lose her husband, the man who shared her passion for singing. The next line of the hymn spoke of piercing the shadows of the tomb. All these deaths in the choir, so soon after John Noble's, must be greatly distressing for her.

As soon as the service had ended, Daisy nodded at Maud and slipped out of the pew and through the church door. Maud, for her part, waited until Captain Farquharson left his pew at the front of the church and was threading his way through the little groups chatting in the aisle. She snatched up her black gloves and small bag with its chain handle, and when he drew close enough, she propelled herself straight into his path.

TEN

'Oh, I'm sorry! I should have been looking where I was going!' Maud clutched her pale blue hat with its dark blue feather as if to steady it and shot the laird a winning smile. 'Captain Farquharson. A most illuminating sermon, don't you think?'

'Yes, Miss... er...' He frowned.

'McIntyre. We first met at the unfortunate scene of Mrs Rankin's accident.'

His brow cleared. 'Indeed. Poor Jane. And you were...' It came back to him. 'You are one of the two lady detectives?'

'That's correct, Captain.'

Just then, they were interrupted by a man standing behind the laird, who addressed him as if Maud were not there. 'Charles, have you time for a wee drink?'

The laird's gaze went from Maud to the man whom she now recognised as Dr Robertson, who had been called to the shoot. She remained standing where she was, smiling politely at both men, as Clara and her family eased out of the pew and other parishioners continued to chat and jostle in the aisle around them.

'Angus, why don't you and, um, the young lady come up to

the castle for a dram before luncheon?' The laird sent an anxious glance at Maud. 'Or coffee?'

Seeing the doctor's doubtful expression, Maud accepted before the laird could change his mind. 'That would be delightful.'

'I just need to have a word with the minister,' the laird said, looking keen to escape the situation he had put himself in.

'Of course, and I like to walk,' Maud said, although she had not been offered a lift in either gentleman's motor car, 'so I will see you at the castle shortly,' she added firmly.

Pleased to have secured herself an invitation for a chat with both the laird and the doctor, Maud smoothed down her blue coat, found Clara and told her she would not be joining the others for tea and a chat with the minister after the service, and left the kirk. She strolled along the footpath leading to the castle, formulating her questions as she went. Under her button boots the fallen leaves rustled, and overhead the sky was a wintry pale blue.

She needed to find out how well the captain had known John Noble and work out the captain's role, if any, in the deaths of Emily Black and Jane Rankin. And what a fortuitous turn of events that Dr Robertson would be there. With a bit of luck, she might learn something about these deaths and that of John Noble, whose demise appeared to have started this horrifying chain of events.

As Maud turned onto the main drive up to the castle some twenty minutes later, she saw ahead of her two motor cars, which suggested the laird and the doctor had already arrived. Remembering Daisy's throwaway remark about the laird and his housekeeper working together, Maud quickened her pace, wondering if the laird and the doctor were involved in some plan, although what it might be she couldn't imagine.

And where was Lord Urquhart? He hadn't been at the kirk and there was no sign of his cream motor car with its green leather upholstery, although of course he had probably travelled up by train as had she and Daisy...

Telling herself she did not need to speak to Lord Urquhart and therefore his presence was immaterial, she reached the huge front door and lifted the brass knocker. She was soon passing once again through the oak-panelled hall, the two black Labradors dancing round her skirts. Crichton shut the dogs in a room at the rear of the house, then led her up the stone stairs and into the morning room.

The two gentlemen were standing companionably in front of the log fire, the doctor in a dark suit, the laird in his kilt and the tweed jacket which Maud noticed was fastened with leather thongs, warming their backsides by the hearth.

'Ah, Miss... er.' The laird stepped forward. 'What would you like to drink?' His gaze travelled to the side table on which had been set an array of bottles.

'It's a little too early for me to take anything strong,' Maud said, 'but a cup of coffee would be most welcome.'

The butler bowed in acknowledgement of her request and withdrew. Maud was about to take a seat when through the window she caught a glimpse of the grounds.

'How beautiful it must be here in the summer,' she said.

'It is quite something all year round,' the laird said earnestly. 'Come to the window and let me tell you about my scheme for the garden.'

Maud followed him over to the window and looked out over farmlands dotted with the houses of what she supposed were tenant farmers, burns and beech woods.

'You can't see from here, of course,' he went on, 'but there are pine forests and mountains to the north and west. Now, there' – he pointed down to the vast lawn stretching from the back of the house and away to trees – 'I'm going to put in a magnificent water feature. There will be a fountain in the centre, with Atlas balancing on his back the weight of the world in the shape of a globe.' He beamed. 'I saw a photograph of the one at Castle Howard in England, although mine will be a smaller version.'

'Goodness,' Maud said. 'That will certainly be a sight to behold.'

The laird nodded. 'And over there, where you see the grand old lime and chestnut trees, I will have a small Greek temple of white marble built.'

'I'm full of admiration for your plans,' Maud said, and she meant it. 'They will be breathtaking when finished.'

'Work starts on the pond tomorrow and I hope to have that completed while the weather holds.'

'With all your plans, Captain,' Maud asked in an innocent tone, 'I imagine you have little time for other interests.'

He frowned. 'Such as?'

'Oh, poetry and the like,' she said airily. More specifically, writing little verses, she thought.

His frown deepened. 'I never touch the stuff.'

He gestured for her to take a seat before pouring two glasses of whisky at the side table and handing one to the doctor. They made themselves comfortable in overstuffed armchairs. Dr Robertson clearly felt at home here, which suggested the two men were old friends. The doctor removed a small silver box from his jacket pocket, opened it and took a pinch of snuff.

'I'm sorry my house guest, Lord Urquhart, isn't here today, as I'm sure he would have liked to see you again,' said the laird politely, 'but he has gone to visit some relations near Inverness.'

After a moment's pause, Maud said, 'This is a beautiful room, Captain. I am very glad to see it again.'

'You've been here before?' asked the doctor, surprise clear in his voice as he slipped the snuff box back into his pocket.

'After the death of Mrs Rankin.' Now Maud had the opening she wished for. 'Such a tragic accident.'

The doctor inclined his head in agreement and took a sip of his whisky.

'And Miss Black's death too. So sad. Is it known what time she died?' Maud gave him an innocent look. She had a good idea of this already, but she wanted to take the conversation in the right direction.

Dr Robertson hastily swallowed his mouthful of drink and looked at her sharply. 'What a strange question to ask, madam.'

'The young lady is a private detective,' put in the laird. 'We should do all we can to aid in her investigation.'

That didn't sound like the comment of a guilty person, Maud thought. Unless it was a double-bluff and he thought that she and Daisy had no chance of solving the case.

'Really? How interesting,' the doctor murmured. 'We now have women qualified in medicine in Scotland, so why not female detectives? I suppose it wouldn't hurt to discuss the matter with you.'

Maud was sure Constable Beggs would strongly dispute that, should he have been here. But fortunately, he wasn't.

'My impression,' the doctor went on, 'when I saw Miss Black's body not more than a quarter of an hour after Charles had pulled her from the water and taken her back to the house, was that she had not been dead for long. But it is difficult to be certain within an hour or two, you understand.'

Given that Emily Black had last been seen alive by the housekeeper at about half past two and then her drowned body seen by Dr Robertson not long after half past four, his opinion was sufficient for Maud.

'Were there any other injuries?' Maud asked.

'Whatever do you mean?'

'Were there any signs of a struggle?'

'No... Her clothing was in some disorder and her hair was down, but you'd expect that to happen when a person is drowning. And when their body is pulled up a bank.'

Maud turned to the laird. 'Captain, can you add anything further to what Miss Black looked like when you found her?'

'The light was fading so I couldn't see much, but her coat and skirt were sodden. It's a wonder she wasn't pulled under the water by the weight of them.' He looked saddened by the memory.

'Was that all?' Maud couldn't allow him to drift in his thoughts.

'She was floating face down in the water. I got her out of the loch and turned her over, but I could see I was too late to save her.'

'So we can't know for sure how long she had been in the loch?' Maud felt the need to keep pushing for something more.

'We can make a reasonable assumption,' the doctor cut in. 'A body in the water starts to sink as soon as the air in its lungs is replaced with water. Once submerged, the body stays underwater for a while before it floats to the surface.'

'So that means Miss Black could have been in the loch for no time at all – or for quite some time?'

'It means she couldn't have been in there for long. How long a body takes to rise again to the surface once it has sunk depends on a number of factors, but it will be days or even weeks later.'

Maud frowned. The doctor had confirmed that Emily had been in the water for only a very short time, but something else was niggling at the back of her mind.

'Of course,' went on Dr Robertson, getting into his stride, 'the situation is different with a body that is dead before it hits the water. In that case, it might remain on the surface, since there would be no way for the air inside the lungs to escape and be replaced with water. However,' he added quickly, seeing Maud readying herself with another question, 'the post-mortem found no marks on the body to suggest foul play.'

Maud had to be careful with the way she worded her next

comment, which was to be addressed to the laird. She was, after all, Alasdair's house guest and the laird was his employer.

'It was fortunate that you were walking your dog at that time and in that area,' she said, keeping her tone casual, but watching him closely as she said it.

The laird's facial expression didn't change and he remained sitting comfortably in the armchair.

'Indeed, it was. I was later than usual that day walking Tessie and Bessie, so I decided to exercise them closer to home, along the banks of the loch. I wanted to be back for tea and crumpets at half past four, you understand,' he added sadly.

The door opened and he looked up. 'Ah! Coffee.' He sounded relieved at the interruption in their conversation.

The elderly butler entered and placed a tray on the small table at Maud's side.

'Would you like me to pour, madam?' he asked.

'I can manage, thank you.'

He bowed slowly and carefully before making his stately way out of the room and closing the door quietly behind him. The laird and the doctor remained silent, staring into the fire. Bother, thought Maud, she was going to have to get the conversation back to the case.

'When you were walking the dogs, Captain, and before you found Miss Black, did you hear a scream or a splash, or anything unusual?' she asked, as she lifted the silver pot and poured the wonderfully aromatic coffee.

'Nothing.' The laird sighed. 'There wasn't a soul about.'

'Is there nothing more you can tell me?' Maud worked to keep the exasperation from her voice.

'I cannot think of anything else. But if you can solve this mystery hanging over the castle, I'd be awfully glad.'

As would she, Maud thought. This was followed by another thought.

Was the laird the killer they sought?

. . .

Back at Clara's house, shortly before lunch, Daisy burst into the sitting room. Maud looked up from repairing the tweed skirt that she'd caught with her heel when she rode out of the quarry.

'Are we alone?' Daisy glanced round the room.

'Clara and Susan are helping in the kitchen as the cook is off, and they wouldn't allow me to lend a hand, so I thought I'd get on with a bit of stitching.' She held up the skirt.

'Just as well,' Daisy said, 'as your cooking skills leave a lot to be desired. But then so do your sewing skills, actually. Oh go on, here, give it to me.'

She was referring to the fact that Maud had never needed to cook for herself until she and Daisy had moved to Edinburgh to start the agency. But, under her friend's direction, Maud was gradually learning how to prepare simple meals.

'No! I must improve.' Maud held the skirt to her chest, narrowly missing stabbing herself with the needle. 'Did you come in to discuss domestic chores?'

Daisy smiled and shook her head. 'I've solved the case of the enamoured elder.'

'Excellent, Daisy!' Maud put down her stitching. 'Tell me everything at once.'

Daisy dropped into a chair on the other side of the fireplace. She held out her hands to the flames. 'I'm as cauld as a gravedigger's bumbaleerie.'

Maud didn't ask how Daisy could possibly know that, given that surely she had never felt one in the flesh, deciding the wiser course was to say nothing.

Daisy was already giving an account of her morning's work. 'I went back to my position on Victoria Street and it wasna long before I saw him come up the road, walking like a man who was awfa content. I went straight up to him and told him who I was and why I was there.' She waited for Maud to say something.

Maud obliged. 'Yes?'

'He said' – Daisy cleared her throat and mimicked the stern voice of the young clergyman – '"There are a number of lodgings in the building, young lady. What makes you think I am the man you seek?" "Because I'm a detective employed to keep an eye on you and you look like an elder who is far too pleased with himself," I told him.'

It was as good an explanation as any, thought Maud. 'So he didn't attempt to deny living with the woman?'

'"Who is employing you?" he said rather sharply. "I'm nae at liberty to say," I replied and he didna like that. When I asked him if he'd like to explain his relationship with the lassie, he said, "It's none of your business, but if you must know"' – Daisy paused, looked at Maud and raised her eyebrows – '"we are married."'

Maud smiled.

'Well,' continued Daisy, 'I said I was sorry and that I hadna kent. "Why should you?" he said. "Now tell me who is it that wants to know my business." So I told him.'

'Oh, Daisy.'

'It just slipped out!'

'But, still...'

'Anyway, he starts talking then.'

'What did he say?'

'He said, "We met and married when I was a student at the university. I didn't tell my father because I knew he wouldn't approve on account of my wife being a barmaid."'

Daisy lifted the tray of matches from round her neck and set it on the floor. She leaned back in her chair and stretched out her legs, the picture of a woman at ease, satisfied with a job well done.

Maud laughed. 'That must be the agency's easiest case.'

Daisy's grin was wolfish. 'I'll type up the report and invoice for his faither when we get back to Edinburgh.'

'Whenever that will be,' Maud said, sober again. 'The clue talks of an explosion tomorrow afternoon and we've yet to identify Mr X or his next victim...'

The need for urgency struck her anew and her heart began to race. She and Daisy must solve the mystery before another murder could take place.

ELEVEN

'What about your morning, after kirk?' Daisy glanced at the skirt lying in Maud's lap. 'You've never spent the whole time stitching? I ken your sewing is about as bad as your cooking, but still—'

'I have been at the castle, interviewing the laird and the doctor.' Maud's voice was indignant. Her domestic skills might be lacking, but they weren't as poor as all *that*.

Daisy's eyes grew larger. 'What did the two mannies say?'

'Not much, actually,' Maud admitted. 'The laird confirmed his finding Emily's body at about half past four and the doctor said there were no signs of any struggle.'

'Och well, everything we learn is a step forward.' Daisy pulled off her dark grey velvet hat and dropped it on the floor beside her chair. 'What if the killer is plotting more deaths? After the one we have the next clue for, I mean?'

'I've been thinking about that too. If we can't catch him before he commits murder this time, perhaps we should tell Clara it's time she took a holiday.'

'Where?'

'Anywhere she likes.'

'Could she stay at the flat?'

'Of course, Daisy. Given the circumstances, I think a stay in Edinburgh would be very good for Clara's health.'

Daisy visibly relaxed and for a moment Maud felt a pang of guilt for not suggesting the move sooner. Yet would Clara go, Maud wondered, with her family here and the competition final fast approaching? It had to be Clara's decision.

After luncheon and when Alasdair and Susan had left the table, Maud broached the subject.

'Clara, would you feel happier if you weren't in Fort William while these threats are being made to the choir members?' And carried out, she thought.

Clara frowned. 'And where would I go?'

'You could stay in our flat in Edinburgh,' Daisy said eagerly.

'You dinna have a cat, do you? I'm nae feart of them like John Noble was, but I'm nae keen on them either.'

Maud and Daisy sent each other a sharp glance.

'Mr Noble was afraid of cats?' Maud asked.

'Aye, Maggie told me he couldna abide being anywhere near one. He had a... what's the word? *Phobia* – that's the one – about cats.'

'I wonder how Maggie knew,' Maud said, keeping her voice light.

'There's a cat at the castle, to keep down the pests.'

There didn't really explain it, Maud thought – unless John Noble visited the castle. And why would he do that?

'We've nae cat, Clara, and you'd be safe in our flat,' Daisy said.

'Safe in a city I dinna ken, surrounded by strangers and goodness knows what? No, I'll stay here, thanks.'

'But you could be in danger!' Daisy cried.

'So could you, for that matter,' Clara retorted.

'The deaths began before we arrived,' Maud pointed out. 'I think whoever the killer is, he won't be interested in *us*.'

Clara shivered. 'Nae matter, I'm nae going to leave Susan and Alasdair. They need me here. And besides, I dinna want to miss the competition and the chance to meet the King.'

'Aye,' said Daisy wistfully, 'dinner at Holyrood Palace with King George...'

'Daisy!' Maud spoke sharply.

'Och, sorry. Maud is right, you ken. You should leave Fort William for your own safety.'

'Maybe I should, but I willna.' Clara stuck out her chin in a way Maud had seen Daisy do when being particularly obstinate. 'I'm nae going to let some sleekit gowp drive me away from home.'

Mr X was rather more than a sly lout, Maud thought, but she and Daisy couldn't insist Clara left. They would simply have to work even harder to keep her safe and unmask the killer.

The three women moved into the sitting room, where Alasdair was reading the newspaper and Susan a book.

Alasdair looked up as they took their seats. '*The Observer* reports that Captain Scott is making progress on his journey to the South Pole. The first two men have been sent back to Cape Evans.'

'That's nice for them,' said Clara, smoothing her skirts.

All the newspapers were closely following the story of the race to the Pole. Sixteen men, two motor sledges, ten ponies, twenty-three dogs and thirteen sledges in Scott's team had set out early in November. A team was to turn back every ten days or so as rations required, eventually leaving four men to continue to the Pole.

Alasdair frowned. 'The Norwegian is twenty-three days ahead of the British expedition, though. It's to be expected, I suppose, since Amundsen's team set out three weeks before Scott's.'

'Let's hope that the British team make it there first,' said Clara, picking up her knitting. 'It would be braw if they won after all the work they've put in.'

Alasdair folded the newspaper and put it to one side. He rose, took his pipe from the mantelpiece and resumed his seat. 'I read about your Laing case in *The Scotsman,* Maud.' From his pocket he took a tobacco pouch and began to fill his pipe. 'You and Daisy must have been relieved when the court ordeal was over, having to testify against your nemesis.'

Maud blinked. Of course – that was how Mr X knew they were detectives and was able to send the first clue so quickly. The success of the M. McIntyre Agency had been in the *newspaper*.

Susan looked up from her book. 'What's a nemesis?'

'An arch enemy,' said Maud. 'But, Alasdair, I hardly think Mr Laing could be described as my nemesis. A corrupt lawyer, certainly, but nothing more I assure you. What made you think to ask at this moment?'

'Oh, it just came into my mind. I expect it was something to do with Clara hoping Captain Scott would win the day, even though the odds are against him. I like the idea we have our very own version of Holmes and Watson within our extended family.'

'Really, Alasdair!' Clara sent her husband a warning glance.

He lit his pipe and Maud recognised with pleasure the slightly sweet, smoky and spicy aroma of Clan tobacco, favoured by her father. 'There's no harm in Susan knowing your cousin and her friend are successful private detectives,' Alasdair said with a smile. 'It's something to be proud of.'

'Well, of course I'm proud of them...'

'Who is Mr Laing, and what about him?' Susan asked.

'Would you like to tell her, Daisy?' Maud said. 'If Clara agrees.'

Clara sighed, made herself comfortable and began to knit. 'Go ahead, Daisy.'

Daisy shrugged, but with a satisfied look on her face, and leaned forward. 'Douglas Laing stole jewellery from house parties, killed a viscountess, and when we were on to him, he tried to murder me and Maud. That's about it.'

Susan's mouth had dropped open. 'What happened at his trial?'

Maud thought she had better explain the matter a little further. 'Laing was charged with the murder of the viscountess, the robbery of her diamond necklace and inciting two other named persons to commit murder.'

Susan's eyes were wide. 'But what about the other jewellery he stole? Daisy said house *parties*, not just the one.'

'He denied those offences and the police were unable to trace the stolen jewels, so there was insufficient evidence to proceed in those cases.'

Susan wrinkled her brow. 'Did he plead guilty to the other charges then?'

'He did not. He claimed that the viscountess's necklace found by the police had been planted by them to incriminate him. He also argued that there was no evidence he had encouraged others to commit murder. Unfortunately, there was only Daisy's and my word that one of the two villains had confessed that Laing had paid them to kill us, as they both died in the motor car crash. The jury found that charge not proven.'

'Oh... Then what about the murder of the viscountess and the robbery of her diamond necklace?'

'Laing was found guilty of the robbery. On the charge of murder, the jury thought Laing's actions were deliberate but that he lacked the intent to kill, and they brought in a verdict of culpable homicide.'

The whites of the viscountess's eyes had shown small areas of bleeding, Maud remembered, which suggested she had been smothered for less than twenty seconds. This had helped persuade the jury that Laing hadn't intended to murder her. Although the Crown hadn't been able to prove murder beyond reasonable doubt, Maud felt the jury was possibly reluctant to return a conviction for murder because of the death penalty. But Laing would be locked away for a good many years, and that's what mattered.

'So it was all right in the end?' asked Susan, looking relieved.

'Yes,' said Maud with a smile, 'it was all right in the end.'

'What are your plans for today?' Clara asked Maud and Daisy at the breakfast table on Monday morning.

Susan had already left for school, but Alasdair was enjoying a plate of eggs and bacon.

The pair had decided the previous evening that they would bicycle to the quarry in the early afternoon, in the hope they might spot anything or anyone suspicious before an explosion could take place.

Rather than worry Clara, though, Maud said, 'On Saturday I noticed a sign to Neptune's Staircase. It sounds intriguing. What is it?'

'It's an amazing feat of engineering,' Alasdair said, looking up from his breakfast. 'A staircase lock on the Caledonian Canal, made up of eight locks and the longest in Britain. It takes a boat half a day to travel up or down it, you know.'

'That must be worth seeing.'

'Aye, it is,' went on Alasdair. 'The locks are operated by capstans, each with four poles, and they have to make seven full revolutions to open or close a gate. And then each gate leaf has two capstans, one to open it and the other to close it. That makes thirty-six capstans on the flight and one hundred and twenty-six revolutions needed for each boat.'

Clara rolled her eyes at her husband's detailed descriptions.

'Those mannies must have braw strong muscles,' said Daisy with a smile.

'The staircase has had its troubles in the last few years, though,' Alasdair added, setting down his knife and fork on the empty plate. 'Repairs had to be made thirty years ago and again last year because there were serious defects in the masonry. Still, it's a sight to see.'

'It sounds perfect,' Maud said. 'We'll visit it this afternoon.'

Alasdair wiped his mouth on his napkin, dropped the linen square onto the table and got to his feet. 'I won't be home for luncheon today, my dear, as the laird will be keeping me busy.' He kissed his wife on her proffered cheek. 'Have an enjoyable day, ladies.'

As soon as Alasdair had left the room, Clara turned to them. 'But aren't you going to investigate the case? Jane's death has proved I was right to ask you to come here and it looks like none of the choir is safe.'

Maud glanced at Daisy before she answered. 'I'm sorry, Clara, but we didn't want to worry you. The clue we received on Friday talks of another death taking place today.'

'Today?' Clara gasped, her hand to her chest. 'Where? Will it be here?' She looked around the dining room wildly.

'Nae, not in this house,' said Daisy. 'Dinna you think we'd have told you if that were likely?'

Clara dropped her hand, looking only slightly less worried. 'Where then?'

'We can't be certain, but we think it will be at the quarry,' Maud told her. 'This afternoon.'

'The quarry? That's where Walter Stevenson works, and Netta's young man. We need to warn them!'

'I have already told Mr Stevenson,' Daisy said. 'He didna seem bothered at all when I warned him his life might be in danger, and he told me in no uncertain terms that he never makes mistakes with explosives.'

'Netta's young man then. He needs to be told.'

'You're right, Clara,' Maud said. 'My first thought was that the fewer people who know about the clues we're being sent, the better, as we don't want to provoke widespread fear. But on the other hand, we wouldn't want to risk any innocent lives. I will inform Netta and also try to reassure her that I believe her fiancé, and the other men employed at the quarry, are safe, as they're not in the choir and so not at risk from the killer.'

Clara shook her head sadly. 'I dinna know who would want to kill off a choir, anyway.'

'We've been asking ourselves the same question,' put in Daisy. 'But I promise you, Clara, we're doing our best to solve these crimes.'

Her cousin looked mollified. 'I'll say naething about the clues.'

There was a soft tap at the door and Netta came into the room carrying an envelope. At the sight of her maid, Clara's face was immediately suffused with a guilty flush.

'Are you all right, Mrs Ross?' Netta asked, looking concerned.

'It's just a wee bit hot in here.'

The three women stared at the letter in the girl's hand. Surely not another clue, Maud thought in despair. A clue meant a death, and at this rate there would soon be no members left in the Fort William choir.

'This has just come for you, Mrs Ross.' Netta placed the envelope on the table. 'Shall I clear away?'

'Not yet, thank you,' Clara told her. 'Perhaps in ten minutes or so.'

The maid left the room.

Clara gazed at the envelope. 'What if the killer is sending clues to *me* now?' she whispered.

'I think that's unlikely, Clara,' Maud said. 'What is the postmark?'

Clara peered at the print across the stamp. 'It's Dingwall.' She let out a breath. 'It must be in answer to my question about their choir.' She tore open the envelope and pulled out the sheets of paper.

Scanning it, she said, 'All is well there... looking forward to the finals... they are sure to win. Ha!' Clara threw the letter onto the table. 'That's what she thinks. Our choir is better by far—'

Remembering again the gravity of the situation, Clara shot Maud and Daisy a sheepish look. 'Anyway, there have been nae deaths there.'

Which was both good and bad news, Maud thought. Good that they had lost no members; bad that it looked like the Fort William singers were indeed the sole target of Mr X.

'How did Netta take the news?' Daisy asked, when she joined Maud in her room and they had settled in the comfortable armchairs.

'Much as you would expect. Horrified, of course, and alarmed, but I hope I've managed to reduce her fears by pointing out that the killer's sights seem to be set on only the choir members. She'll tell her fiancé and ask him to let the other men at the quarry know, and to warn them to stay vigilant. Now then,' Maud went on, 'let us try a new approach to what we already know. Who had the knowledge necessary to commit each murder and who had the opportunity to do so.'

Daisy pulled her notebook and pencil from her cardigan pocket. 'I kent we'd be discussing the case this morning, so I'm prepared.' Turning to a new page, she wrote *Knowledge* and underlined it.

'We'll start with John Noble. We now know that he was

deeply afraid of cats. Who in the choir – or closely associated with the choir members – knew of this phobia?'

'Maggie the cook and Clara, obviously. Nae doubt Mrs Wilson the housekeeper,' said Daisy, scribbling in her book. 'Maybe the laird...?'

'Especially if John Noble was a regular visitor to the castle.'

'We need to find that out.'

'Presumably John's wife also knew about the phobia. It's not the kind of thing you could hide from your wife.'

'Aye, Beatrice.' Daisy added her name.

'Have we left out anyone?'

They both considered the matter for a moment.

'Nae, I think that's it.'

'Next victim then,' went on Maud. 'Who knew of Emily's Sunday afternoon walks to the loch?'

'The laird, Maggie the cook, Mrs Wilson the housekeeper...' Daisy looked up at Maud. 'There's a wee bit of a pattern forming.'

'That's what I was hoping for,' Maud confirmed. 'We need to see whose name appears most frequently.'

'Next,' Daisy went on. 'Who kent Jane was to be one of the guns at the shoot?'

'The laird.' Really, thought Maud, his name does crop up rather often. 'Very likely the other guns and possibly the loaders. Also, Alasdair.'

Daisy shot her a look.

'We did agree he should be included, I believe?' Seeing her friend's glum face, Maud added, 'I really don't suspect your cousin's husband, Daisy. He should be on the list merely for the sake of completeness. But also, whether we like it or not, he must have known Emily Black. She was, after all, a member of the laird's household and he would have come into contact with her more than once.'

Daisy nodded and added Alasdair's name to the list.

'Now, moving on to *Opportunity*,' Maud said and waited while Daisy wrote the fresh heading. 'Who was on the spot when, or close to the time when, each victim died?'

'John Noble – Beatrice,' Daisy said, as she wrote down the names. 'Emily Black – the laird. Jane Rankin – everyone at the shoot.'

'Hmm. That last is rather a large category. Hopefully, all will become clearer as we go on. Next—'

'Still under *Opportunity*?'

'Yes. Who has a cat or access to one?'

'I'm nae sure about the word *access*. A cat canna be persuaded to do what it doesna want to.' Daisy shrugged.

'Write down the laird, the cook, the housekeeper.'

'I canna see any of them picking up the castle's cat and carrying it to John Noble's house, if that's what you're thinking,' Daisy went on.

'True, but he or she could have put it in a bag.' Maud wondered if it were possible to get a yowling cat into a sack without drawing attention.

'Next,' she continued, 'under the same heading. Who was free on Sunday afternoons?'

'Probably everyone, apart from Maggie and the house-keeper. Clara's told me the laird gives them Saturday afternoons off so they can attend choir practice. Ivy Fraser's tea shop is closed all day on Sundays. I ken that from when I was chatting to her.'

'Last entry then, for the present at least,' Maud added. 'Who could shoot and was present when Jane was killed? If we note those we think most likely, and bearing in mind our knowledge list, we have the laird, Harry Affleck and the three loaders.' Maud didn't mention Alasdair because he was with Jamie Gillespie the gamekeeper, but the fact that she didn't see him again until after Jane was shot jumped uncomfortably into her head.

'We need to interview Mr Affleck and those loaders,' said Daisy, bringing Maud out of her thoughts.

'I agree. We'll ask Alasdair about them this evening.' Maud nodded at Daisy's notebook. 'Now, whose name appears most frequently there?'

Daisy glanced at the two lists and looked up at Maud.

'The laird.'

TWELVE

At luncheon, Daisy chatted brightly. Maud was grateful to her friend for covering the silences at the table, so as not to worry Susan or arouse any concern.

Once the meal was over, Maud and Daisy changed into their cycling costumes, mounted the bicycles and pedalled towards the quarry. Their warm breath puffed out in front of them in the chilly air, and from somewhere in the woods the smell of smoke from a bonfire hung in the stillness.

'Maud,' said Daisy, 'what if we canna prevent this next murder happening?'

'We mustn't think that.'

'But we *have* to think of it.'

'The quarry workers have been warned, Daisy. Now we as detectives have to keep our minds and wits clear so that we can act to prevent it happening if we get the opportunity. So let's just get there and see what's what.'

'You didna tell me this hill was so steep,' Daisy said breathlessly, as they toiled up the incline. 'You ken I'm allergic to strenuous exercise.'

Maud laughed. 'You're not allergic to it, my friend. You simply prefer not to do it.'

'Right enough,' Daisy said through gasps.

'At least the pedalling is keeping us warm,' Maud added.

'There's an even better way of doing that – in front of a braw fire.'

Maud pictured the two men yesterday warming themselves in front of the flames in the laird's morning room. That was certainly a lot easier than bicycling up this hill. But that wasn't an option. They had a job to do: to prevent a person being killed in an explosion.

Something stirred in the back of Maud's mind: a connection between the laird and an explosion... What was it? She frowned as she pedalled.

Daisy caught sight of her face. 'So you're finding it hard going too?'

'Hush, Daisy, I'm trying to remember something...' Maud stopped abruptly in the middle of the road and put her foot down to steady herself. 'Oh, Daisy. I'm very much afraid that we have the wrong place for the explosion!'

Daisy's bicycle came to a screeching halt. 'You mean nae the quarry?'

'Think what the second clue said...'

'Something about *TNT or dynamite*? That's got to be the quarry.'

'Remember how the rhyme goes on...' Maud wracked her memory for the exact wording. '*It will give them quite a fright.*'

'Aye, well, it will give a fright when the person's blown up.'

'But what if it's a place where an explosion wouldn't *normally* take place? The next line says *Where will this event occur?*' The words were coming back to Maud now. 'That suggests it will be somewhere other than the quarry, don't you think?'

'Where else do you think the explosion will be? I mean, what would anyone around here want to blow up?'

Not taking the time to explain, Maud turned her bicycle around and jumped back into the saddle. 'We must hurry, before it's too late!' She pedalled off down the hill, the peak of her flat cap fluttering in the breeze from the bicycle's momentum.

'Wait for me!' Daisy flew after her. 'Where are we going?'

'To the laird's garden!'

'That doesna make sense!' Daisy called after Maud as they shot down the hill.

'Oh, but it does, Daisy, it really does!' The road levelled out and they resumed their furious pedalling side by side. Now Maud explained: 'When I was at the laird's house yesterday, he told me he was planning major improvements to his grounds, including excavating for a fountain – and starting work today.'

'Michty me. You think he's going to *blow up* the land to make his muckle pond?'

'We've been told by Clara that the laird is eccentric, and Joseph Watson informed you that the man is accident prone. So yes, Daisy, I'm very much afraid that is exactly what he intends to do and someone is going to get badly hurt.'

They cycled frantically along the empty country road. The morning frost had melted in the weak midday sun and Maud would have enjoyed the exercise, were it not that her heart pounded with the fear they would not get there in time.

'The fountain is being dug at the rear,' Maud gasped, as they turned their machines into the driveway to the castle. 'This way!'

She pedalled faster, taking the service road round to the back of the building. Maud had a fraction of a moment to take in the scene, bustling with workers, before an explosion split the air.

. . .

Jolted by shock, Maud lost control of her bicycle and found herself sprawled on the grass, skirts and legs in disarray.

A man's breathless voice said, 'Miss McIntyre, let me assist you.'

She looked up and saw Lord Urquhart holding out his hand towards her. Had he caught a glimpse of her legs and a flash of cotton and lace undergarments? No matter; she couldn't think of that now. She was not hurt, she admonished herself, so she must get up and help anyone who was.

A cloud of dust danced about them. Coughing, she took his hand and allowed him to help her to her feet.

'I saw you and Miss Cameron cycle into the garden, seconds before the explosion,' he said, 'and I came running over. Are you all right? You might have been killed.'

'I might have been,' she croaked, looking about for Daisy, 'but I wasn't.'

The wide lawn at the back of the house now contained a gigantic crater pouring with smoke. Lumps of earth had been flung hither and yon. All around the huge pit people ran about in confusion. In the midst of the mad scene, one figure stood alone and still. Maud recognised the closely-clipped greying hair and faded kilt of the laird, his eyes fixed on the site for his fountain. Around it the grass had withered and turned brown.

Where was Daisy?

'Maud!'

She spun round. Some distance away from the others a dark shape lay on the ground, with Daisy bent over it. Maud raced across to her friend.

'It's Joseph Watson,' Daisy said, looking up at Maud. 'Or... it *was* Joseph Watson.'

Certainly, part of the man was there. But what was left bore little resemblance to the poor man. Maud looked around for something with which to cover his remains.

Lord Urquhart appeared beside her and began to remove his coat.

'I'll find something,' Daisy said to him. 'You must be getting short of coats by now.' She ran over to a nearby wheelbarrow and returned with a tarpaulin, which she placed over Joseph Watson.

Maud could hear Daisy's words, but they were muffled, as though they were underwater. She looked around and saw some of the labourers climbing to their feet, shaking their heads to clear their ears. Clouds of soil and stones were scattered about the ground. It could have been much worse.

'We need to speak to Captain Farquharson,' she heard herself say, as though her voice was not her own.

'He's there.' Lord Urquhart gestured to where the laird still stood, gazing at the enormous hole in his lawn.

As the three of them approached the laird, the muffled ringing in Maud's ears gradually dissipated. The laird was speaking to himself. 'In all my war years I never saw such a sight.' Oblivious to their presence behind him, he continued to stare at the crater. 'It's made a much bigger hole than I expected, but it is rather splendid.'

Lord Urquhart went to his side. 'Charles, a man has died.'

'Did you see that, Hamish? The blast was tremendous. I'm pleased I had my fingers stuck in my ears to deal with the noise.'

'Charles. I'm afraid we need to call the constable out again...'

'I think he'll be on his way already, old man. I bet you could hear that blast all the way to Inverness.'

'Still, I think we had better telephone him to come.'

'Why would we do that?' The laird turned to them and frowned, sending dust slipping from his brow onto his equally dusty old tweed jacket.

'A man has been killed,' Lord Urquhart said.

'Killed?'

'I'm afraid so.'

'Killed, you say? How?'

'The explosion.'

'What? But everyone was standing behind the line.'

'Well, *he* couldna have been,' Daisy snapped.

'Who was it?' the laird asked, aghast. 'Who's been killed?'

'I'm afraid I don't know.' Lord Urquhart looked to Maud for help.

'Joseph Watson, one of your forestry workers,' Maud told the laird.

'Watson? But he was standing over by the...' The laird looked in the direction of the covered shape on the ground and his face fell. 'He asked me if he could watch the explosion and I told him he could, as long as he kept his distance. I don't see how he could have been harmed that far from the site of the explosion.'

'Perhaps he was thrown there by the force of the blast?' Maud suggested.

'That can't be the case, as others were standing closer to the hole.'

'You saw where Mr Watson was standing?'

'I made sure everyone was safe before I lit the fuse on the dynamite.' The laird glanced again towards the man's body. 'Watson was standing in almost that exact spot.'

'It's Mr X again,' Daisy murmured.

The large door of the castle opened and a gong sounded from within.

'Tea,' said the laird. 'I think we are ready for it.'

Daisy gaped. 'Joseph Watson is *deid* and you talk about tea. Are you mad?'

'Do I appear mad?'

Three pairs of eyes stared at the laird's dirty face. His moustache appeared to be smouldering and his eyes were blazing with excitement.

'Aye, you do,' said Daisy, forgetting all decorum and folding her arms across her chest.

He frowned. 'Well, of course, there are things that need to be done in such a situation, but perhaps we can discuss the matter over a nice cup of tea.'

'Come, Charles,' said Lord Urquhart, 'you are not thinking straight.'

'Tea is ready. Everything else can wait until later.' The laird set off at a lope towards the castle.

'I must apologise on Charles's behalf,' Lord Urquhart said. 'Sometimes the fever of his war experiences returns to him.'

'And what were they?' Maud asked.

'There were a number, I'm afraid. His first was back in 1879; the Battle of Isandlwana. It was the first major conflict in the Anglo-Zulu War. Charles was in his late twenties at the time. Old enough to be able to cope, you might think. But looking out from the stockade, surrounded by twenty thousand warriors, must have been a frightening experience.'

'Father mentioned something to me once about less than two thousand British soldiers holding out against the great Zulu nation.'

'That's the very battle I'm referring to, I'm afraid.'

'Oh my goodness,' said Maud. 'The laird was there?'

'He was.'

'But father said only five hundred British troops survived.'

'Serves the British right for starting it,' said Daisy darkly.

Lord Urquhart inclined his head in agreement. 'Unfortunately, Miss Cameron, it didn't go well for the Zulu nation afterwards. The British Army took a much more aggressive approach in the war and it resulted in the destruction of King Cetshwayo's hopes of a negotiated peace.'

Daisy huffed. 'I'll see what can be done about the remains of Joseph Watson,' she said and walked away.

'Charles Farquharson is not a bad man,' Lord Urquhart said to Maud, 'but he is sometimes troubled.'

'I would have thought he would dislike explosions after his war experiences,' Maud responded.

'You would think so, but we are all different. It has made him determined to carry out his plans, whatever they are, as who knows what the future may bring?'

Did that mean the laird *was* Mr X? Maud wondered. The afternoon was wearing on and the sun low in the sky. She looked about her again at the clods of earth and the stones deposited over the grass, and at the covered mound of Joseph Watson. She looked back at the laird as he disappeared through the open door into the castle. He didn't *appear* to have the brains to be Mr X.

'I think he's a little upset, too, by the death of John Noble,' Lord Urquhart added, breaking into Maud's thoughts.

She turned her head to look up at Lord Urquhart. 'The laird knew Mr Noble?'

'Yes, he did.'

'Did they know each other well?'

'Oh yes. Don't you know? John Noble was Charles's soldier-servant during the war.'

THIRTEEN

The conversation over dinner that evening was naturally concerned with the shocking death of Joseph Watson. Alasdair was at a loss to explain how such a thing could have happened, as the laird was certain Watson was standing at a safe distance from the explosion. 'His poor family,' murmured Clara. Susan sat wide-eyed throughout the talk.

Realising she and Daisy were learning nothing new, Maud casually asked Alasdair as soon as she was able to if all the laird's house guests were still there or if they had returned home.

'All have departed for home,' Alasdair told her. 'All apart from Lord Urquhart, that is.'

'Is that why you asked, Maud?' Clara said with a small smile. 'He is a very pleasant young man.'

'Not at all.' Maud couldn't stop a slight warmth come to her cheeks and was grateful that the flickering light of the oil lamps would hide her embarrassment. 'I knew Lord Urquhart had not yet left. I asked Alasdair because I hadn't noticed anyone from the shooting party, save his lordship, in Captain Farquharson's garden this afternoon.'

Daisy helped herself to a second portion of roast pheasant. 'Who were the loaders on the shoot, Alasdair?'

'That's not an easy question to answer, I'm afraid. All the guns had their own men...' Alasdair paused and shot a quick look at Susan, who appeared to have lost interest in the conversation once the topic of the explosion had been exhausted.

He returned his steady gaze to Daisy. She held it for a moment, and an unspoken understanding passed between the four adults; Alasdair clearly had more to say when Susan was not in earshot.

It was not possible to speak to Mr Affleck, thought Maud, but he was not high on their list of suspects as he had no connection with the choir. On the other hand, it seemed that an interview with at least one of the loaders, if not all of them, might well be profitable.

When the meal was over, Clara rose. 'Coffee in the sitting room,' she told them.

The others got to their feet. Clara took Susan's arm and began to chat to her, determinedly leading her out of the dining room. Maud and Daisy lingered until they had gone. Quickly and quietly Daisy closed the door.

'Well?' she said to Alasdair. 'What have you got to tell us?'

'It's a funny thing...' Alasdair looked uncomfortable and not at all amused.

'Aye?' prompted Daisy.

'Well, the truth is, Mrs Rankin's loader seems to have... disappeared.'

Maud drew in a sharp breath. 'Disappeared?'

'And you didna think to tell us before?' demanded Daisy.

'Really, Daisy, give me some credit. I've only recently learned this. The laird mentioned it in passing over tea this afternoon. Clearly he didn't think it was important, and I'm afraid its significance has only just occurred to me now.'

'Who was Jane Rankin's usual loader?' Maud asked.

'I don't know. The guns usually bring their own loaders. If a guest arrived without one, the gamekeeper would ask one of his men to act as loader. When Mrs Rankin joined a shoot, she always brought her own man. It would be someone from the town and the laird himself paid the fellow as Mrs Rankin was' – Alasdair cleared his throat and looked embarrassed – 'more often than not short of funds. It was rarely the same loader who came, as she could be a little impolite—'

'Crabbit,' amended Daisy.

'Quite.' Alasdair went on with barely a pause, 'As a result, no one took any notice of her loader. It was when I asked Gillespie for the fellow's name to arrange to pay him that I discovered there is no one in town called Chi Smith.'

'Chi?' Daisy wrinkled her nose.

'I assumed it was an abbreviation of Christopher.'

And you are right, Alasdair, Maud thought. Thanking him for the information, she encouraged him to join his family in the sitting room and took hold of Daisy's sleeve before she could follow.

'It's Mr X again,' Maud whispered.

'I've nae doubt it is.'

'Daisy, it's the name – Christopher. In Greek, the language of the New Testament, the word *Christo* or *Christ* begins with the letter *x*, which is pronounced *chi*.'

Daisy's eyes widened. 'Our killer isna exactly the modest type. If this hunch of yours is right, he must be fairly well educated as well.'

'Indeed,' Maud said dryly. 'And now we know that X was at the shoot and standing immediately behind Jane.'

'Which means he canna be the laird.' Daisy sounded disappointed.

'I suppose it also means he's *Mr* X, after all,' Maud said slowly.

'Nae necessarily.' Daisy brightened. 'X could be a woman, dressed as a man, just like we were.'

'You're right, my friend. So we are looking for a man, or a woman dressed as a man.'

'Maybe she only dressed like a man on that one occasion,' Daisy added.

'I'm not sure I can believe that, Daisy. Think how long it took us to get a manly swagger in our walk.'

'I think you're talking about yourself, Maud McIntyre,' Daisy said with a grin. 'I don't remember having any trouble at all.'

The following morning Maud came downstairs to find Daisy finishing a bowl of porridge.

'The next clue,' Daisy said, gesturing with her spoon to the now-familiar square envelope which lay on Maud's side plate.

Still feeling subdued by the events of yesterday, Maud slid into her seat and poured herself a cup of tea. 'Open it, Daisy, and let us know the worst.' She handed her the note.

Daisy dropped her spoon into the empty bowl, ripped open the small white envelope and pulled out a single sheet of paper.

'Here we go again,' she said. 'Pencils and paper...'

Over the top of her teacup, Maud sent her a severe look. 'Just read it out. We've really got to solve this one in time, Daisy.'

'I ken, Maud.' Chastened, Daisy cleared her throat.

> *Do they like to eat wild food*
> *Where angels gather in the wood,*
> *Destroying the peacefulness that's there?*
> *Will they then become aware*
> *That if they start to feel unwell,*
> *There's no one near for them to tell?*

X.

'It's another conundrum,' Maud said, as she took the note and read it for herself. 'It's on the same good quality notepaper. Perhaps this clue won't be as misleading as the last one.' Maud couldn't keep the doubt from her voice.

'It sounds more difficult to me.' Daisy nodded at the paper in Maud's hand.

'Let's get down to it, take it bit by bit.'

Maud quickly finished her tea and Daisy set aside her bowl. Moving their chairs closer to one another, they put their heads together. The rhyme passed from Daisy's hand to Maud's and back again more times than they cared to count. The tall clock in the hall struck the quarter hour. When it struck the half hour, they were still struggling with the verse.

'You ken, it's this angels business that's hard,' declared Daisy for the tenth time. '*Where angels gather in the wood.*'

'I have a feeling that if we could just solve that line, it would all become clear,' Maud agreed.

'Whoever heard of angels gathering in a wood?' Daisy said scornfully. 'Everyone kens they live in heaven.'

'The Archangel Gabriel came down from heaven...'

'Aye, but nae in Fort William.'

Maud sighed. 'What about a church?' she asked suddenly.

Daisy wrinkled her brow. 'A church in the middle of a wood?'

'Forget the wood for a moment, Daisy. Let's focus on angels and where they might be.'

'A monument in a burial ground.'

'That's a start,' Maud said, imagining an ornate column of stone with an angel carved at the top. Was there such a gravestone in or near the town?

'Inside a church,' went on Daisy.

'There will certainly be an angel featured in a stained-glass window.'

'It's an idea when we havena got any good ones.' Daisy slumped back in her chair.

'Although I'm not sure about this third line: *Destroying the peacefulness that's there*. Whatever could that mean?'

'The kirk is always a peaceful place, but if an angel came down it would cause a bit of a stushie, right enough,' Daisy said.

'And what about the connection with the victim starting to feel unwell?'

'I suppose a visitor from above might make a few people start to feel a wee bit peely-wally.'

'That's not very helpful, Daisy,' Maud said with a smile. 'But I take your point. The church idea doesn't sound very probable, after all. Perhaps, though, the graveyard...'

'I'm keeping an open mind. You ken me, open-minded to a fault.' Daisy grinned. She poured out another cup of tea for Maud. 'Drink this. It'll perk you up.'

'At this rate we'll be here until luncheon without solving the clue.' Maud took a sip of her second cup and found the tea had cooled. 'Let's leave the puzzle for a bit and go for a walk to clear our heads.'

'A walk?' Daisy shuddered. 'I dinna feel *that* scunnered.'

Maud's thoughts were going round and round, much like the wheels of a bicycle. She left Daisy with a notebook and pencil, trying to work out the clue in front of the fire in Daisy's bedroom. As she pulled on her coat, hat and gloves in the hall, Maud heard a deep sigh and looked down to see the Ross's yellow Labrador sitting at her feet and watching her closely.

'Would you like to come with me for a walk, Ellie?' she asked.

The dog wagged her tail hard.

'I take it that means yes?' Maud laughed. 'Very well, let me tell Netta and then we'll go. You wait here.'

She found the maid dusting in the dining room.

'I'm sure Mrs Ross won't mind at all, Miss McIntyre,' Netta said, pausing in her work. 'Mr Ross is visiting a grain supplier in Inverness, so he couldn't take Ellie to work with him today. The dog's leash is hanging on the hall stand.'

Maud returned to the hall where the dog waited patiently. She took the leash from its hook, and she and the dog went out into the crisp morning air.

'We'll take the lane to the banks of Loch Linnhe, if that suits you?' she said cheerfully to Ellie.

The dog looked perfectly happy with the decision and they set off. Maud wasn't sure how well-behaved Ellie was around sheep, so she kept an eye out. There were no sheep in the fields, so she let the Labrador run ahead. Before long the dog's nose was to the ground, following a scent or two, hoping to sniff out a rabbit. There was a pale sun but a chill in the air, so Maud kept up a smart pace to keep warm.

The loch was a melancholy place in the winter: the silence, the bare trees clinging to the top of the banks. A patch of grass – green in the winter landscape – sloped down to the dull grey surface of the water. Maud was the only person there. According to her wristwatch, the walk had taken her twenty-five minutes. Add on another five minutes for the laird's house and it would have taken Emily Black half an hour to reach the loch, confirming what Mrs Wilson the housekeeper had said. Maud looked about the bank for any signs of a struggle, such as snapped branches. There were none she could see.

She gazed at the water for a time, trying to imagine what might have happened to Emily on that fateful day. Did she meet her lover here? Did they argue, and did she fall? Or was she pushed? Did he – Mr X, Maud supposed – keep their assignation with the specific intention of drowning her? Given the poems alerting her and Daisy to the later murders, there had been a great deal of premeditation by Mr X. Unless, of course,

Emily's secret lover was not Mr X but a different person entirely. And John Noble. Where would he fit in if Jane Rankin and Joseph Watson were murdered to put the police off X's trail?

Maud let out a sigh that hung in the clear air. There were too many unknowns. She pulled her woollen coat more tightly around her, her thoughts buzzing as she continued to gaze at the cold dark water.

It was impressive to think that Loch Linnhe was one of a string of major lochs in the Great Glen, which stretched from Fort William to Inverness. At the other end of the glen to Loch Linnhe was Loch Ness, the longest, deepest and most famous of all the lochs. Maud's thoughts went back to the *each-uisge*. St Columba was said to have seen a large beast appear from the depths of the water to attack a man who was swimming there. The saint raised his hand and in the name of God commanded the monster to return to the loch. It obligingly did so; but over the centuries there had been folk who swore they had seen the beast. Maud could at least be certain that Emily Black hadn't been taken by the water horse. Which was just as well, because that would present a case that no one would be able to solve. Anyone claiming to have seen such a beast was no doubt blootered, as Daisy would say, Maud thought with a smile.

She turned and picked her way gingerly up from the bank and along the frosty path, twigs snapping under her boots.

'Ellie!' she called, and they set off back to Clara's, the dog trotting beside her.

Maud let them both into the house through the back door. Before she could stop Ellie, the Labrador had nosed the kitchen door open and disappeared into the hall.

Maud hastened to remove her muddy boots on the doormat and dashed after the dog into the sitting room, where she found Clara seated by the fire and reading *Milady's Boudoir*. Clara looked up from her magazine as Ellie slumped in, dirty and tired.

'Look at you,' exclaimed Clara, staring at the dog, 'covered in clarts! Where on earth have you been?'

Maud followed her gaze to the lumps of mud clinging to the dog's legs and undercarriage. 'I'm so sorry...' she began.

Clara smiled at her. 'Dinna worry. You've saved one of us having to walk Ellie, and she's obviously had a braw time.'

The dog wagged her tail and flopped down on her blanket in the corner of the room. She stretched out and closed her eyes. Her tail thumped on the rug and within seconds she was snoring.

Maud glanced at her wristwatch. Over an hour had gone by since she'd left the house. 'Would you mind if I joined Daisy upstairs, Clara? We're in the middle of working on a new clue.'

A shadow passed over Clara's face, but she said, 'Just let me know if you need anything.'

Maud removed her coat, gloves and hat, and hung up the leash. In her stockinged feet, she raced upstairs and entered Daisy's bedroom. The fire was burning low and Daisy was napping in an armchair.

'Wake up, Daisy,' Maud said gently. 'The cold air has cleared my head and I'm ready to throw myself back into the clue with renewed vigour.'

Daisy stirred, groaned and levered herself to a sitting position. 'I was just resting my eyes.'

'I know you were.' Maud took the seat opposite her friend and picked up the notepad and pencil which had fallen to the floor. 'First line, Daisy. *Do they like to eat wild food?* Wild food.'

'Eating what you can gather?'

'What sort of thing would that be?'

Daisy thought for a moment. 'Flowers, fruit, leaves, nuts, seeds.' She pulled a face and groaned as she stretched her limbs.

'What can you forage for in November?' Maud persevered.

'The days are getting shorter and the weather colder, but it might still be possible to find nuts and berries. Bullace plums in hedgerows, perhaps...'

'I ken the cook at your faither's place used those plums to make braw jams and wine,' put in Daisy, 'but I dinna think they grow in the Highlands.'

'Hmm, you're probably right. What else?'

'Pines?' Daisy hazarded a guess. 'Canna the needles be used to make tea?' She grimaced. 'Though why anyone would want to is beyond me.'

'And pine seeds can be eaten raw or roasted,' Maud continued, ignoring Daisy's comical facial expression. 'I seem to remember my governess saying sweet chestnut trees were introduced to Britain by the Romans and have been an autumn and early winter favourite ever since. Father has quite a few of them on the estate.'

'Och, aye, a muckle favourite.' Daisy nodded without enthusiasm. 'They can be baked, roasted or boiled.'

'I also remember my governess saying it was important to cut a cross in them, otherwise they explode when cooked.'

'Well, if we come across any, we'll be sure to mark them with a cross,' Daisy said dryly. 'We've had enough of explosions for the time being.'

'We don't have to eat the wild food mentioned in the rhyme,' Maud reminded her. 'It's simply part of the clue.'

'Aye, so it is. We're nae getting on very fast. What's the second line again?'

'We're back to angels in the woods.'

'Wait a minute!' Daisy's face lit up. *'Where angels gather in the wood.* It doesna mean where angels get together to sing or whatever it is angels usually do in groups.'

'What then?' demanded Maud. 'You think he's alluding to carvings on kirk pews?'

'Nae, I dinna. Food is nae allowed in the kirk. I think it

means there's a clearing in the trees where things grow like nettles or what have you.'

'We'd have no chance of ever finding the right woods and the right clearing, though. And anyway, Daisy, why would the victim go there with Mr X?'

'For a picnic?'

'In November?'

'Well...'

Maud stared at her friend. A clearing in the woods where edible plants grow. 'You may be right, Daisy.'

Daisy beamed. 'That nap did me good.'

'Where do angels gather their wild food?'

Daisy's face fell. 'I thought you said it was a good idea.'

'It was. It *is*,' Maud said firmly. 'We are another step closer to solving the clue. Let's deal with the next line. *Destroying the peacefulness that's there.* Where is the nearest peaceful wood?'

'I'm guessing all woods are peaceful,' said Daisy, 'but the nearest one? We'd have to ask Clara or Alasdair.'

'Glen Nevis must be the closest forest. Note that down, Daisy.'

Turning to a fresh page in her notebook, Daisy began to write.

'Foraging by angels in Glen Nevis,' she read out, before looking at Maud and raising her eyebrows. 'It sounds like a book title.'

Maud ploughed on. 'Now let's consider the final part, about starting to feel unwell. *Will they then become aware That if they start to feel unwell, There's no one near for them to tell?*'

'A sweet chestnut that didn't agree with the angel?' suggested Daisy.

Maud stared at her. 'That's it!' She threw her friend a huge smile. 'Oh well done, Daisy! The angel – that is, the next victim – will be poisoned.'

'Poison!' exclaimed Daisy, getting to her feet. 'What gowps we were not to think of it earlier!'

'Something only seems obvious when you know the answer. You may as well sit down again, Daisy. The murder—'

'*Attempted* murder,' cut in Daisy. 'We're going to stop it happening this time.'

'As it's not due to take place until Friday and today is Tuesday, we have three days yet.'

'Three days? How are we supposed to find where angels gather in just three days?'

'Since angels don't exist...'

Daisy took in a sharp breath, her eyes wide as she stared at Maud.

'We need to work out where exactly in Glen Nevis this poisoning is to take place,' Maud went on, 'and the type of poison.'

Daisy huffed back down in her seat. 'How on earth are we supposed to find that out? It'll be like looking for a haggis amongst a bunch of rugby balls.'

FOURTEEN

Once again Daisy flipped back to the beginning of her notebook and read aloud as she turned the pages. 'Victims, theories... Och, here we are: prime suspects. One of the guns by accident, one of the guns on purpose...' She looked up at Maud. 'They're the suspects for the shooting.'

'Didn't we narrow it down?'

Daisy returned to her notebook. 'Aye, we had one of the guns on either side of Jane – they were the laird and Mr Affleck, or one of the three loaders.'

'With Alasdair's information, it points to Jane's missing loader being X.'

'I ken it *looks* that way, Maud,' said Daisy slowly, reluctant to give up on her theory, 'but I think it's the laird. I thought so then and I think so now.'

'It's true that he was the one to spot the second victim, Emily Black, and pull her from the loch...'

Daisy sighed. 'But the problem is the first victim. Mr X canna be the laird, as John Noble hadna a connection to him. At least not that we ken of.'

'I have news for you, Daisy. After you went off to see about

Joseph Watson's remains, Lord Urquhart informed me that Mr Noble was Captain Farquharson's soldier-servant in the Anglo-Zulu War.'

'Crivvens! So there's a connection there too then.' Daisy looked pleased.

'Such relationships often develop into long-lasting friendships, I believe, especially as the two men stayed in the same town.' Maud looked at Daisy. 'But as he isn't in the choir, do you really think the laird is about to poison another of their members? And if you do, could you explain to me what reason he might have for wanting to ruin the choir's chances of winning the competition?'

Daisy shrugged. 'No, I canna, but why would any person want to do that?'

'Hmm.' Maud frowned. 'Let's consider the laird. Emily Black worked as one of his housemaids, Jane Rankin was a friend of his and, like Emily, Joseph Watson was employed by him. Mr Watson wasn't a gardener, though, but a forestry worker. It might have been a case of plain bad luck for Mr Watson.'

'That he'd been in the wrong place at the wrong time?' Daisy shook her head. 'The clue warned us there was going to be an explosion. I dinna think the killer would take any chances in getting the wrong victim. Somehow or other, Mr X must have known Joseph Watson would be there. Mind,' she added, 'everyone working for the laird probably kent about how he intended to make that hole. Men are mad about those sorts of things. Motor cars, train engines, explosions and the like.'

'And no doubt Mr Watson had told all the other men in the choir.'

'We could find that out from Lord Urquhart.' Daisy saw the frown on Maud's face and added, 'Only if you think it would help.'

'It may, Daisy, but I think there are more pressing things to attend to first. We need to put the victim's safety at the forefront of our actions right now because the one thing we can be reasonably certain of is that the next victim, the one to be poisoned, will be a soprano.'

Daisy gazed at her. 'If we include John Noble and his heart attack—'

'I think we have to.'

'There's a pattern.'

'I think there—'

'Nae, don't tell me. I see it too. We've had bass, soprano, alto, bass again...'

'Exactly. We are looking for a soprano with the voice of an angel.'

Maud tried to remember who had been described as such. One of the sopranos, undoubtedly, but which one?

'Come on,' Daisy said, hopping with excitement, 'let's visit the sopranos.' She pushed back her chair.

'Daisy,' Maud's voice was soft, 'you realise that one of them is you, and another is your cousin?'

Daisy blinked. 'Aye. I can take care of myself, but Clara...'

'We should start with Clara, then visit Beatrice Noble. There's nothing to suggest Mrs Noble might be a target of Mr X, but I have promised to keep her informed of events. And she's leaving today to visit her sister.'

'I'll let Netta know we won't be back for luncheon,' said Daisy, 'because after we've spoken to Clara and Beatrice, we can eat at Ivy Fraser's tea shop and hopefully get a chance to speak to her there.'

They found Clara working on her scrapbook in the dining room. An assortment of photographs, prettily coloured drawings and various pieces of writing, plus a glue pot, were arranged on the oilcloth covering the table. She looked up from cutting out a picture from a society magazine and gave them a welcoming smile.

Daisy immediately crossed to where her cousin sat and looked over her shoulder. 'Lily Elsie.' Daisy sighed. 'She's beautiful.'

Maud glanced at the picture. The English singer and actress gazed dreamily into the distance. Yes, the woman was beautiful, thought Maud, but she was not the reason they were here to speak to Clara.

Clara gestured to a letter lying amongst the other items. 'I've heard from the Cambus o'May choir and all is well with them too.'

'Dinna tell me you're going to put that letter in your scrap-book!' Daisy said, straightening.

Clara laughed. 'Of course not. But I will include the news-paper article when you and Maud have solved the crime.'

'The letter you've received confirms our need to focus on the Fort William singers,' Maud told her.

Daisy added, 'And we've come to tell you we've worked out that the next victim will be a soprano.'

Clara dropped the scissors onto the table. 'Oh... Do you ken which one?'

Maud shook her head. 'I'm afraid not.'

'But we think it's one who sings like an angel,' put in Daisy.

Clara managed a shaky laugh. 'Well, that's me out then.'

'Are you sure you dinna want to change your mind about our Edinburgh flat?' Daisy asked anxiously.

'I'm staying here.' Clara's voice was firm. She picked up the scissors again and began to trim the edges of Lily Elsie's portrait. 'Now, off you go and find the killer.'

'It willna happen until Friday afternoon,' Daisy said, 'so all the sopranos are safe until then.'

Beatrice Noble was working in her front garden when Maud and Daisy arrived. Her slight figure was muffled in a large woollen coat that had seen better days, and on her head she wore a straw hat secured against the chilly breeze with a scarf. She straightened from moving one of the flower pots by the door of her cottage and looked with surprise at them as they climbed off their bicycles and wheeled them up the hedge-lined path.

'Maud and Daisy, our two new recruits!' she exclaimed. 'What a pleasant surprise. And you are just in time to catch me. I can only give you ten minutes, I'm afraid.' She looked down at her muddied shoes. 'I need to get cleaned and changed, and I will be leaving after a quick luncheon.'

'We're sorry to interrupt your work.' Maud indicated the two large terracotta pots with attractive markings.

Beatrice followed her gaze. 'I'm rather fond of these pots, but they are not frost-proof and so I must store them in the greenhouse over winter. Not that my dahlias would appreciate being left outside either! I've moved two of the pots and when spring returns all I need to do is bring them back outside, water and fertilise them, and they will bloom again!' She smiled. 'Isn't nature wonderful?'

'Aye,' said Daisy without enthusiasm.

'But the weather can change so quickly here,' went on Beatrice. 'Winter comes upon us all of a sudden. One must take the necessary action.'

She suddenly seemed to recollect her manners. 'But you didn't come here to talk about gardening, I am sure. Would you like to come in?'

'Yes, thank you,' said Maud.

She and Daisy leaned their bicycles against the house wall, as Beatrice peeled off her gardening gloves. She lifted the latch on the door and led them into the cottage.

Pausing in the tiny dark hall, she turned to them. 'Would you mind if we went into the kitchen? It's not where I would normally entertain visitors, you understand, but needs must.'

'Of course,' said Maud.

They moved through to the kitchen at the back of the house, which smelled of stale cooking. Beatrice untied the scarf and removed her hat. In the poor light her face looked almost as grey as her hair.

The room faced west and they stood there looking out upon a rather gloomy wooded landscape. A thin plume of smoke rose from a small bonfire of leaves, adding to the dreariness of the scene. But the room was clean and tidy, with a dresser displaying crockery on its shelves, a black cast-iron range at the far end, and in the centre of the room was a wooden table with two chairs.

Beatrice dropped her hat and scarf onto the dresser. Her eye fell on a book placed on the table. She crossed the room, lifted her crochet work from one of the chairs and placed it on top of the volume. Her manner appeared casual, but Maud wasn't so sure. The book was covered and it was impossible to see the title.

'You find me quite unprepared for visitors,' Beatrice said with a smile.

She sat, bent forward and unlaced her muddy gardening shoes. By the side of her chair sat a pair of felt slippers, each with a pom-pom on top, and these she drew on. All the while, Maud and Daisy stood, feeling slightly uncomfortable.

Beatrice rose and sent them an enquiring look. 'Have you come to let me know how your investigation is progressing?' She crossed to the deep sink, turned on the tap and began to wash her hands.

Maud had no intention of informing her of what they had learned or even suspected, other than to pass on the warning. 'We are afraid that there may be another death.'

'Another death?' Beatrice's shoulders tensed. 'Have we not suffered enough?'

'Dinna worry, Beatrice,' Daisy put in. 'We *will* prevent this one happening.'

'Thank goodness!' she said over her shoulder. 'But how will you do that?'

'That's for us to deal with,' Daisy told her.

'I only hope that you can. So you really think these deaths are related in some way, that they are not accidental?' She dried her hands and turned to face them.

'We at the M. McIntyre Agency dinna believe in coincidence when it comes to death,' Daisy said, pride shining in her face.

'But who do you suspect is causing these deaths?'

'It's better that we dinna name names at this stage,' went on Daisy.

'Yes, of course. I can see that it must be a delicate matter,' Beatrice said.

'We think that the killer intends to target another of the sopranos,' Maud said, picking up the conversation, 'which means you may be in danger.'

'*Me?* But why would anyone want to kill me?'

'There seems to be little reason as to why anyone would want to kill any member of the choir. At least not one we have found to be feasible.'

'So you *do* have an idea?'

'Not one I'd wish to reveal at present. But we wanted you to know that you need to take care, especially as you live alone.' As soon as she had spoken, Maud realised this was a little insensitive, so soon after Mr Noble's demise, but it had to be said if Beatrice was to understand the severity of the situation.

'With three unexplained deaths in quick succession' – Maud chose not to include John Noble while speaking to his widow – 'I think we would be wise to tell everyone in the choir that these were not accidents.'

'Oh,' said Beatrice, the colour draining from her face. 'I won't be here for the next few days. I expect you'll tell the others what you've told me.'

'We'll be visiting Ivy Fraser shortly, then Maggie and Mrs Wilson at the castle, as any one of them could be the next victim.'

'Or Daisy or sweet Clara... Oh dear.' Beatrice wrung her hands.

Daisy lifted her chin. 'Dinna worry about me or my cousin. There's enough of us in the house to put off any murderer.'

Beatrice gave Daisy and then Maud a keen look. 'When do you think the killer will strike again?'

Out of the corner of her eye, Maud saw Daisy open her mouth, doubtless to say 'Friday.' Maud wished not to reveal too much to anyone else. Quickly she said, 'We can't be sure, but I promise we will be ready.'

'Well' – Beatrice gave a nervous little laugh – 'I hope you will look after my choir ladies while I am away.' She made it clear their visit was at an end.

'Remember, ladies, to keep practising your parts. *I love a lassie, a bonnie bonnie lassie,*' Beatrice trilled, 'and *By yon bonnie banks and by yon bonnie braes.*' She sighed as she ushered them through the hall. 'Such a sad and beautiful song. I will see you on Thursday. *Chi mi thu ma bhios sinn beo.*'

If I am spared. Maud remembered Ivy translating this Gaelic saying of Beatrice's.

'Now to Ivy Fraser's tea shop,' said Daisy, as the door of the cottage closed behind them. 'I'm ready for luncheon.'

Maud smiled. 'I don't know how anyone as petite as you, Daisy, can eat as you do and stay the same.'

'It's just my bad luck.' Daisy shook her head as they walked down the path. 'Nae matter how much I eat, I never grow any taller.'

Maud laughed. 'Perhaps Ivy Fraser will have a cake like the one Alice ate in Wonderland, with the words *Eat Me* marked out in currants.'

'In that case' – Daisy grinned, taking hold of her bicycle – 'lead on, Macduff.'

'Lay on.'

'Pardon?'

'The quote is actually "Lay on, Macduff".'

Daisy frowned. 'What's that supposed to mean?'

'It's what Macbeth says to his enemy Macduff when they confront one another for the last time. Macduff challenges Macbeth to yield and he refuses. "Lay on, Macduff" means to go on and strike.'

'Then lay on, Mr X!' declared Daisy.

'I hope not, Daisy, for our sakes.'

'Why?'

'Because Macbeth is then *killed* by Macduff.'

'That Macbeth sounds like a bit of a daftie.'

'It's complicated.' Maud mounted her bicycle. 'But you're right in that the net around Mr X is surely tightening.'

Although who exactly they would catch, Maud still didn't know.

FIFTEEN

A fifteen-minute bicycle ride brought Maud and Daisy to the High Street and Ivy Fraser's tea shop, Bide-A-While. They parked their machines in a side road and walked back, peered through the tea shop window and saw there was one table vacant.

'Quickly, Maud,' said Daisy, 'before anyone else can take it.'

She pushed open the door, darted in, caught the waitress's eye and nodded at the table, all before Maud could tell her it was a good idea. She joined her friend and they perused the light luncheon menu.

'Curried eggs for me,' declared Daisy. 'The food is good at Clara's, but there's nae much real taste to it for my liking. I need something a wee bit spicier.'

'I know what you mean, Daisy. I think I'll have the same.'

They placed their order, along with a glass of water each should the curry prove hotter than was comfortable.

'With two cups of tea to follow, please,' Maud added to the waitress.

'Did you see how Beatrice Noble lifted those garden pots?'

said Daisy, when the waitress had gone. 'They were full of earth and whatever else goes into the things.'

'Compost, bulbs...'

'Aye, those. Well, they must have been awfa heavy. To be honest, I wouldna have thought she was that strong.'

'She certainly doesn't look it.' Maud stared at Daisy, who seemed to be waiting for her to work out what she meant. 'Are you thinking about what we said regarding strength being required by Mr X?'

Daisy nodded.

'That was when we assumed muscle must have been needed to bring about an explosion. Now we know that wasn't necessary because a stick of dynamite is not a heavy item to carry, or to throw.'

'I'm thinking that's what happened with poor Joseph Watson. Mr X was hiding somewhere and when he saw his victim standing alone, he flung the stick and dunted half of Joseph's heid off.'

'It's the only plausible explanation.'

'Here comes our luncheon.' Daisy looked up eagerly as the waitress returned bearing a laden tray.

Two plates of hard-boiled eggs in a spicy sauce on a bed of rice were set before them on the table. Maud looked at her meal and tried not to think of Joseph Watson's head. She took a quick gulp of water, picked up her cutlery and began to eat.

'Mmm,' said Daisy, 'this is good.'

Maud nodded and took another gulp of water.

'What's the matter, Maud? Is it too hot for you?'

'Just a little,' Maud lied and managed another forkful.

'Anyway,' Daisy continued, 'even if strength isna a require-ment for the murderer, we can't rule out Beatrice.'

Maud put down her knife and fork on her plate with a clat-ter. 'Daisy, I believe you have shone a light on our investigation.'

Daisy frowned. 'I dinna really think Beatrice Noble is our killer, but—'

'I'm not suggesting that because Beatrice can move big pots around her garden that it's got to be her. But, Daisy, we've been blind. We briefly considered that Jane Rankin's loader might have been a woman dressed as a man, but mainly we've been working on the assumption that X is *Mr* X. Why could it not be Mrs or Miss X?'

'You mean a wifie?'

'I do indeed mean a female.'

Daisy put another forkful of egg, sauce and rice into her mouth and chewed with a satisfied smile on her face.

'Clara told us that Emily Black was not a tall young woman,' Maud continued. 'It wouldn't have taken a lot of force to push her into the water.'

'Especially if she hadna been expecting it,' Daisy managed to say through her mouthful.

Maud nodded. 'Jane Rankin was shot, so again no special strength was required, apart from dealing with the recoil from the gun as it was fired. Joseph Watson we've just discussed.'

'And John Noble died of a heart attack, maybe caused by a fricht, so nae muscle needed there either.'

Maud resumed her meal. 'Another step forward, my friend.'

'Although we've now got *more* suspects than we had five minutes ago.'

'Exactly! We have widened the net' – Maud paused – 'if only we could be sure of the motive.'

'It's got to be the competition final,' Daisy said. 'X wants to stop the choir winning. It canna be anything else.'

'I'm inclined to agree, but why does he – or *she* – want to prevent them winning?'

Daisy puffed out her lips. 'It keeps coming back to this.'

'It does. We must think hard, Daisy. Why does X feel so strongly about the matter that he is prepared to risk hanging?

For that is what will happen when we solve this case and the court finds him guilty.'

'Something happened in the choir that really upset him,' Daisy mused, 'really, *really* upset him.'

'Yes...'

'What if,' Daisy exclaimed suddenly, 'Mr X wanted some sculdudrie with Beatrice, but she wasna having any of it and threw him out the choir?'

'Hmm. We haven't considered that possibility...'

Daisy beamed.

'But would he kill so many for such a reason?'

Daisy shrugged. 'We ken he's off his heid.'

'Not a very helpful observation, my friend, but we will bear it in mind.' Maud continued to ponder the matter aloud. 'I feel sure the killer is one of the choir; the fact that the clues are presented to us in rhyme is a clue in itself. And it must be relevant that he is choosing one from each voice section in turn.'

'And he's started working through them again. When there's only one choir member left, we'll ken who he is.'

They ate without speaking for a while, to the sound of cutlery on plates and the other diners chatting around them.

After a while, Daisy said, 'X must be a man, if he got Emily up the spout.'

Maud gave a start, but ignored Daisy's idiom. 'You are right again!'

Daisy looked puzzled. 'Everybody kens only a man and a woman can make a bairn, Maud.'

'Yes, but we have been assuming that Miss Black was with child simply because of a malicious comment made by Jane Rankin. We've heard nothing to say that was actually the case.'

'But we do ken that she was walking out with a fellow.'

'I think we can assume that is true. The laird's housekeeper, Mrs Wilson, told me that Emily went out every Sunday afternoon in her prettiest blouse to meet her young man. The question is: who is he? Why hasn't he come forward and expressed his grief at her death, which is what you would expect?'

'Because he was the one who pushed her in the loch?'

'It certainly looks that way. So the next question is: what sort of a man are we looking at here?'

'A deil who was already married!' Daisy exclaimed.

A devil indeed, Maud thought.

The startled waitress, who had just appeared with a tray, almost spilled their cups of tea as she placed them on the table.

'Thank you,' said Maud. 'Is Mrs Fraser here?'

'Yes, miss,' the girl whispered, 'but I'm very sorry your tea nearly ended up in your saucer. Please don't make a complaint about me.'

'Goodness, no,' Maud said with a smile to reassure her. 'My friend and I are acquainted with Mrs Fraser and would just like to have a quick word with her, if that is possible.'

Not entirely convinced, the girl loaded the tray with their empty plates, and went off towards the kitchen. Maud and Daisy sipped their tea while they waited, and before long Ivy Fraser came bustling across to their table. She had as plump a figure as Maud felt those who ran a tea shop should possess, was cheerful-looking, wore her black curls pinned in a cottage loaf pompadour and smelled like the sweet concoctions she sold.

'Miss McIntyre and Miss Cameron, how pleasant to see you at my little establishment.'

'We thought we would ask for you while we were here,' Maud said. 'Do you have time for a little chat?'

'Of course.' Ivy Fraser drew out the third chair at their table and sat down. 'Was there anything you particularly wanted to talk about?'

'You know that we are private detectives,' Maud began, her voice low, 'and that there have been a number of... let us say *unusual*... deaths over the last fortnight or so?'

'With poor Joseph Watson's only yesterday.' Ivy Fraser gave a sad shake of her head. 'I can't believe he's no longer with us.'

'This is a difficult thing to have to tell you,' Maud continued, 'but my assistant and I believe that one of the sopranos may be targeted next.'

Ivy wrinkled her brow. 'Targeted? You mean the deaths are not accidental?'

Maud took a silent breath. How could anyone still think that? 'That is correct, Mrs Fraser.'

'Does the constable know?'

'He doesn't believe the deaths are unusual, not yet at least, but we have reason to think there will be another, and that the next victim might be poisoned.'

Ivy gave a start. 'Poison?' she whispered. 'Poison? Are you suggesting—'

'No, Mrs Fraser, we are not. Nothing of the sort.'

Her generous bosom rose and fell beneath her high-necked blouse. 'If you even mention the word poison to anyone here, that would be the end of my position at Bide-A-While.'

'Your position here, Mrs Fraser?' Maud said. 'I was under the impression it was your own business.'

'Och, no. I don't own it. I just run the establishment on behalf of the owner.'

'And who is the owner?'

'I thought you knew. It's Captain Farquharson.'

Daisy drew in such an audible breath that Ivy Fraser turned to look at her. 'Is that a problem?' she asked.

'Not at all,' Maud hastened to tell Ivy. 'It's not a problem.'

'Far from it,' murmured Daisy.

Before Ivy Fraser could put two and two together and perhaps start to spread the news that the detective pair thought the laird was a murderer, Maud took her napkin from her lap and placed it on the table.

'You must be very busy, Mrs Fraser, and we have finished

our luncheon, so we should take our leave. But before we go, may I ask if there is a Mr Fraser?'

Ivy puffed out her bosom. 'Of course there is!'

'Then my advice is to make sure you stay with Mr Fraser whenever you're not here in the tea room.'

Ivy scoffed. 'How will that make a difference? He's not exactly Louis Cyr,' she said, referring to the Canadian strongman who could lift a quarter of a ton with one finger.

'Nae matter,' said Daisy, 'he is *your* man.'

'So far,' Maud explained, 'the murderer has killed only members of the choir. As Mr Fraser isn't one, I think he'll be safe. And if he's safe, perhaps you will be too.'

Understanding crossed Ivy Fraser's face. 'I see.'

'Good. Well, we had better be going.' Maud rose, followed by Daisy and Mrs Fraser. 'We must warn others to be vigilant. Thank you for your time – and please remember our warning. Come, Daisy.'

As soon as Maud had paid their bill at the counter and they were back on the street, Maud said to Daisy, 'We must take care. We don't want news to reach the laird's ears that he is one of our suspects.'

'It might make him feart and then he willna kill any others.'

'That would surely be a good thing. Or he might stop sending us clues and then we'll have little chance of exposing him for the murders already committed, and even less chance of preventing any future ones.' Maud took Daisy's elbow and guided her round the corner. 'We'll go to Linnhe Castle next and speak to the last two sopranos on our list.'

They collected their bicycles and set off along the High Street. What with hoots from the occasional motor car, the clip-clopping of horses' hooves, exclamations from cart drivers and shouts from a boy selling hot pies, they were unable to exchange another word on the subject. Once away from the town, however, Daisy drew alongside Maud.

'It does look like the laird is the guilty person though, don't you think, Maud?' Daisy asked as they pedalled.

'There is only one certainty, Daisy.'

'What's that?'

'That nothing is certain.'

Daisy glanced across at Maud. 'That's awfa clever.'

'I can't take the credit. It's a famous quotation. Before you ask, it was Pliny the Elder, a Roman scholar, who said it first. He was killed during the eruption of Vesuvius in 79 AD, although it's not known if he suffocated from the volcanic gases or died of a heart attack.'

'The things you ken,' Daisy said in astonishment.

Maud smiled. 'Let us hope that one day such titbits of information will be useful in an investigation.'

They fell silent as they cycled round the corner and turned into Parade Road.

'Talking about dying of a heart attack,' Daisy said, catching up with Maud again, 'and now we ken that John Noble and the laird were pals of a sort, we should find out if Mr N visited the castle often.'

'I agree.'

Before long they reached the driveway to Linnhe Castle.

'We'll go round to the back door,' said Maud, 'as our business is with the housekeeper and the cook. I know I spoke to Mrs Wilson on the way home from choir practice on Saturday, but we hadn't seen the pattern of deaths then. And I didn't get a chance to speak to Maggie.'

They took the road to the rear of the house and came to a halt by the low door. Maud turned the metal ring and pushed open the door. There was no one about but they could hear talking, so following the voices they made their way along the passage and entered the kitchen.

Maggie and the kitchen girl looked up in surprise from the preparations for the evening meal.

'Och, you did give me a start, coming in like that!' Maggie paused in her stirring of a large saucepan. 'Why have you not used the main entrance? I'm sure the captain would be pleased to welcome you there.'

'Nae doubt, Maggie,' said Daisy, sticking a finger into a bowl on the large central table and scooping out a blob of thick, creamy mixture. The maid, a small, thin girl with colourless hair and large scared eyes, let out a gasp and looked at the cook. Daisy popped the dollop of cream into her mouth. 'But it's you we'd like to have a wee chat with today, Maggie.'

'If you do that again, Daisy Cameron,' the cook said, wiping a hand on her apron, 'I'll skelp you, private detective from the big city or no.'

Daisy laughed and Maggie nodded at the open-mouthed kitchen maid. 'Get into the scullery and prepare the vegetables to go with the rabbit stew.'

As soon as the girl had gone, Maggie balanced the large wooden spoon across the top of the pan she'd been stirring and gave them her attention. With the back of her hand, she brushed a loose strand of brown hair from her flushed forehead. 'I can spare five minutes.'

Once again Maud said that she and Daisy had reason to believe one of the sopranos was likely to be killed – poisoned – by the person who was targeting the choir members. She received a response similar to that made by Ivy Fraser.

'Poisoned? I can't believe it!' said Maggie. 'Why would someone want to do that to any of us?'

'If that were an easy question to answer, we would find ourselves much closer to discovering the killer.' Maud felt a weight settle on her chest.

Maggie seemed to be reconsidering her comment on poison. 'The castle is full of rats, as you can imagine, especially in the kitchen, so they have to be dealt with. But I take great care only to put the strychnine where a few potatoes are stored. As bait, you know. The rats love tatties...'

At that moment a large black cat stalked into the kitchen and jumped up onto the scrubbed table.

'Shoo, you dirty creature!' Maggie went to flick it off with the towel resting on her shoulder, but it was too quick for her and it jumped down, stalked to a patch of sunlight on a rocking chair in the corner of the room and settled there.

Was this the cat that had frightened John Noble to death? Maud wondered.

'For two pins I'd poison that animal,' said the cook, giving it a threatening look. The cat watched her from its cushioned seat. 'It's lazy, hardly stirs itself, at least not in the daytime. I've only ever known one day, not long ago, when it wasn't to be found on that chair.' She sighed. 'I shouldn't complain, I suppose; the creature helps to keep the mice down, right enough. It cornered a rat once and was bitten, so now it gives rats a wide berth, but it's still a good mouser.'

'Poor wee pussy cat,' said Daisy, going over to the animal and stroking it behind an ear, eliciting a purr. 'Did you get injured in the line of duty?'

'You like cats, do you?' asked Maggie.

Daisy stood. 'I dinna mind them.'

'That John Noble hated them.'

Maud and Daisy exchanged glances.

'Did he?' said Maud.

'Personally, I think he was plain scared of them.' Maggie went on as if she hadn't heard Maud. 'Can you believe that? A grown man feared of a cat?' She shrugged.

'How do you know that, Maggie?'

'Why, because when he visited the captain, he would some-times come down here and I'd find him chatting to—'

She stopped, pressing her lips closed.

'Chatting to?' Maud asked encouragingly.

'I shouldn't speak ill of the dead.'

Why not, Maud thought, if they deserve it?

'It canna do him any harm now,' put in Daisy.

Maggie turned back to the stew pot. 'Chatting to the kitchen girl. She's just a scrag-end of a thing. I think it amused him to torment the girl. He liked to watch her go bright red.'

'He doesna sound a pleasant man.'

'He wasn't.' Maggie put the lid on the saucepan with a thump and turned back to them.

Before she could speak further, the housekeeper appeared at the open door.

'I thought I heard your voices,' she said to Maud and Daisy. 'Can I offer you both a cup of tea in my room?'

'That would be most welcome, Mrs Wilson.'

Goodness, thought Maud, she was turning into a tea jenny, but it was an excellent way of making an interview seem like a friendly chat.

SIXTEEN

Maud and Daisy followed Mrs Wilson, the plait of her greying hair tightly pinned to her head. At the end of the passage, she ushered them into her domain. A tiny room with a tidy desk, two small armchairs and a few of Mrs Wilson's personal things: a picture postcard from Inverness, a framed photograph of a young man in soldier's uniform...

The housekeeper followed Maud's gaze. 'My husband. He was killed at Khartoum, when the city fell.'

'I'm so sorry,' Maud said in a soft voice. 'War is such a terrible thing.'

Pray God there would not be war with Germany, she thought. But the threat of war was far from over, that was obvious.

Mrs Wilson gestured for them each to take an armchair and she sat in the wooden chair at her desk. 'I couldn't help but over-hear what Maggie said about John Noble being an unpleasant man. She's right, you know. I believe he was of great help to Captain Farquharson in the war, but I think it's fair to say that here he was not universally liked.'

'Why was that?'

'Some of his opinions were objectionable.'

'Such as?' asked Daisy.

Helen Wilson gave a wry smile. 'Such as matters I suspect you two young ladies would take issue with.'

Daisy raised an enquiring eyebrow.

'Suffragettes,' Mrs Wilson explained. 'He used to complain about the problems that women are causing these days. He'd say it with a laugh, but I am certain he was deadly serious.'

'He's certainly deid,' put in Daisy.

Surely John Noble hadn't been killed for his anti-suffragette opinions? If he had, which she could not believe, wouldn't that mean all the others had been killed for the same reason? That notion was preposterous.

'"Problems caused by women?" I once asked him,' went on Helen Wilson. '"With their antics," he said. "Their marches and so forth. Give the vote to them? Women haven't the minds to know what to do with the vote. Most of them can't even write their own names." Well, you can imagine what I said to that! "Of course women can write their own names. They've been able to since school fees were abolished and they've been given the schooling."'

The housekeeper spoke in such a haughty voice, and with her upturned nose giving her a naturally superior look, Maud had to suppress a smile, although there was nothing amusing about John Noble's views.

'What did he say then?' demanded Daisy.

'He said, "Maybe *you* can write your own name, Mrs Wilson, but you're an exceptional woman."' The housekeeper snorted. 'He was always ready to turn on the charm when it suited him. "Most women haven't the time or inclination to write at all," he told me. "The vote is a bad idea, and it won't happen."'

"What a muckle gowp!' Daisy said in disgust.

Maud was impressed that her assistant had confined herself

to a relatively innocuous term. Daisy must be seething with anger, she thought, because Maud herself was furious to hear such an ill-informed speech.

A soft tap on the door announced the arrival of the kitchen girl carrying a large tray with their tea things. As soon as she had set it down and scurried from the room, Helen Wilson went on.

'When I told John Noble we are equal and that women should have the same rights as men, he scoffed. "Equal? I don't think so."'

'I have to agree with him there,' Maud said. 'In my experience, women are *superior* to men.'

The housekeeper smiled. 'He was quite a short man and you know what they say about short men.'

Daisy opened her mouth. 'That their—'

'No,' said Mrs Wilson, blushing deeply. 'I meant that they have a chip on their shoulder.'

Maud felt herself flush too. She wasn't certain what Daisy had been referring to but felt it best not to ask. 'That explains why we've heard people talk of poor Emily, Jane and Joseph, but never poor John,' she said. 'No one liked him.'

Mrs Wilson nodded. 'No one likes to speak ill of those who have passed, but I'm afraid sometimes these things have to be said.'

Once they had made their goodbyes, they mounted their bicycles and were back on the road. The hawthorn hedges were cheerful with their crimson fruit, which the birds ate thankfully. The branches of the trees were almost bare and the peak of Ben Nevis glistened with snow. Somehow the changing of the season reminded Maud of the urgency of their investigation.

They drew to a halt outside Clara's house.

'Maud...' said Daisy, dismounting and avoiding Maud's gaze.

Maud climbed off her own bicycle. There was a nip to the afternoon air. Winter was definitely on its way, she thought, as she waited for her friend to speak.

'About the poison,' Daisy began at last, with a glance at the downstairs window where an oil lamp had been lit.

Maud looked at her. 'Yes?'

'Gamekeepers use poison to kill rats.'

'They do.' Her father's gardener used cyanide to control rodents, but there might be a number of different types of poisons for that purpose. 'You think X has access to a gamekeeper's storage of pest-control poisons?'

Daisy nodded.

'Perhaps the laird's gamekeeper, Jamie Gillespie?'

Daisy frowned. 'Or his factor.'

Maud smiled. 'I can't see your cousin's husband as a multiple killer.'

Daisy chewed her bottom lip and now looked at Maud. 'I'm serious, Maud. We need to consider every possibility.'

'Of course, Daisy.' Suddenly alarmed, she added, 'Has anything occurred that you haven't told me?'

Daisy shook her head.

'We will also bear him in mind, but it might be wise *not* to write him on our list.'

'In case he or Clara should find our notes?'

'Aye.'

'But I can't believe Alasdair has anything to do with this case, other than providing hospitality to two detectives. Daisy, think about it. Why would he allow us to stay here, given we can ask all sorts of questions about his whereabouts?'

'Why would a murderer send us clues?'

'To show how clever he is; to pit his wits against ours. There can be no other reason. As to Alasdair, apart from having no motive, when would he have the time? The laird keeps him busy from morn till night.'

'And there's that name again. The laird, Captain Farquharson, who can easily help himself to the estate's rat poison.'

Maud frowned, ruminating on what Daisy had just said. 'Apart from the laird, who else might have access to the estate's store of poison?'

'The cook said the castle was full of rats, so Maggie and all the other servants.'

'Rodents are fairly common in most rural houses,' Maud pointed out.

'But dinna you think the laird's estate would have *more* of the stuff?'

'Hmm. I wonder how much would be required to kill a person, as opposed to a rat?'

Daisy had no answer to Maud's question.

'Tomorrow, Daisy, first thing,' Maud went on, 'we'll visit the public library and see what we can find out about every kind of poison that might be readily available to anyone who wants to purchase or,' she added, remembering the *wild food* part of the rhyme, '*pick* it.'

The following morning, Maud dressed in her lilac wool wrap-over dress, the cream blouse with its high-necked lace collar underneath, and the small amethyst and pearl earrings. Daisy had agreed to accompany Clara to visit an old friend, after Maud had assured her that she could manage to visit the library on her own.

'In fact,' Maud had added, 'one is probably better, as you know how librarians forbid anything other than essential talking.'

'Our talking *would* be essential,' Daisy had said with a grin.

'But I doubt they would see it that way.'

After breakfast Maud set off on foot, feeling rather stylish in a new pale pink hat with a wide white and pink bow she had bought in town the previous afternoon. Clara had told her that she would find the Cameron-Lucy Reading Rooms in Monzie Square, just off the High Street.

'They were gifted to the town in memory of Mrs Cameron-Campbell of Monzie. She was a gey generous woman who donated money to good causes,' Clara had added proudly.

The lane between the factor's house and the town was lined with trees, before the foliage changed into hedgerows of hollies, their berries glowing amongst the glossy leaves in the low wintry sun. Underfoot the lane was rutted from carts travelling up and down, and the ruts had frozen a little in the night. The morning was fresh and crisp, the sounds bright and clear: a robin's song; the soft sigh as a red squirrel jumped from one spruce to another, its branches dancing with the animal's movement.

Maud reached the town and saw the spire of the Free Presbyterian Church pointing towards heaven. Clara had mentioned the building as a landmark to guide Maud towards the reading rooms. She turned into Monzie Square. Dogs lay idly on the doorsteps of cottages, a few children bowled hoops and played games, and bicycles were propped against walls.

The reading rooms were housed in a pleasant stone building. It was not as grand as the public library in Edinburgh, but Maud hadn't expected it to be. Edinburgh was late in having a library, it not being finished and opened until just over twenty years ago, but it had been worth the wait. As with the Cameron-Lucy building in Fort William, another philanthropist, Andrew Carnegie, had donated money to build the city library. The Edinburgh building was designed in the French Renaissance style and looked like pictures Maud had seen of great chateaux in the Loire Valley. *Let there be light* was carved into stonework above the Edinburgh library entrance, and who could argue with that, Maud thought.

Now Maud pushed open one of the large double doors of the Fort William reading rooms and gazed around at the huge bookshelves and the oak card indexes with their brass plaques which were set on tables in the middle of the room. A counter ran round the centre of the room to prevent the public touching the books. The reader had to consult cards in the small drawers to see what books the library had. Once a book was selected, the reader was to approach the desk. An attendant stood behind the counter, charged with bringing the volume to the reader. Maud sighed, thinking of the small library in her father's country house and the pleasure it gave her to be able to browse freely shelf after shelf.

Not knowing the titles of any books on poisons, Maud told the attendant what she was looking for, then she took a seat at one of the tables to wait. A few people were in the room, heads bent over publications, but clearly a Wednesday morning was not a busy time, and the place had a suitably peaceful air.

Maud removed her gloves and placed them and her small bag on the table. Before long, a neat little woman in a black dress with a high collar brought her two slim volumes and set them down carefully on the table in front of Maud.

'This is all we have on poisons, miss,' the attendant whispered, giving her an odd glance before turning to go.

'A moment, please,' Maud whispered back. 'Has anyone asked to consult these books in the last few weeks?'

'Besides yourself? Certainly not.' The look she sent Maud was now distinctly disapproving. 'I think you'll find it's not a common subject for study.'

Maud thanked her, then opened the top volume. The contents were arranged in alphabetical order and she leafed through first to the section marked A.

Arsenic, she read, was a highly poisonous white powder.

Very cheap, had little or no flavour and could be bought from a local chemist or grocer to kill rats and mice. Since 1851 every sale of arsenic had to be recorded. Which meant that if X had bought any, she realised, the details would be entered in a book kept for that purpose.

But that didn't really help their investigation, Maud thought, leaning back in the chair, because any of the residents in this rural town could have a genuine need to control rodents. Besides, as she and Daisy had discussed, the poison could have been taken from another person's supply.

Maud sat forward again to continue her research. What about the other poisonous substances?

Cyanides, like arsenic, were found in natural substances. When sold as a white powder, she read, they could smell like bitter almonds. They were fast-acting, and in large doses their effects could be seen within seconds.

This sounded more promising. Maud scanned the page which detailed the signs of exposure: weakness, confusion, headache, nausea, difficulty breathing, death. That sounded fairly comprehensive. She couldn't immediately think of any cyanide murder cases in Scotland, though, so perhaps this poison wasn't the best option available to the killer. On the other hand, because it hadn't been reported as being used in that way before, it might be *precisely* what X had decided to use.

Maud turned next to the page on strychnine, another form of pest control. In humans it caused frothing at the mouth and muscle spasms, which grew worse until the victim died from suffocation. She knew this had been the poison used by Glaswegian Dr Thomas Neil Cream. He murdered at least eight of his patients, mostly women, in Canada, America and England before finally being convicted and hanged in London in the early 1890s.

The main natural source of strychnine is found in a

plant... Maud sat up straighter – at last, here it was... Oh, a plant that grows in southern Asia and Australia. She sank back into her chair in disappointment. That plant would not be found growing in woods in the western Highlands.

Once again Maud's thoughts returned to the question of *why* X was targeting the choir members. The final of the competition must be relevant. It was also fast approaching. They now had only a little over a week to solve the case.

Daisy seemed to believe there might be a connection between the deaths and the Empire Theatre in Edinburgh. Did something happen at the semi-finals to cause such hatred? She didn't think so, but she owed it to her assistant at least to investigate that line of enquiry. She would ask to see the relevant newspapers.

SEVENTEEN

Leaving the books on the table so that she could return to them shortly, Maud picked up her gloves and bag and followed the sign to the news room, mounting the staircase to the next floor. Here there were long tables with chairs in the centre of the room and tall windows to admit the light. Daily newspapers were displayed on huge mahogany stands.

When had the theatre fire taken place? Maud searched her memory. It was a few months ago... The early summer, she was sure. April? No, that could not be described as early summer. It must have been May.

She approached the desk and made her request.

'The entire month of May?' asked the woman.

'I'm afraid so,' said Maud. 'Perhaps I could start with the middle fortnight?'

Maud slid onto one of the hard wooden chairs near the end of a long table, set down her gloves and bag and waited. The only other person in the room, an elderly man, was seated further along the table on the other side and engrossed in the day's copy of *The Times*.

An attendant wheeled over to her a trolley holding a pile of

newspapers. Maud thanked her and reached for the first publi-
cation. *The Scotsman*. Briefly wondering, not for the first time,
why not simply *The Scot*, she scanned the pages looking for any
story on the semi-finals of the competition.

She reached the end of the newspaper and closed it with a
sigh. Nothing. If there was nothing about the competition in
The Scotsman, there was unlikely to be anything on it in the
other journals.

Maud picked up the next day's edition and flipped through
the pages. There at last she saw the report she was looking for.
On the previous afternoon, it stated, nine choirs from around
Scotland had taken part in the semi-finals. She read on, but
there was nothing to ring any alarm bells.

Maud leaned back in her chair and gazed up at the tall
windows. A watery sun shone through the glass. They need
cleaning, she thought idly. But what she was really concerned
about was the daunting thought of interviewing the members of
the five other choirs who had taken part in the semi-finals.

As Maud considered this, she was aware of a tall man
sliding onto the end chair beside her.

'Good morning,' he said.

For a moment her brain went away. Then it came back. She
turned to look at Lord Urquhart. He was far too big for the
simple wooden seat... although she couldn't deny that his shape,
and his face, were pleasing.

'What are you doing here?' she said, keeping her voice low.

'I bumped into Mrs Ross with Miss Cameron on their way
to visit a friend and she told me you were in the library.'

Clara seemed to like Lord Urquhart, so of course she would
have told him where Maud was.

'She didn't tell me *why* you were here, though,' he went on.

'As you very well know, because we have had this conversation before, I cannot discuss a client's business without their

approval,' Maud told him primly. 'But why are *you* in the library?'

'Oh, books and things help to pass the time,' he said airily.

Lord Urquhart was a man without purpose in life and she had no time for such a man. He appeared to be interested in the detective business and she would suggest he start his own agency, but she didn't want him in competition with her. Clients were, annoyingly, inclined to want a man at the helm.

But she wished Lord Urquhart did not look at her with that steady gaze from his dark eyes. It was unsettling. Perhaps there was more going on in his brain than she'd thought. Her colour rose at the idea.

She needed to keep Lord Urquhart in his place, or at the very least out of hers. In a dismissive gesture, she picked up the next edition of the newspaper and placed it on the table, although she had no interest in reading any further.

There on the front page was the story of how, on the previous evening, that of Wednesday the tenth of May, three thousand spectators had packed the Empire Palace of Varieties in Edinburgh's Nicolson Street. The Great Lafayette, the principal attraction, came on just before eleven o'clock. Dressed in a satin costume, he entered to a trumpet fanfare and proceeded to shake dozens of birds from a sequined cloth and then produced a goat from the folds of the material.

Lord Urquhart looked at the newspaper in front of her. 'Are you here to read about the fire in the Empire? The poor fellow and his assistants were burned to death on the stage that night.' He turned to her. 'Good Lord! Don't tell me you are investigating the death of the Great Lafayette?'

'*Wheesht!*' The elderly man seated further down the table looked up and glared at them.

Sorry, she mouthed back. For goodness' sake, why was she apologising for Lord Urquhart?

'Of course not,' she addressed him in a low, cross voice. 'It is the date that interests me.'

He leaned towards the newspaper and her. Unnecessarily close, she thought.

'Is there something wrong with your eyesight?'

'My eyesight is fine.' He grinned.

The elderly man gave an impatient rustle of his newspaper as he folded it. 'And, sir, there is nothing wrong with my hearing.'

He rose from his seat, tucked the newspaper under his arm, picked up his bowler hat and walked in a marked manner to a table further away.

'There, isn't that better?' said Lord Urquhart. 'Now we can discuss the case without fear of being overheard.'

'Really, Lord Urquhart, you are incorrigible.'

'Agreed, but what would be the point of changing?' He gave Maud a look of innocent enquiry.

'Do you really want me to answer that?' She drew a breath and opened her mouth to give him a list.

'That was a rhetorical question,' he added hastily.

She closed her mouth and smiled at him. At least he had a degree of self-awareness. A little humility was good in a man. But then he moved the newspaper so that it lay between them and said, 'We should get started.'

'I already have.'

'And what have you learned so far?'

'That you are *infuriating*.'

'I know,' he said. 'I honestly can't help it.' He raised an eyebrow. 'But let us not waste any more time in idle chit-chat...'

Maud snorted.

'... and put our combined brains to use on the investigation.' He bent his head over the newspaper. Her heart gave a little skip. He really did have an attractive profile. She looked at his face: dark eyebrows, long straight nose, slightly curved lips, strong chin...

He turned to Maud. 'Are you going to help or not? There is only so much a man can do on his own.' He smiled.

He'd caught her studying him, she was sure. Quickly recovering her composure – something detectives had to be good at, she thought – she drew the newspaper back towards her. Keeping her voice soft out of consideration for the other library user, she read:

A beautiful princess survives a shipwreck, only to be given the choice of joining the Pasha's hareem or being thrown into a cage with the royal lion. On the stage an African lion paces in a cage while fire-eaters, jugglers and contortionists perform. Walking slowly, the princess enters the cage. The lion roars and rears up. The animal's head is ripped off to reveal The Great Lafayette – her lover, the Persian envoy – who has mysteriously changed places with the lion.

'You read that beautifully,' said Lord Urquhart with a sigh.

'The illusion took twenty-five minutes to perform,' Maud went on, ignoring his comment. 'It must have been spectacular.'

'It says here,' Lord Urquhart continued, 'as the Great Lafayette took his bow, a great mass of flame burst out on the stage. The audience thought the ball of fire was part of the performance. It was only when the fire curtain was rapidly lowered, and the orchestra played "God Save the King", that they realised what was happening.'

'So desperately sad...' Maud murmured.

For a moment she was silent, remembering Clara telling her that the choir members watching the show, not then realising one of the oriental lanterns hanging above the stage had fallen onto the scenery, thought the pipe-smoking Walter Stevenson was to blame.

This would not do, Maud told herself. The comment about Walter was meant as a joke, surely?

Irritated by her lack of progress on the case, she turned to Lord Urquhart. 'Don't you have some pressing work, such as counting the number of birds recently shot?'

Listen to yourself, Maud McIntyre, she thought. As if dead birds from a shoot would be counted a week later.

'I'm not that keen on shooting,' he murmured. 'And I missed a few birds on purpose...'

'Well then, you must have something else to do, such as ensuring your cravat has been pressed in exactly the correct way.' She heard her own sharp intake of breath. What could have possessed her to utter such a thing?

A shadow crossed his face, so fleeting that Maud couldn't be sure it had even been there.

'I'm sorry, I must go,' she said. 'I have a lot to do, so if you will excuse me.' Gathering her gloves and bag, Maud got to her feet. She looked down at him, still perched on his seat at the end of the long table. 'I need to get by,' she said firmly.

'Oh, certainly.' He rose gracefully and took a step back.

She held on to her beautiful pink hat and eased past him – goodness, the spacing between tables was remarkably *cosy*. That must be what was causing the heat to wash through her in waves. And then there was that faint scent of lime, lemon and lavender...

Maud pulled herself together. 'Would you be so good as to arrange the return of the newspapers, Lord Urquhart? I cannot stay any longer. There is a case to be solved.'

'So, X either has to have easy access to a poison or he'd need to buy it from the chemist saying he has a rats' nest under his house,' Daisy said, as they discussed the case that afternoon over a cup of tea at Ivy Fraser's tea shop. 'Then again,' she added, 'could it be that he kens a lot about poisonous plants?'

'It's possible.'

'What did you manage to learn about them?'

With a sinking heart, Maud realised she had not returned to the ground floor of the library.

'What is it?' Daisy put down her teacup.

'I'm so sorry, Daisy, but I forgot to consult that book.'

Daisy frowned. 'How could you forget to do that?'

Too easily, it would seem. 'Lord Urquhart came into the reading rooms and... well, he did his very best to distract me.'

'It worked,' Daisy said with a smirk.

'The building is closed this afternoon, but I'll return tomorrow.'

'Nae matter, I'll go next time. We dinna want you getting diverted by his braw lordship again, in case he's loitering about hoping to accidentally bump into you.' The smile on Daisy's face faded. 'You dinna think he was trying to interfere with your work on the case, do you, to prevent you solving the murders? You ken how we thought in the early days of the agency that his lordship might be working with the villains?'

'No, I honestly don't think that,' she said.

Daisy's brow cleared. 'Nae, neither do I. Any ideas on where X is getting the poison from?'

'I'm inclined to go with your third suggestion. That he or she has knowledge of poisonous plants.'

'And what about the fire at the Empire, the day after the choir sang there?'

'I am struggling to think of a link there,' Maud admitted.

'Unless it was a member of one of the choirs who didna make it through to the final and who kent some of the Fort William folk would be at the theatre.'

'That's pure supposition, Daisy.'

'One of them losing choirs,' Daisy persisted, 'might have

been crabbit enough to arrange for that lantern to fall onto the stage.'

'That's far too much of a long shot.' Maud sighed. They were getting off track. She couldn't believe in Daisy's theatre fire retribution theory; her assistant was working hard to make the evidence fit. But was she in danger of doing the same thing? She mustn't allow herself to make her own theories fit the case. Fitting a theory to the crime was the wrong way round for a detective. As Sherlock Holmes said in *A Study in Scarlet*, it was a mistake to theorise before one had all the evidence as it biased the judgement.

'Could we have misread the clue – gone wrong somewhere?' she said.

'I dinna think so, but let's go over what we've found out so far. We might get lucky this time.' Daisy produced her notebook from the bag at her feet. 'I copied the clue into here.'

They bent over the notebook and studied it carefully.

'How is the investigation going?'

They looked up to see Ivy Fraser.

Daisy hastily closed the book. 'Nae too bad,' she said.

'I saw you both here with your heads together and thought I'd ask. You don't mind, do you?'

'Not at all,' Maud said, 'but you do understand that we're not at liberty to discuss the case with a third party?'

A frown marred Ivy Fraser's usually cheerful face. 'Even though I knew all those in the choir who are with us no more?'

'Even though,' Maud agreed.

'Och, well, no harm in asking.' She saw their tea things on the table. 'Can I get you anything to eat?'

Daisy opened her mouth, and Maud waited for her to order some bread and butter, or a slice of cake.

'Nae thanks,' Daisy said, 'I'm stapped.'

'Are you feeling well?' Maud asked Daisy, once Ivy Fraser

had left. 'I don't think I've *ever* known you to refuse the offer of food.'

Daisy gave her a pained look. 'I didna want to give her a chance to interrogate us any further. And anyway, we've not long had luncheon, you ken.'

'Ah, of course.' Maud suppressed a smile.

She and Daisy looked around to make sure no one was near the corner table they had chosen for privacy. Satisfied, Daisy opened her notebook again.

'We can't have gone wrong,' Maud declared. 'Unless the entire verse is a hoax.'

'It canna be. There's nae reason for it.'

'There's no reason for any of it – the writing notes for us, or murdering the choir members one by one – that we can be sure of. But the other clues have been genuine, so it is best to assume that this one is too.'

Daisy gave a nod of agreement.

'Very well.' Maud went on. 'Assuming we have deciphered the clue correctly, what are we looking at? *Wild food* and *start to feel unwell* – it must mean eating something poisonous. That can't be wrong.'

'But what about *where angels gather* and *destroying the peacefulness*? We canna just ignore those two lines.' Daisy frowned as she stared at her writing in the notebook. 'They must mean something. X didna put them in for naething. He doesna make mistakes.'

Maud studied the clue with equal concentration. They must solve the clue this time. She couldn't bear the thought of failing another victim.

Presently she looked up at Daisy. 'I can't see that it means anything but something poisonous growing in the woods.'

'I think that too.' Daisy groaned. 'So, what are we missing with the angels?'

'Now might be a good time to consider motive, means and opportunity,' suggested Maud.

Daisy cheered up. 'Aye.' She turned to a new page and at the top wrote *Motive*. 'Right.' She looked at Maud.

After a pause, Maud said, 'We'll start with the laird.'

Daisy smiled.

'Motive. The laird.' Maud acknowledged the smile with one of her own. 'John Noble... put a question mark. We now know that the two men knew each other well, but there's nothing to suggest their relationship had soured in any way.' She paused and waited for Daisy's pencil to catch up.

'Emily Black,' Maud went on. 'Another question mark. We no longer believe that the laird had got her with child and wanted to put a conclusive end to her hope that he might marry her, or at least acknowledge the babe as his own.'

Daisy scribbled in her book. 'Next, Jane Rankin. Had there been some kind of a stushie between her and the laird?' She looked up at Maud. 'They might have argued in the past over who had shot the most birds.'

'That's possible, but wouldn't someone have mentioned that to us by now?'

'Nae if they liked the laird and not that besom.' Daisy continued to write furiously.

'And Joseph Watson.' Maud thought for a moment. 'Had he... I don't know... demanded higher wages than the laird was willing to pay?'

Daisy nodded. 'Now we need to look at means for the laird. We canna comment on John Noble until we ken if the laird visited him at home on the day he was found deid. What about Emily Black?'

In *The Fordwych Castle Mystery*, Maud thought, Miss Duplessis found the murdered body of her maid and allegedly important papers stolen. Enter Lady Molly of Scotland Yard, who discovered that the papers were a fabrication and the murderer was none other than Miss Duplessis herself.

'The captain was the one to find her body,' Maud said. 'That's often significant.'

'Aye. Now, Jane Rankin. She was standing next to the laird at the shoot.'

'You had better add *nota bene*—'

'What?' Daisy looked up sharply from her notebook.

'Note well. I'm thinking of the concern we have that someone, whether a loader, gun or beater, would surely have noticed if the laird shot Mrs Rankin. And the same applies if he had thrown a stick of dynamite to where Joseph Watson was standing. The laird was very visible in both cases.'

Daisy sighed.

'Shall we look at Walter Stevenson next?' Maud said.

Daisy wrote his name on the list. 'I'm nae sure about motive for him. We've heard naething to suggest he wants any of his fellow choir members deid.'

'True, but what about means? I know we're jumping ahead here, but he works at the quarry and so he does have knowledge of explosions.'

'Opportunity too,' Daisy said. 'Couldna he have taken a stick of dynamite and chucked it at Joseph Watson?'

'The problem with that is he would have had to be present at the time of the explosion, when his absence from work at the quarry would have been noticed.'

Daisy wrinkled her brow. 'If it had to have been someone there—'

'Actually, perhaps not, Daisy,' Maud cut in. 'The killer could have used an extra-long fuse.'

'And been hanging about well away from the folk in the garden? Is that possible?'

Maud shrugged. 'I don't know.'

'What does the other stuff mentioned in the clue – TNT – look like? Maybe that's easier to set off from a distance.'

'Bother!' Maud said. 'I should have looked up TNT and dynamite at the reading rooms this morning.'

Daisy laughed. 'That would have raised an eyebrow or two.'

Maud smiled. 'I'm pretty sure the assistant already has me marked as suspicious because I wanted books on poisons.'

'We can ask Alasdair this evening over dinner,' Daisy said. 'He kens why we're here and willna be surprised at the question.'

'Good idea.' Maud nodded at the notebook on the table in front of Daisy. 'Who else should be on the motives, means and opportunity list?'

Daisy pulled a face. 'It takes longer to say those three words than it does to repeat the names of our suspects.'

Maud had to smile at her friend's comment. It was no smiling matter, though, as Daisy was correct. They had almost nothing to go on.

'The only connections between all our victims are the choir and the laird,' she said. 'Who could possibly want to kill four—'

'Five,' put in Daisy, 'if you count the planned poisoning, that is.'

'Which we must, of course. Five very different people, but all with the same aim – to be the winning choir in the finals.'

'Maybe that's the answer,' said Daisy. 'They dinna all want to win the competition.'

'What do you mean?'

'It's obvious, dinna you think? One of them wants to sabotage their chances.'

Maud stared at Daisy. 'You could be right, my friend, but which one and why?'

And if they had the answer to that question, Maud thought, they would have their murderer.

EIGHTEEN

'Alasdair,' said Daisy over dinner that evening, 'what's the difference between TNT and dynamite?'

He put down his knife and fork. 'That's an extraordinary question for a young lady to ask during dinner.'

'Nae really,' put in Clara. 'Nae when you consider poor Joseph was blown up.'

Daisy nodded. 'I want to ken the difference between the two types of explosives.'

Alasdair picked up his cutlery and frowned at her. 'Let me first say, Daisy, that I'm glad Susan is at a friend's house this evening and not here. It would be too upsetting for her to know what's going on in Fort William.'

'I suspect she already kens – or at least guesses,' Clara said. 'She's nae as blind or as deaf as you seem to think.'

'Well...' Alasdair cut off a piece of rabbit pie, the savoury aroma of meat and gravy wafting around them. 'Excellent pie, my dear.'

'I will tell cook. Meanwhile, answer Daisy's question, do.'

'Very well. Let me think how best to explain it. TNT looks like pieces of broken tablet—'

'Those sweeties?' cried Daisy in astonishment.

Maud was equally surprised. Tablet was a confection made from sugar, condensed milk and butter, boiled and then allowed to crystallise. It was very sweet, far too sweet for Maud's taste.

'Where is TNT used?' she asked.

'Mainly in military shells, bombs and hand grenades.'

'Hand grenades?' This could be relevant. She and Daisy exchanged a glance. 'What sort of container would be used for the explosive?' Maud asked.

'It could be any sort of metal, really,' Alasdair said, 'to enable it to be thrown into the enemy camp. Hand grenades have been known of in France since the sixteenth century, although of course TNT and metal canisters weren't used then.'

'Hand grenades in France?' Maud asked in curiosity. 'Is that where the word *grenadiers* comes from?'

'I don't know, I'm afraid, but if you wish to know more Captain Farquharson might be able to help you. He's interested in army history. Well, I suppose he would, as he was in the army for so long.'

Daisy glanced at Maud, before turning back to Alasdair. 'Now, please tell us about dynamite.'

Alasdair took a sip of his beer. 'That's used mainly in mining, quarrying and construction.'

'And demolition,' Maud added.

'Aye, that too.'

'What does it look like?' Daisy asked.

'It comes in cardboard cylinders about eight inches long and just over an inch in diameter.'

'So it's easy to carry then, as it's nae heavy?'

'I believe each stick weighs about six and a half ounces.'

Both TNT and dynamite would be easy to transport, Maud realised, but a thrown stick of dynamite must have caused the explosion that killed Joseph Watson.

Alasdair looked worried as he addressed his house guests. 'I know you two ladies are private detectives, and I applaud your initiative in starting your own agency, Maud, but do take care, won't you? I hate to think of either of you getting into situations you're not naturally equipped to deal with.'

Maud was both touched by his concern and irritated by having a man talking to her in a way he would not to a male detective. Had the admittedly fictional Miss Gladden had to put up with such an attitude? Not that Maud could remember. Had the very much real-life Big Rachel of Partick received such comments? Undoubtedly not. Although it could be said that at an impressive six feet five inches and seventeen stone, the special constable employed during the Glasgow riots was more likely to toss a man into the Clyde than she was to engage him in conversation. There had to be a middle way...

Clara broke into Maud's thoughts. 'It's Jane Rankin's funeral tomorrow morning, if you'd like to go.'

Maud glanced at Daisy, who gave a nod.

'We didna like the wifie, but we'll pay our respects,' Daisy said.

And it was a good opportunity, Maud realised, to see who else was there. Didn't she read somewhere that a killer always attends the funeral of his victim?

The funeral service took place early the following morning. Alasdair drove Maud, Daisy and Clara in his Ford. He stopped the motor car in the High Street outside the Episcopal church.

'She was a Piskie?' asked Daisy.

'Aye,' Clara said. 'Some must be.'

The Church of Scotland was governed by representatives of the congregation, but the Episcopal Church by bishops. Maud knew this did not sound like a major difference, but when Charles I tried to impose bishops on the Church of Scotland, all hell seemed to be let loose. Those days were thankfully long gone, but back then church governance had literally been a matter of life and death.

Surely Jane Rankin's death had nothing to do with religion? Maud wondered, as they all climbed out of the motor car and walked through the lychgate. The laird, she knew, was a member of the kirk, the Church of Scotland, but was it possible the two of them had argued over some ecumenical matter? Possible, but not likely.

They walked up the path to the large stone church with its towering spire. The oak doors of St Andrew's stood open, and they entered. The church was almost full and Alasdair directed Maud and Daisy to two spaces in a pew close to the front, while he and Clara slipped into a pew on the other side of the aisle.

Maud gazed about discreetly while they waited for the service to begin.

'Is there anyone you recognise?' she whispered to Daisy above the subdued conversational hum of the congregation. 'I can see the laird and Lord Urquhart, and seated between them a man who must be Mr Rankin.' Maud gave a tiny nod to the front pew, where a short, thin gentleman sat ramrod straight. He had removed his gold-rimmed spectacles and was dabbing at his eyes with a large white handkerchief.

Daisy swivelled round in her seat.

'Daisy!' Maud hissed, 'don't make it so obvious.'

'Dinna worry yourself,' Daisy said cheerfully, turning back. 'It's natural to want to see who's at a funeral. Nae doubt there are plenty of busybodies, but I've spotted the two McDougall brothers together, and Maggie the cook and Mrs Wilson from the castle.'

'That makes sense. Whatever their opinion of the lady, they are all fellow members of the choir.'

'And they all work for the laird,' Daisy added.

'He must have given them the morning off to come to the service.'

'If they've been telt to come, there goes the theory that the kill—'

'Hush,' Maud murmured.

Ivy Fraser hurried past the end of their pew, the inexpensive sweet-scented perfume she wore wafting towards them, and squeezed into a pew behind Clara and Alasdair.

'Anyone else here?' Maud whispered.

Daisy turned round again, and Maud gazed at the large stained-glass window behind the magnificent altar. The early morning sun coming through the blood red pieces of glass cast a watery pink light on the three men in the front pew. Maud raised her eyes again to the splendid window. Was there an angel depicted in it? She was examining it when Daisy faced to the front again.

'Walter Stevenson is right at the back,' Daisy hissed, 'and the four altos are sitting next to each other in a pew on the other side.'

The four altos, Maud thought, with a sudden shock. She had not given these women – the three sisters and Anne Ritchie – anything like enough consideration. Perhaps she and Daisy should turn their attention to the elderly Faith, Hope and Charity Moffat, and the young Anne. But Maud had discounted them for a reason. Anne was employed as a housemaid in the town, the three sisters had never worked and still lived together at the family home, and none of the four women had a connection to the laird.

'So all of the choir are present?' Maud asked.

'Aye, minus Beatrice Noble, who's away.'

Maud had to admit that, apart from the doctor seated in front of them and the policeman across the aisle, she had no idea about the other members of the congregation. There seemed to be no family members supporting the bereaved husband, so the remainder must be local people and perhaps other members of the laird's household and his estate servants.

Not as well liked as the packed church would suggest then, thought Maud.

The organist struck up the introduction to "Lord of All Hopefulness", and as the funeral service began, Maud herself took the opportunity to glance around. There was no one acting strangely or suspiciously, as far as she could tell. She wasn't sure what she had expected – the murderer breaking down with emotion and guilt to confess all would have been rather nice – but everything went off quietly. Every eye in the church was dry, with the exception of Mr Rankin, Jane's husband.

From the church a small procession of motor cars travelled at walking pace the short distance to the little graveyard by the chapel on the edge of the laird's estate. They were followed by others on foot. The minister had told them this was Mrs Rankin's wish and the laird was pleased to be able to grant it. All those who could come were welcome, he added.

Alasdair's Ford could manage no additional passengers and the four of them were amongst the earliest mourners to arrive.

'I wonder why the captain has agreed to have Mrs Rankin in his private cemetery?' Daisy muttered to Maud as they stood and watched the rest of the procession come along the road. 'Guilt?'

'Friendship?' Maud suggested.

Daisy snorted.

Jane Rankin's coffin had been taken from the glass-sided hearse a short distance away and was now resting on a farm wagon with her husband leading the horse.

'Extraordinary...' Maud murmured.

'She must have hated the wee man to make him do that.'

'He must have loved her to agree to do it.'

'Puir wee daftie.' Daisy sighed.

They joined the tail end of the line of mourners following the minister behind the wagon, bowing their heads in respect. When it reached the graveyard, the wagon halted and the coffin was lifted off. The laird and Lord Urquhart shouldered the heaviest end, two men Maud didn't recognise positioned themselves at the foot, and Mr Rankin and the doctor took the middle positions. Each pair was matched for height, although their burden sloped alarmingly at the rear.

The congregation followed the coffin to the graveside. Once it was lowered, those standing closest to the grave each dropped a small handful of earth onto the coffin, and the minister finished his prayers. Everyone began to move away.

'So that's that,' said Daisy, as soon as they were out of earshot of the other mourners.

'I don't know that we've learned anything...'

'I wouldna say that. I mean, Jane Rankin being buried in the laird's private graveyard?'

'True. We should find out the reason for that, but take care, here comes Clara.'

Clara approached them. 'We're going home now. Would you both like a hurl?'

'Is there nae a purvey?' asked Daisy.

'If there is, we're nae invited.'

'Och well,' said Daisy, disappointed at the lack of a funeral tea, 'then a hurl would be braw, thanks.'

The three of them walked to Alasdair's motor car and he drove them back to the house. On their return, he took the Ford round to the garage.

'Any chance of a cup of tea before I visit the reading rooms?' Daisy asked her cousin as they walked up the path.

'You're going to the reading rooms?' Clara halted, affecting surprise. 'That doesna sound like the Daisy Cameron I know.'

'That was the *old* Daisy Cameron.' Daisy grinned. 'The new one is a book-reading, cosh-carrying private detective.'

'Cosh-carrying?' Clara's surprise this time was genuine. She came to a halt.

Daisy laughed. 'Nae really. Although Maud here has a cosh.'

'It's not a cosh, Daisy, as you very well know, but an Indian club. A pair of Indian clubs, to be exact, for purposes of exercise,' Maud added. 'I have never used them to hit anyone over the head.'

'Nae yet,' put in Daisy. 'So, tea?'

'You havena changed in that respect, Daisy Cameron,' Clara said, patting Daisy's hand fondly.

'And nor will I. Thank the Lord for tea. We couldna manage without it, could we?'

They resumed walking up the path.

'Maud,' went on Clara, 'wasna one of Queen Victoria's prime ministers supposed to have put tea in his hot water bottle before he took it to bed?

'So it has been said about Mr Gladstone.' Maud couldn't help but smile.

'There, I kent you'd have the answer. Our Daisy does well to be working for you.'

'With me, Clara. We're a team.'

'She's come right since she joined your faither's household, so she has.' Clara opened the front door. 'Now, I'll get Netta to put on the kettle.'

'And I'll change out of these mourning clothes. I canna stand dreich colours,' Daisy told Maud, as Clara went off to the kitchen.

'I'll come with you to the reading rooms, if you have no objection,' Maud said.

'Four eyes are better than two, and two brains are better than one.'

'I need to think of something other than the funeral. It reminded me of my Aunt Sophy's burial and has made me feel rather sad.' Maud was grateful to her aunt for bequeathing the money which enabled her to buy her very own motor car, a smart Napier Tourer, but she was sorry that it had come about in such a way.

'Of course, Maud.' Daisy gave her a sympathetic smile. 'I'll see you in the sitting room in a wee while.'

Refreshed by the tea at home and both wearing brighter colours – Maud in her lilac cashmere jumper and a pretty floral brooch, and Daisy in a red top with white polka dots – they entered the reading rooms later that day.

Seeing the assistant's worried look, Maud gave the woman her most charming smile and asked to see the book on poisonous plants.

'Unfortunately, I did not get time to read it when I was here yesterday,' she said.

'You should have returned the books to the desk and not left them on the table,' the neat little woman chastised her. 'Fortunately, a nice gentleman brought them back to me.'

Maud flushed. 'I'm most dreadfully sorry. Of course I should have done that. I assure you that my friend and I will take great care of the book today.'

Mollified, the assistant told them to take a seat and she went away to find the volume. Maud cast a glance around and, seeing no Lord Urquhart, or indeed anyone apart from the assistant, gestured to Daisy to sit at a table as far from the desk as possible.

The book was placed before them, the woman gave them a warning look, and Maud and Daisy were left to consult the volume.

'Where to start?' Daisy whispered. 'There must be poisonous nettles, berries and all sorts.'

Maud opened the book to the first page. 'Plants used in medieval medicine,' she read. 'Belladonna, foxglove, hemlock, lords-and-ladies, monkshood...'

'We nae looking for remedies, but *poisons*.'

'Many plants can be used for both purposes, Daisy. It's the dose that is important.'

'Kill or cure?'

'Something like that. But as those plants can't be considered wild food, we can discount them.' Maud moved her forefinger further down the list of contents. '*Amanita phalloides*,' she said in a low voice. 'Commonly known as the death cap. The deadliest fungus known. No antidote exists.'

'Michty me,' Daisy exclaimed softly. 'What do they look like?'

Maud turned to the relevant page and they bent their heads over it.

'The caps are greenish in colour with a white stipe and gills,' she read.

'So what's a stipe?'

'It must be the stalk, as the description mentions the cap and the gills, which are the parts under the cap that resemble ribs.'

'Right,' said Daisy. 'So it's a pale green mushroom.'

'It says here that the cap colour is variable – it can be white – and it's one and a half to four and a half inches across.'

Daisy frowned. 'Now it sounds like an ordinary mushroom.'

'Not in its effect, though. Look at this.' Maud tapped her finger on the lines. 'One small cap is enough to *kill* an adult human.'

Daisy read the text and shuddered. 'Deid after a week of excruciating pain. Six to twenty-four hours after swallowing, you boke, do the back-door trot and get awfa bad gut pain...'

'Followed by jaundice, seizures, coma and death from kidney and liver failure,' Maud finished.

Daisy looked at her. 'I'm nae going to eat another mushroom.'

'These are not ordinary mushrooms,' Maud reminded her. 'Which lets us know that X must be very confident about identifying fungi, if he doesn't want to pick a harmless one and risk the failure of his plan. Apparently, the fungus comes up in the same area every season, which must be useful to know.'

'These *Amanitas* have a mingin smell, which would help X get the right one.'

'In what way mingin?'

'It says here a sickly sweet smell.'

Maud's eye fell on another variety of fungi. 'There's also *Amanita citrina*, often referred to as the false death cap, which is not seriously toxic.'

'Och, that's a comfort.'

'That also has a pale green colour, but it smells of potato.'

'Imagine having to get down on your hands and knees to sniff a mushroom to see if it smells of tatties or not before you pick it.'

Maud immediately imagined it. 'Let's see if the book says where these fungi can be found.'

She found a map at the front of the book and they examined it.

'It looks as though the death cap is not common in the Scottish Highlands,' she said, 'although it does grow in one spot – the ancient oak woods on the Ardnamurchan peninsula. That's the most westerly and remote part of mainland Britain, but it wouldn't take X too long from here if he caught the ferry.'

In the silence of the reading rooms, they heard a creak and both looked up. There was no one in the room or behind the desk.

Daisy shrugged and they returned to the map. Another creak, this one closer.

Daisy leaped from her seat. 'There's someone else here.'

'It'll be the librarian...'

'She's invisible, is she?' Daisy looked round wildly.

As they waited, each holding their breath, Daisy's chair

toppled backwards. She screamed at the sound and ran to the door.

The library assistant hastened from her office to the desk. 'What was that noise?' she demanded. Her voice was low but surprisingly fierce for such a small woman.

'There's a bogle in the room!' Daisy hissed from the doorway.

She and the assistant, both white-faced, held their respective breaths.

Maud broke the silence. 'There are no such things as ghosts,' she said in a firm tone.

'Och, miss, you mustn't say that,' whispered the assistant. 'You will bring the *buidseachd*.'

'What is that, pray?' Maud bent to pick up the wooden chair.

Daisy and the assistant gasped in unison. 'You may be well to pray,' went on the library assistant, 'as it's a curse. The town of Fort William has not always been a peaceful place. It was the scene of many a violent struggle, from the invasion of Cromwell to the Forty-Five, and the aftermath of the Battle of Culloden. Terrible retribution was inflicted on the defeated Highlanders.'

Daisy remained standing by the door, her colour slowly returning. Maud set the chair back on its feet and turned. She sent Daisy an encouraging smile before focusing her attention on the assistant. 'What is this about the *buidseachd*?'

'An old oak tree had stood outside the fort walls for three hundred years. It was the hanging tree, put to frequent use by the governors of the old fort to hang Highlanders. Then it was cut down to make way for these reading rooms.'

'I see,' Maud said.

'Many folk predicted that it would fulfil the ancient prophecy – the curse of ill omen,' went on the assistant, staying behind her desk as if for protection. 'The morning after the rooms opened to the public for the first time, I found the door unlocked and inside chairs were knocked over, books strewn across the floor and there were mysterious bangs.'

'And what did you do?'

The librarian looked affronted. 'What do you think I did? I fled.'

'That's all very well,' Maud pointed out, 'but it meant that you failed to find the culprit.'

The other woman drew in a long breath through her nostrils. 'If you have quite finished with that,' she gestured towards the volume lying on the table, 'perhaps you would have the goodness to return it to me?'

'Certainly.' Maud could see that nothing sensible could be had from the woman. She closed the book and carried it over to the desk.

'Thank you,' the woman said stiffly.

'Not at all,' replied Maud.

Gathering up her and Daisy's gloves and bag, she strode towards the door.

'Come, Daisy. We have finished our work here for the day.'

NINETEEN

'I hope you have all been practising your parts in my absence.' Beatrice Noble gazed around the choir members in the village hall that evening.

'Aye!' called Maggie. 'And how was your wee holiday in Arisaig?'

Beatrice flushed. Goodness, thought Maud, the woman really doesn't like personal questions.

'Only I told my cousin who lives in Arisaig to look out for you,' went on Maggie, 'but she didn't see you.'

'It was a worthwhile trip,' Beatrice said with her tight smile. 'That is, my sister was pleased that I could visit. And now,' she continued, 'we will start with the usual voice warm-up exercise of a small rhyme about ourselves over the last few days. Perhaps you would care to start, Maggie.'

The cook thought for a moment, cleared her throat and sang: '*I often cook and sometimes bake. I really like to make a cake.*'

Each of the other choir members took their turn.

'Lord Urquhart?' said Beatrice, looking at him. 'What do you have for us?'

He gave a lazy smile, opened his mouth and sang. '*My name is Urquhart, and I sing from the heart.*' He placed both hands over the left side of his chest and bowed.

'Bravo!' Beatrice appeared to be genuinely charmed.

Oh really, Maud thought, if that was the best he could do...

She turned her mind back to more important matters. She had learned nothing of interest from this evening's rhymes. What was she expecting, she wondered: the killer to confess in rhyme? They moved on to practise "I Love a Lassie" and "The Bonnie Banks o' Loch Lomond".

At the end of the session, Beatrice said, 'A little bird has told me that one of our number has a birthday tomorrow.' She smiled at Ivy Fraser. 'Are you having a celebration?'

Ivy smiled. 'I'm taking the afternoon off work and will enjoy putting my feet up for a wee while.'

'That sounds delightful,' Beatrice told her. 'Everyone, we will finish this evening by sending Ivy our best wishes in the usual way.'

Ivy beamed as they all sang 'Happy Birthday' before breaking into small groups to chat before making their way out of the village hall and homewards. Today the subdued conversations were all about the murders: who could be doing such a thing and who would be next? Now that it was time to leave the safety of the group, the women glanced around, trying to assess their situation. None wanted to walk home alone. Daisy was talking to Clara and Ivy Fraser.

Maud turned to see Lord Urquhart approaching and immediately remembered his performance at the beginning of the session.

'Lord Urquhart,' she said, looking gravely at him, 'I believe you were showing off earlier.'

'I believe I was.'

She drew in a sharp breath. The man had no shame. 'Sir,

there are a number of nervous females here who would appreciate your escorting them home.'

'I had intended to offer that service to you.'

'But I am not, as you know, a *nervous* female. Your attention would be better directed towards the Moffat sisters.' Maud glanced at the three elderly ladies, hovering and twittering in the corner.

One of them – Maud could not be certain if it was Faith, Hope or Charity, as they looked so alike – caught Lord Urquhart's gaze and sent him a hopeful look. He bowed to the inevitable and to the three ladies.

'Of course,' he murmured and made his way over to the sisters.

Daisy returned to Maud. 'Clara's walking home with Ivy Fraser. I told her we'd be following nae long behind.'

Maud and Daisy lingered for a little while longer to ensure all who wished for company on their walk home were provided for, then they prepared to leave.

'Maud and Daisy,' said Beatrice, calling them back. 'I have to be away early this evening. Would you mind putting out the appliances and locking up? You can leave the key under the stone outside the door when everyone has gone.'

Maud thought it strange that Beatrice had not asked Clara, but she agreed to help. 'Yes, of course we will.'

Beatrice smiled, nodded her thanks, gathered up her coat and gloves, and let herself out of the building. Some five minutes later, the hall was empty and silence descended. Maud and Daisy went round turning off the gas lamps and the oil heater. The room was in darkness, save for an oblique patch of cold moonlight thrown upon the wooden floor from the window.

'I dinna like this,' Daisy murmured, glancing nervously around. 'I have a bad feeling.'

'There's nothing to be afraid of, Daisy. Your mind is simply playing games because of Jane Rankin's funeral this morning and then what you heard in the library about the ghostly happenings after the hanging tree was cut down.'

'*Wheesht*. Dinna mention that in here. You might bring back the bootchach or whatever it was called.'

'The *buidseachd*.'

Maud heard a creak. Shadows gathered at the edges of the room. The sound came from a corner opposite the door into the hall. She glanced over at Daisy, whose wide eyes confirmed that she had heard it too. They stood in silence. A second creak. Then a third.

'There's someone in here,' whispered Daisy.

Maud placed her forefinger on her lips to gesture silence. They stood very still, waiting to hear more. But there was no sound. Whoever it was must have gone, she thought. But then came another creak, louder, closer.

They stayed perfectly still, staring into the darkened corner of the hall.

'Who is there?' called Maud, a tremble in her voice.

The corner remained in blackness. Nothing moved.

Before Maud could speak again, there came a low scratchy voice, whether male or female she could not tell, but it was singing:

> *We'll meet where we parted in yon shady glen,*
> *On the steep, steep side o' Ben Lomond,*
> *Where in purple hue the Hieland hills we view,*
> *And the moon looks out frae the gloamin.*

Daisy stared at Maud, her face lit deathly white by the shaft of moonlight.

'Who's there?' Maud demanded, her voice stronger this time.

No answer, just total silence.

Daisy grabbed Maud's sleeve. 'Let's go.'

It's a funny thing, Maud thought, that in daylight you can tell yourself there is no such thing as ghosts and believe it, but it's a different matter in the dark when there are footsteps and...

In the dim corner there were two small circles of red light, like a pair of spectral eyes. Maud straightened her back. Whatever they were, they were not the eyes of a ghost.

'Maud, come away!' hissed Daisy, her hold on Maud's sleeve tightening.

'There is someone there...' Maud said in a firm voice.

'That's what I'm feart of. Only that it's nae a person, but a bogle.'

'I can make out an outline of something black...' Maud stepped closer to peer, while Daisy tried to pull her back.

A sudden gust of wind caused the window to rattle. Daisy screamed and dropped her hand. They both spun round.

'It was just the wind,' Maud said. 'There is no one there.'

They turned back. The dark shape had gone.

'I'm getting out of here.' Daisy set off towards the door, then turned back. 'Are you coming?'

'In a moment.' Maud moved slowly forward, her arms out before her, until she reached the shadows in the corner. 'There's definitely no one there.'

'Aye, that's what I said. A bogle.' Daisy hopped from one foot to another. 'Hurry up. I dinna want to wait to be murdered.'

'A ghost cannot murder a person,' Maud stated with conviction.

Her arms still stretched out, she followed the wall until she reached the door to the scullery and wrenched it open. Lacking a window, the little room was even darker than the hall. Nothing moved. She felt her way through the scullery to the back door and turned the handle. The door was locked.

'Maud, are you all right?' Daisy called anxiously from the hall.

'Yes, Daisy, I'm fine,' Maud said, stepping out of the scullery. 'Whoever was here must have left through the rear door and locked it behind them. We'll have a look at the back of the building, but whoever it was will have gone.'

They left the hall and walked round to the rear but, as Maud had expected, there was no one to be seen.

'The trees make an excellent cover for an intruder to slip away.' She turned back towards the main door to lock it behind them.

'Wait for me!' Daisy hurried after her.

'There is no such thing as ghosts,' Maud said. 'Someone is trying to frighten us.'

'Then they've succeeded.' Daisy caught her up at the front of the building.

Maud gave Daisy a stern look. 'A detective must rise above her fears.'

'I ken that—'

'Hello again.'

Daisy shrieked at the sound of the voice. They turned to see Beatrice Noble standing in front of them.

'I'm sorry if I startled you, Miss Cameron,' Beatrice said. 'Is everything all right?'

'Nae, it's not. And what are you doing here?'

'I was almost home when I remembered that I had left my sheets of music behind. So silly of me.'

Daisy spoke in a rush. 'There was a bogle in there, with burning red eyes—'

'Really, Daisy!'

'And it *sang*.'

'It sang?' Beatrice let out a breath and sank against the door.

'Beatrice? Are you unwell?' Maud moved forward to support the older woman.

'I just feel a little faint. I'm sure I'll be all right in a moment.'

Gradually Beatrice's breathing steadied as she fingered the silver cross around her neck.

Someone expected Beatrice to be here and not Daisy and me, Maud thought. Whoever it was, he was playing an unkind trick on the recently widowed woman.

'Who was it, do you think?' Beatrice asked in a whisper.

X, Maud was about to reply before she realised that Beatrice was asking whose ghost had appeared.

Thinking to reassure the woman, Maud said, 'It was not a ghost, Beatrice. It is foolish to believe in them.'

'I believe in souls,' Beatrice said slowly, regaining her poise. 'We enter heaven or hell when we die; but lost souls, those who have died violently, are left behind.'

This was not the time or place to debate the matter, but the lyrics of 'Loch Lomond' came back to Maud: the dead soldier who took the low road would soon be home in Scotland. Did Beatrice Noble think her dead husband had returned?

'I wonder if it was my dear John, wanting to tell me what occurred on the day he died.'

'Or it might be Emily, Jane or Joseph,' put in Daisy.

Beatrice frowned. 'I suppose it might be.'

'I have locked up,' Maud told Beatrice, bringing common sense back to the conversation. She was about to place the key under the large stone by the door, when Beatrice held out her hand towards Maud.

'Thank you for doing that for me,' she said, her dizzy spell apparently completely passed.

Maud placed the key on Beatrice's open palm.

'You canna go in there by yourself,' said Daisy. 'Nae self-respecting detective would let you after what we've just experienced.'

'Daisy, my dear, if it is a ghost, I can't think I will come to any harm.'

'I think it more likely it was an assailant. The murderer perhaps?' said Maud.

'My dears, I know that Clara has brought you here with the best of intentions, but I think she is suffering from an overactive imagination.'

Daisy came to Clara's defence. 'So how do you explain that two more people who also sung in this choir have come to unexpected ends since we arrived? You canna put that down to Clara's imagination.'

'Accidents, my dear.'

'But—'

'If we can't convince you,' said Maud, cutting Daisy off in case she was about to mention the poems, 'we can at least come in with you while you get your music.'

'No need, I assure you.' Beatrice stepped past Maud to unlock the door. 'I'm not afraid of ghosts and I can't think of one reason why anyone in the choir would want to murder me. Goodnight.' She let herself back into the hall and swiftly closed the door behind her.

'Do you think she's gone back inside to speak to her mannie?' asked Daisy.

'She's gone back inside for some reason, although I'm not sure it's anything to do with her husband or music sheets.'

'Would you say the bogle that was singing was a mannie or a wifie?' Daisy asked.

'There are no such things as ghosts, Daisy. As far as I'm aware, there are three explanations for such occurrences: a change in temperature, a human trick or a hallucination. The window rattled because of a sudden gust of wind; the singing and the red circles, supposedly eyes, were a human trick, deliberately done to frighten Beatrice...'

The door to the hall opened and Beatrice stepped out clutching the music sheets. 'Good heavens, you two are still here.'

'Would you like us to walk you home, Beatrice?' Maud asked.

'Thank you, but there's absolutely no need.' Beatrice gave them a curt nod and walked smartly away down the lane.

Maud took Daisy's arm and they followed her at a distance to ensure she got home safely. How strange, Maud thought, that Beatrice was not afraid to be alone in the dark, given what had just taken place.

'As to your question,' Maud murmured to Daisy, 'I'm not sure if the singer was a man or a woman. Whoever it was, they had disguised their voice. If it was the killer, and the little performance staged to frighten us rather than Beatrice, then perhaps we're getting closer to discovering just who X really is.'

TWENTY

On Friday morning, Maud performed a couple of half-hearted basic *pliés* and *relevés* and did a desultory swing or two of her Indian clubs before going down to breakfast.

'We've still not managed to identify the victim or location for today's murder,' she said to Daisy, as she took her place at the table. She was thankful that Clara had eaten earlier with her husband, which meant she and Daisy could discuss the case freely.

'Do you want to go for a walk to clear your head?' Daisy asked dubiously.

Maud laughed. 'That's kind of you to suggest it, knowing how much you dislike the exercise.' She thought for a moment. 'It's not a bad idea, Daisy.' Feeling sorry for her assistant, she added, 'We could go via Bide-A-While and drop in to wish Ivy Fraser many happy returns of the day.'

Daisy cheered up. 'Aye. And maybe have one of those wee cakes of hers with pink sugared roses on top.'

'Aye, maybe.' Maud smiled. 'If you have room after breakfast.'

'I'm sure I can manage one of those. They're really wee.

One bite and they're gone. Hardly more than a mouthful, really.'

They ate their porridge in silence. This case was proving their most difficult yet, Maud thought. What did they have? she asked herself for what seemed like the hundredth time. A series of unfortunate accidents? No, they had eliminated that possibility a while ago, but had that been the right thing to do? Were they on a wild goose chase?

But then there were the rhymes. She brushed back her hair, ruining the front of her cottage loaf pompadour, and sighed. They were solving the clues too late, rather than making their way along a planned path. They had gone over and over the facts they knew, but the identity of X eluded her. Yet they were making progress, Maud felt it in her bones.

'We can't eliminate Beatrice Noble,' Maud declared, placing the spoon neatly in her bowl.

Daisy had finished her porridge and was now spreading butter on a slice of toast. She looked up and frowned. 'Why do you say that?'

'Her behaviour last evening was strange, don't you think? Granted she seemed genuinely shocked at the notion that her husband had returned as a ghost—'

'That sounds natural to me.'

'Yes, but was it because she was afraid he had returned to exact retribution?'

'Get his own back on her, you mean, for doing away with him?'

'Perhaps.'

'I dinna ken. Even if Beatrice had killed her husband, what about the murders of Emily Black, Jane Rankin and Joseph Watson?'

'John Noble must also have known something about explosives when he was a soldier.'

'Aye, but he's deid, so he couldna have thrown a stick of dynamite at Joseph Watson.'

'I meant couldn't Beatrice have learned something about such things from her husband while he was alive?'

'Maybe, but what about X's other two victims?'

Maud sighed. 'I don't have an answer regarding them. There could well be a connection between her and the other victims. We haven't found it yet, that's all.'

She stared out of the window. It was a crisp winter's morning, wispy clouds sailing across a pale blue sky. She gave herself a shake and turned to address Daisy.

'Come on,' she said, rising from the table. 'We'll take that walk, Daisy. It's an excellent idea. Let's fetch our outdoor garments and meet in the hall in ten minutes.'

Before long, Maud and Daisy were walking along the lane, each dressed in thick tweed skirts and coats. Their breath puffed out, feathered in the air and vanished. The hawthorns were almost bare, stripped of their fruit by hungry birds.

'What a beautiful morning!' Maud exclaimed. 'So fresh and crisp it makes you glad to be alive and in the countryside,' she added mischievously, seeing her friend's crestfallen face.

Daisy pulled her dark green coat more tightly around her and shivered. 'I bet Jenners is hoatching even as we speak.'

'Indeed, my friend,' Maud said cheerfully. 'How much more pleasant it is out here than in a department store in the city!' She relented a little. 'You will enjoy shopping there all the more when we return.'

Daisy grunted. 'Where are we going now? It's a bit cauld for a stravaig.'

'Then let us put purpose into our walk and stride out.' Maud increased her pace.

'My legs are shorter than yours,' Daisy huffed, 'so I have to walk for longer to cover the same distance.'

'I don't think that follows.'

'Well, I'm nae following you at this pace when there's nae need, so slow down a wee bit.'

They passed a steading, its doors open and cows visible inside. A stooped old farmer was setting out the feed of hay in front of them. He paused to lift a hand in greeting to Maud and Daisy.

They continued past what must have been acres of old pine forest. Daisy peered into the frosty woods. 'I'm nae going in there.'

'Beatrice Noble mentioned on Tuesday when we visited her that the weather changes so quickly here,' Maud said. 'I agree. Winter does seem to be upon us all of a sudden.'

'I've been thinking about what you said earlier, about Beatrice, and you're right. She was acting a bit odd last night.'

'And what makes you think so?'

'Well, she didna seem to be afraid of going in the hall after I told her about the bogle.'

'She obviously believes ghosts can't harm you.'

'Nae, but a person can. So if you were right that it might be the killer, why wasna she feart to go in by herself?'

'Perhaps she doesn't believe there is a murderer, Daisy. Any more than I believe in your ghost.'

After a while they found themselves close to the banks of Loch Linnhe. A faint mist hung over the low ground by the water. The frost on the grass crunched under their feet.

'Poor Emily,' murmured Daisy, 'to have met her end here.'

'All the more reason for us to solve this case, Daisy, so that others don't have to die needlessly.'

'You're right,' Daisy said. 'I'm sorry for being so crabbit. Let's go back and really put our minds to the clue.'

Maud smiled, noticing that her friend's nose in the frosty air was almost as red as her hair. 'Yes, let's.' The cold had seeped through the soles of her boots and her feet were growing numb. 'It's even colder out here than it looks.'

They were about to retrace their steps, when through the white strands of mist, a figure in the distance waved to them.

'Is that Maggie?' Daisy said, squinting.

'I think it is.'

The figure came hurrying towards them, her mouse-brown hair escaping from beneath a dark brown hat.

'I thought it was you!' Maggie gasped breathlessly on reaching them.

'A bracing morning for a walk,' Maud replied with a smile.

'I'm out looking for mushrooms for the laird's steak pudding tonight, but it's just a wee bit too late in the season to collect many.' Opening the cloth bag she carried over her shoulder, she showed them a handful of mushrooms. 'This is all I've been able to find and I'm already frozen to the bone.'

'I hope they're nae the poisonous kind,' said Daisy, peering nervously into the bag.

'Of course they're not.' The cook sounded insulted as she drew it away from Daisy's gaze. 'I should hope I know my mushrooms by now.'

'I'm sure you do,' Maud said in a soothing voice. 'It's just something we are curious about, having recently read something about deadly fungi.'

Maggie's face brightened. 'Och, I know what you mean. You have to know what you're doing. Death cap is fatal. There's another poisonous mushroom... I can't remember the name, but it's one of those fungi you need to wear gloves to pick, it's that deadly, although I can't imagine why anyone would want to pick it.'

'Really?' said Maud, sending a swift glance at Daisy.

'Just a moment... it starts with *ama... Amanita virosa*, that's it. Now, let me see if I can remember its common name.' She screwed up her face in concentration. 'I know it's a pure white one with a sickly smell like old honey... destroying angel, that's it!'

Daisy squeaked.

Maggie turned to her. 'Are you all right, Daisy?'

'Aye, yes thanks.' Daisy swallowed.

'Destroying angel is an unusual name,' Maud said, doing her best to keep her voice calm while her heart thudded inside her chest.

'Misleading, too, in a way. I mean, angel sounds soft and pretty, and it looks harmless, but the destroying part – well, it causes diarrhoea, nausea and stomach pains after a few hours. Then the symptoms usually fade away for several hours, or even a day or two, fooling the person into thinking they're recovering. Och, but that's a cruel trick. The symptoms return even worse and then the person falls into a coma and... and *dies*.'

'I hope they dinna grow round here,' said Daisy, her voice wavering a little. 'Plump white mushrooms with a sweet smell,' she added, as if committing the information to memory.'

'The destroying angel likes mossy soil under beech trees, so I think you're safe. And it's probably too late in the year now to find any specimens. They need to be freshly picked, you know.' Maggie gave them a friendly smile. 'Excuse me, but I must be getting back.' She hastened away.

It suddenly came to Maud. 'The next victim is Ivy Fraser,' she said.

Daisy gazed at her in amazement. 'How do you ken that?'

'Beatrice described Ivy as having the voice of an angel.'

'And it's her birthday,' Daisy said, realising the significance.

'The case of the poisoned food parcels.'

Some years earlier, parcels had been sent to families in Brighton, a town on the south coast of England, bearing the message: *A few home-made cakes. You will guess who this is from*. What the note hadn't said was that the baking was laced with strychnine.

Maud nodded. 'Ivy is going to be given a gift of—'

'Cakes?'

'Something edible, anyway. Hurry, Daisy, there is no time to lose!'

They scrambled up the crisp white grass of the embankment, slippery with frost, and ran along the lane, clutching their hats with one hand and holding up their skirts with the other.

'I'm getting a stitch in my side,' puffed Daisy.

'That is nothing to the pain Ivy will suffer if we don't reach her in time.'

'Ivy won't be eating cake until tea time,' Daisy gasped.

'That is when she is *expected* to do so, but we cannot be certain,' Maud said sharply.

'You're right,' Daisy panted, running to keep up with Maud. 'I'd have a finger in the icing as soon as the box was open.'

They hurried past a farm, brown fields and bare hedges. A cold wind had sprung up and it began to drizzle. Maud wondered if it would turn to sleet by nightfall, or even snow. They turned up the collars of their coats, secured their hats more firmly and hurried on.

They reached the laird's estate. After the gloomy loch side, the cottages dotted about looked cosy and festive with their softly glowing windows. At the far end of the avenue, two or three windows of Linnhe Castle were lighted.

They came to Ivy's cottage, opened the garden gate and walked up the path. On the front doorstep sat a colourful square biscuit tin. Daisy snatched it up.

'What are you doing?'

They turned at the sound of the sharp voice.

'I don't know what that is, but it doesn't belong to you.' Ivy Fraser stood on the path behind them in her hat and coat, her round, usually cheerful, face wearing a frown.

'I'm sorry, but we didn't hear you behind us. I must apologise for my assistant,' Maud went on, 'but she has your best interests at heart. We both do.'

Ivy stared at them. 'Whatever do you mean?'

'It's about the recent spate of deaths. We think you may be the next victim and the method of death is in that tin.'

Ivy looked aghast. 'You had better come into the house – and bring that with you.' She gestured to the tin in Daisy's hand.

She led them into a pleasant little sitting room, set down her bag and removed her gloves. They all stood around rather awkwardly.

Daisy held out the McVitie & Price biscuit tin, printed on the lid with a charming classical scene of mother and child. 'You had better have a keek inside.'

Ivy went to take it, but then pulled her hands back. 'I'm not sure that I want to.'

'I dinna think it's anything that's going to bite you. More like it's something you'd want to bite *into*.'

Puzzled, Ivy accepted the tin and slowly prised it open. 'Oh.'

Maud and Daisy crowded around her. Inside was something wrapped in a muslin cloth.

'Hand it over and I'll open the cloot,' Daisy said. 'Dinna worry, Maud, I won't touch what's inside. I've still got my gloves on, Ivy hasna.'

'Don't touch it,' said Maud. 'I also am wearing gloves and I'm the one who should take the risk.'

Ivy set the tin down on a side table as Maud took over. She carefully unwrapped the contents and said, 'It smells like cheese.'

'Something mingin,' confirmed Daisy.

Maud held a wedge of blue cheese on the opened cloth. 'A blue cheese.'

'One of my favourites,' said Ivy, her face pale.

'Is there a note with it?' Maud asked.

They all peered into the tin. At the bottom was a distinctive small square envelope.

'It is probably best that you don't touch that either.' Maud directed this statement at Ivy. Would you like to open and read the note to us, Daisy?'

Daisy removed the envelope in her gloved hands and read aloud from the single sheet of white paper, as Maud replaced the cheese. *Many happy returns of the day. I wonder if you can guess who this is from?'*

'Dinna eat the cheese!' Daisy blurted out. 'It's poisoned. It has to be. Who'd send an anonymous gift if they're a good friend?'

Ivy's mouth fell open.

'I'm afraid it's true,' added Maud. 'Daisy and I received a message telling us that someone was to be poisoned by a deadly mushroom. And as the other murders have taken place in the afternoon...'

'But that's cheese, not a mushroom, and it's only luncheon time,' whispered Ivy, clearly unwilling to believe her gift could be so deadly.

'The symptoms make themselves known a few hours after ingestion,' Maud explained. 'If you had eaten the cheese at luncheon, by tea time you would know you were dying.'

Ivy's face turned white. 'How could a murderer know what my favourite cheese is?'

'That's what we'd like to ken.' Daisy placed the note back in the tin.

Maud picked up the cheese once more, taking care to keep it on its cloth base. She held it up and studied it.

'Look, there are holes made from some implement.' She angled it so that Daisy and Ivy could see. 'It's been cleverly done, the puncture marks made to coincide with the blue veins, but if you look closely, small pieces of what seems to be pale flesh have been pushed inside.'

'A poisonous mushroom?'

'I think that's a safe guess, Daisy.' Maud replaced the cheese in the tin and peeled off her gloves, thankful she and Daisy had each brought a spare pair with them. She dropped the gloves into the tin, indicating to Daisy to do the same, and secured the lid firmly. 'We should wash our hands thoroughly before we do anything else.'

Ivy nodded and led them into the kitchen.

'We didn't know who the murderer's next victim was to be until a short while ago,' Maud told Ivy, as she and Daisy soaped their hands. 'I'm very sorry. It's a horrid birthday gift.'

Ivy took a deep shuddering breath. 'I think I need to sit down.'

Daisy quickly dried her hands and helped Ivy onto a kitchen chair at the table. 'Where are your drinking glasses?'

Ivy nodded at a cupboard. Daisy filled a glass with cold water and handed it to Ivy.

'Thank you.' Ivy took a long drink. She put the glass down on the scrubbed wooden table. 'You've saved my life, both of you.'

'Think naething of it,' said Daisy with a pleased smile.

'Would you mind if we take away the tin and its contents?' Maud asked. 'I'd like to make sure the contents are properly disposed of with no further risk to anyone.'

'Do what you like with it. I never want to see it again. Who would want to do such a thing to another person?'

'We don't know yet,' Maud told her, 'but I promise you we *will* find out.'

As Ivy walked them to the front door, Maud asked, 'Will you be all right here on your own until your husband returns?' She was certain the murderer wouldn't try again to kill Ivy, at least not at present, given X couldn't yet know his attempt had failed.

'Yes, he will be back from work within a few hours,' Ivy said in a shaky voice. 'I won't open the door to anyone until he gets home.'

'It would be better if you didn't go out of the house, so as not to alert the murderer we are on to him, until choir practice tomorrow,' Maud added, as an idea came to her, 'and then arrive as late as possible.'

'Maud,' Daisy said, once the two of them were down the path and through the garden gate, 'do you think Maggie left the poisoned cheese? She kent all about the mushrooms—'

'If Maggie is the killer, it would be foolish of her to reveal to us her knowledge of fungi.' Maud closed the gate behind them. 'And I think we can be certain that X is not a fool.'

'Och, well, we have a few more things to put in your notebook.'

'Indeed we do, Daisy. Under *Knowledge*: who knew of Ivy Fraser's birthday?'

'The answer,' Daisy said with a sigh, 'is all the choir members.'

'And Beatrice.'

'Aye, that goes without saying.'

'Daisy, nothing goes without saying in the detective business.' Maud took a breath of the wonderfully fresh air as they walked along the lane, realising how close Ivy Fraser had come to being poisoned. A gleam of pale wintry sun shone on fields of brown ploughed land and the dull green of winter pasture. In the distance snow-capped mountains rose steeply. It was good to be alive, she thought.

'And under *Opportunity* in my notebook,' Maud continued, 'I will add: query who was able to travel to wherever *Amanita virosa* grows. Maggie said the destroying angel likes mossy soil under beech trees...'

'And that it's too late in the year now to find many, and they have to be freshly picked.'

'Which means we must also consider who has very recently visited another area...'

Maud and Daisy looked at each other.

'Beatrice,' Daisy said.

'We need to find out if the fungi can be found in Arisaig. Beatrice is a strong suspect for the murderer, but she's not the only one.'

Daisy took a deep breath. 'What about the pretend bogle?'

Maud smiled. 'So you accept ghosts don't exist?'

'Maybe nae that one.'

'I see. Well, we need to know who had access to the village hall at that particular time to play the ghost.'

'Anyone, as everyone kens the key is kept under the stone by the door.'

'Beatrice appeared soon after the apparition disappeared, but that's too obvious a connection to make.'

'We havena got the murder of Joseph Watson on our list yet,' Daisy suddenly said. 'As soon as we get back to Clara's, I'll add his name as well as Ivy's.'

'Thank you, Daisy. The question there is who knew Joseph would be present at the pond excavation, given that he wasn't employed to do any of the work? The laird would know, the two McDougall brothers because they work for him, and possibly Maggie the cook and Mrs Wilson the housekeeper.'

'And Alasdair?'

Maud stopped walking and looked at Daisy. 'Do we honestly believe he is our X?'

'Nae, but he doesna seem that keen on our investigation,' Daisy said doubtfully.

'I'm sure that's because he's concerned for the safety of his wife. I will put his name down if you feel I must, but only lightly.' Maud smiled.

Daisy looked relieved and the pair walked on again.

'One other question under *Knowledge*, and still considering Joseph,' Maud continued, 'is who knew enough about explosives to kill him in that way?'

'That would be the laird as it was his garden and he was in the army. Beatrice probably kens something about them from her husband, and Walter Stevenson works in the quarry.'

'Agreed. And finally, under *Opportunity*, who was in a position to throw a stick of dynamite at Joseph Watson?'

Daisy huffed. 'Och, the world and his dog,' she said, exasperated.

'Or... the *murderer*.'

TWENTY-ONE

On Saturday morning, Maud and Daisy were deliberately late down to breakfast to be certain of having the room to themselves. Having saved Ivy Fraser from a diabolical death, their spirits were high.

Just as they had finished their scrambled eggs, Clara's housemaid entered the dining room, a familiar white envelope in her hand.

'This came for you, miss.' She bobbed a curtsy to Maud.

'Thank you, Netta.'

As soon as the girl had departed, Maud held up the envelope to show Daisy.

Daisy sighed. 'I didna think we'd hear from X again after we foiled his attempt to kill Ivy.'

'Ivy must have done as we'd requested and stayed indoors, so he doesn't yet know she's alive and well.' That was good, as Maud intended to watch the reaction of the other choir members when Ivy walked into the hall this afternoon.

Maud opened the envelope, slid out the sheet and studied the writing. There was a moment's silence as she scanned the words and then she read them out.

Is it near or is it far?
Will you go by foot or car?
Up here you can see the signs
And join them up, using lines.
Mind your step and where you go
Beware the scree and rocks below.

Daisy sat back. 'Crivvens!'

'To work then,' Maud said briskly.

'Wait.' Daisy put out a hand. 'There's something written on the back.'

Maud turned over the sheet of paper. '*This is the last clue*,' she read aloud. '*It's been fun, but I must stop some time. Au revoir. X.*'

'Goodbye?' said Daisy. 'He doesna think we'll solve the clue and catch him?'

'On the contrary, Daisy. The literal translation of *au revoir* is *until we see each other again.*'

A chill flowed down Maud's spine. She glanced at Daisy and saw her friend shiver.

'More to the point,' she went on, 'why is he stopping *now*?'

Daisy frowned. 'He says he's had his fun.'

'He says it's *been* fun, which is not quite the same thing. It seems he had a purpose, and after this one last murder his mission will be complete.' Maud frowned as she turned the paper over again.

'Let's list the forms of transport first,' suggested Daisy, retrieving her notepad and pencil from her cardigan pocket. 'It might make things clearer.'

She noted down *by foot or car?* They both stared at the four words.

'As clear as a coo-pat,' murmured Daisy.

'Let's start at the beginning,' suggested Maud. '*Is it near or far?* That's not at all helpful.'

'If we look at the next line, that might help.'

'*Will you go by foot...*'

'He hasna sent us very far with the other murders, and he must ken we dinna have a motor car, so maybe this one is the same. How far can someone walk?'

Maud smiled. 'A man, a woman or you, Daisy?'

'An average person,' Daisy said huffily.

'Very well. An average person – by that I mean not a woman in one of those ridiculous hobble skirts – can probably comfortably walk three miles in an hour.'

'Shall we say the clue is taking us nae more than three miles?' Daisy asked hopefully.

'That sounds credible.'

'So we dinna need to worry about how far a motor car can drive?'

'That could almost be an infinite distance, so I think we can safely ignore that part of the clue.'

'Why do you think X put it in then?'

'Hmm, good point.' Another thought came to Maud. 'Perhaps *will you go by foot or car?* doesn't exclude other forms of transport.'

'You mean someone could also go by bicycle, train, horse or boat? That doesna help much either.'

'No, you're right. I mustn't complicate matters. It does sound, though, as if you have a choice. That *both* of those modes of transport would get you there.'

'So nae just one of them? That it's got to be somewhere with a footpath and a road.'

Daisy lifted the teapot in its knitted cosy and poured them both another cup of tea. She added a little milk to each from the pretty flowered jug.

'Thank you, Daisy.' Maud took a sip from her cup.

'If it has to have a path, though, doesna that mean a person could also travel by bicycle or horse?'

'You'd think so...' Maud agreed slowly.

'Third line?' suggested Daisy.

'It talks about *up here*, so it's at the top of something. In Inverness-shire there are many tops. For example, there are more than fifty Munros—'

'Mountains over three thousand feet high?' Daisy paled. 'I'm nae climbing any of those.'

Maud smiled. 'Most are too far for X to be referring to. The closest one to Fort William is of course Ben Nevis.'

'Aye, I ken, the highest mountain in Britain,' said Daisy with a sigh. 'What height is that one?'

'Something over four thousand feet.'

Daisy snorted. 'I'm *definitely* nae climbing that.'

'Don't you remember when those two ladies climbed Salisbury Crags three years ago?'

'Aye, but that's in Edinburgh and only... I dinna ken how tall it is.'

'Getting on for six hundred feet.'

'There you are then.'

They both returned to the clue.

'If nae a mountain,' Daisy added, hope in her voice, 'what about a house? It only needs to be something higher than a normal building. A castle, maybe?' She looked at Maud.

'I'm not sure it's the laird behind all this, you know, Daisy.'

'I never said it was! At least I've nae said it recently.'

'If we continue with a tall building, what else have we got besides a castle?'

They sat silent for a moment.

'An observatory,' Daisy suddenly said. 'I'm sure Clara told me in one of her letters there used to be one nae far from the High Street. But it closed more than five years ago because they ran out of money.'

An observatory? Maud thought of the one in Edinburgh. Thomas Short, Maud's father had told her, was a scientific

instrument maker and after he died, a woman called Agnes
Short claimed she was his natural daughter, his only child, and
therefore the owner of his Great Telescope. The claim was
never proved, but luckily – Maud's father had added with a
smile – she was a good businesswoman. She opened an observatory in a wooden hut next to the Nelson Monument on Calton
Hill. There were continuous disagreements with the local coun-
cil, which resulted in the observatory being pulled down, but a
few years later she moved her business to the High Street.
There she added two extra floors and a viewing platform with a
dome housing the camera obscura, which afforded excellent
views over the city. The building had been renamed The
Outlook Tower and it was still there. Maud liked the story of a
woman succeeding despite the obstacles men had thrown in her
path.

'Mind, I think Clara said the upper observatory is now an
hotel,' Daisy went on.

Maud looked up. 'There were two observatories?'

'Aye, one at sea level and the other on top of Ben Nevis.'

'Daisy, I believe I've got it!'

'Then dinna keep it to yourself.'

'Look.' Maud tapped the letter with a slim finger. 'Lines
three and four could be referring to that.'

'*Up here you can see the signs. And join them up, using
lines.*' Daisy looked at her. 'Signs and lines? What's that
supposed to mean?'

'The constellations, perhaps. The imaginary lines that
connect a group of stars and form an outline representing a
subject. The signs of the zodiac.'

'You mean the sign you were born under, Gemini and the
like?'

'Yes. You can see the zodiac constellations in the night sky,
but not all at the same time or from the same place of course.'

'So that's what you'd observe from an observatory?'

'There are also meteorological lines. I don't know exactly how it works, but they are something to do with taking readings of the weather, and that's done at an observatory.'

Daisy sighed. 'It all fits in, doesna it?'

'Perhaps we won't have to climb as far as the summit of Ben Nevis.'

'I hope not. I dinna like the sound of those last two lines.'

'Mind your step and beware the rocks below? Nor do I, Daisy.'

'It's *Mind your step and where you go Beware the scree and rocks below*. You forgot about the scree.' Daisy got to her feet and placed their teacups on the tray with the teapot. 'Maybe you should show me how to do some of your ballet and Indian clubs exercises. I might be needing some extra strength in the near future.'

'Ha! I knew you'd come round to exercising sooner or later.'

'We've done nothing but exercise since we got here. My legs are aching from all the walking and riding of bicycles.'

'Then you should make the most of an excellent start, Daisy.'

'Just show me what I need to do, and I'll take care of the rest.'

That afternoon, preoccupied with the thought of climbing Ben Nevis, no matter how short a distance they might have to ascend, Maud walked with Daisy and Clara to the village hall. She had earlier told Daisy she would be watching Beatrice when Ivy Fraser made her late entrance and she asked Daisy to keep an eye on the others in the choir.

They entered the hall. Beatrice was there, arranging her sheets of music while chatting to the three Moffat sisters, all dressed in their customary black.

'Ah, ladies,' she said, briefly glancing at them. 'I think we are now complete and can begin the session.' With a satisfied swish of her black crêpe skirts, Beatrice took her place at the front of the choir.

How could Beatrice say the choir was complete? Maud thought. Had Ivy already arrived?

Maud joined the altos, while Daisy and Clara made their way to the soprano section. She looked across to see if Ivy had indeed arrived and was standing with the other sopranos, but she wasn't there. Good, thought Maud.

Lord Urquhart was standing with the basses. The men were clustered together, practising their part. Ever competitive, Maud thought. The choir was supposed to work as a whole, not... He looked up and shot Maud a smile.

The hall door opened and even in the flickering light from the gas lamps, Maud saw Beatrice look up with a start. Ivy burst in.

'I'm sorry I'm late, Beatrice!' Ivy called breathlessly. 'Because I was away from the tea shop yesterday afternoon, I had a few things to catch up on this morning.'

Maud saw Beatrice pale.

'Of course.' Beatrice looked as if she might faint. 'Well, we're very glad to see you here.'

As Ivy removed her coat, hung it with the other coats at the side of the hall and took her place, Maud hastily reviewed what she and Daisy knew of their two main suspects.

A number of things seemed to point to the laird being the killer: his knowledge of John Noble's fear of cats, his finding the body of Emily Black in the loch, standing next to Jane Rankin when she was shot, allowing Joseph Watson to be at the site of the explosion when he had no role there. But there was nothing to suggest he had given Ivy Fraser a poisoned cheese.

Maud now thought that perhaps *Beatrice* should take the laird's place as their prime suspect. Hadn't she been the one to find her husband's body and wouldn't she have known of his cat phobia? He knew something about explosives, and wives often pick up knowledge from their husbands. Beatrice was a keen gardener and had not long returned from Arisaig. Was that where the deadly fungi grew? And had she been the one to push tiny slithers of poison into Ivy's birthday gift? But this was all speculation; it seemed there was nothing to connect her to the murders of Emily or Jane.

Of course, there were other considerations: Beatrice enjoyed rhyming, which the laird showed no interest in, and she had an interest in crochet work. Maud pictured the crochet hook on Beatrice's kitchen table and wondered if such an implement could be used to insert the pieces of mushroom into the veins of the cheese.

But why, thought Maud, would Beatrice jeopardise her own choir's chances in the fast-approaching competition?

TWENTY-TWO

On Sunday morning, Maud and Daisy attended church with the Ross family.

'Today we have lit the second blue Advent candle on the evergreen wreath,' intoned the minister, 'to recognise the virtue of love. Nothing is more important to a human being than love.'

Love, thought Maud, as the minister continued his sermon. It can drive people to do the most extraordinary things, both good and bad.

She glanced down towards the front of the kirk where Lord Urquhart sat, taller than the rest of the congregation, next to Captain Farquharson. Then she looked across the aisle to the pew where Beatrice sat; her face had a strange, closed expression. Daisy noticed this too and she shot Maud a look.

When the service was over, most of the congregation, including Lord Urquhart and the laird, Maud noticed, went to take tea in the vestry. Daisy made their apologies and hurried Maud out of the kirk.

'We must search that woman's house right now, before she's finished tea and blether with the minister.' Daisy pushed her arm through Maud's and hastened her along the road.

Maud came to a halt. 'I'm not sure we should break into another person's house and especially not on the Sabbath.'

Daisy snorted. 'You were going to climb through the window of that MP's house in Edinburgh to retrieve those letters back in the summer – and then you were dressed as a clergyman.'

Maud couldn't deny that it was true.

'Besides,' Daisy added, 'Beatrice doesna snib her door.'

That also was true, so perhaps it wouldn't strictly be housebreaking, Maud thought. She allowed herself to be propelled forward again. 'But what do you expect us to find, Daisy?'

'If I kent that, we could point the finger at her. We need *evidence*.'

Maud couldn't deny that evidence was essential to a detective. 'We had better hurry, then, as we've probably got no more than half an hour.'

'That's what I said, only nae in those exact words.'

They kept up a smart pace and before long reached the cottage on the edge of the laird's estate.

It looked as before, minus the decorative pots in the front garden and the plume of bonfire smoke rising from the back. A pale sun shone in the hard blue sky. There was no one in sight and all that could be heard was the occasional burst of song from a robin.

They entered through the front gate, hurried up the path and were about to lift the latch on the door when another sound broke the quiet. The squeak of a bicycle in need of a squirt of oil. Maud's heart sank.

'Quick,' Daisy hissed and pulled Maud into the bushes.

They stood there, rooted to the spot in the greenery, and watched the young postman park his bicycle before walking jauntily up the path. From his bag he produced a couple of letters, opened the cottage door and dropped them on the hall table. He shut the door. But instead of retracing his steps and going on his way, he pulled a small tin from his pocket and, whistling snatches of "Roamin' in the Gloamin'", proceeded to roll a cigarette. He leaned against the cottage wall, puffing and gazing at the sky.

Maud silently ground her teeth. Would he never go about his lawful duties? Eventually he pushed himself away from the wall, stubbed out the remains of the cigarette and closed the tin. He retrieved his bicycle and disappeared down the lane.

Maud's spirits rose again. She peered out from the bushes.

'Now,' urged Daisy in a low voice, 'before anyone else comes.' She gave Maud a shove.

It was the work of a moment for them to dash into the cottage and close the door behind them. They stood together in Beatrice's hall, breathing heavily.

'I'll look upstairs,' Maud whispered, 'while you search downstairs. And keep an eye and an ear out for Beatrice's return.'

'All right.' Daisy looked up the dark stairs and went in search of the sitting room.

Maud took hold of the banister and ascended the staircase. There were only two rooms up there, one each side of the stairs at the end of a very short corridor. She carefully turned the handle of the nearest door. Beatrice's bedroom. Maud walked in.

She looked about her. An antique rug of red and browns on the floor, books on a small shelf, three botanical prints in oval frames on the far wall, and on the mantelpiece a grey and blue china figurine of a couple dressed in Regency costume. Crocheted blankets were folded over the arms and back of a chair and at the bottom of the single bed. Under the window stood an oak desk.

Was that where Beatrice wrote the clues? Maud hurried over to the desk, its top covered in dark green leather. On it sat an unlit oil lamp, a wooden letter rack, a small bottle containing black ink and a pen. Everything had been placed just so. She would have to take care to ensure she didn't disrupt the perfect symmetry.

Maud examined the fresh sheets of white paper and envelopes in the rack with her fingertips. They appeared to be of the same quality as those sent to her and Daisy. More importantly, the envelopes were also small and square.

Maud straightened. That type of envelope was not uncommon, and she knew something more was required.

On the nightstand stood a book with a crocheted cover. Maud picked up Beatrice's Bible and admired the woman's intricate handiwork, which included a depiction of the cross on the front. She frowned, finding it difficult to reconcile the image of a devout Beatrice with the merciless killer.

Crossing to the bookshelf, she considered its contents. A mixture of romantic novels and books on horticulture. She selected one of the latter and turned to the contents page. There was a section on fungi.

Maud replaced it on the shelf. The books, like the envelopes, were circumstantial. Had she been expecting a page – *Amanita virosa*, the destroying angel – to be marked by a slip of paper? That only happened in detective stories.

Giving one last look, Maud let herself out of Beatrice's bedroom.

John Noble's bedroom appeared to be untouched, left as it had been since last occupied. Her first thought was that it was a shrine to the dead man, and she immediately felt ashamed at the idea of entering. She stood in the doorway.

It was a plainer, smaller room than Beatrice's opposite. On the floor by the single bed had been placed a pair of tweed slippers, matching oval hairbrushes were arranged on the tallboy and in a corner stood a porcelain washstand. A large painting hung on one wall.

Maud stepped into the room and walked towards the

picture. She recognised it as a reproduction of *Sleeping Venus with Cupid*. The French artist Poussin had depicted the goddess of love, sleeping naked in a sensual pose under trees. At her feet was her son Cupid with his bow and arrow. The brightly painted body of Venus, set against a darkly painted rural background, showed two men gazing lustfully at her from behind a tree.

The painting spoke of shadows and secrets. Did John Noble have secrets?

Maud looked at the bed. The pillow had been plumped, the cover straightened. In the shaft of cold sunlight coming through the window, something caught her eye on the Paisley patterned eiderdown. Something so small she could easily have missed it, caught down one of the stitched squares. Maud eased it out. A tiny clump of short black hair. She examined it closely. It didn't look like human hair. Was it... from a *cat*? Had John Noble been frightened to death by the animal he feared most?

Maud's gaze travelled over the bed. The threads of the quilted cover looked as though they had been pulled. Could they be the claw marks of a cat?

Her thoughts went immediately to *The Hound of the Baskervilles*. In that Sherlock Holmes story, a spectral canine haunts Dartmoor at night, howling for blood. One night Sir Charles Baskerville is found dead from a heart attack, his face twisted in stark terror, frightened to death by the hound of hell.

The Nobles' cottage was hardly the Grimpen Mire, nor the cat in the laird's household a ghostly hound, but to the victim it could cause the same extreme fright. Maud imagined John Noble having his post-luncheon nap, the curtains pulled across the window and the room dark. She pictured him being woken suddenly by something warm and heavy on his chest, kneading and clawing, inches from his face, the feline's dusty odour and its unblinking yellow eyes staring at him. Yes, she thought, that could cause a man's heart to fail.

Maud moved around the room. The bookshelf here contained a selection of detective stories that she was familiar with: Sherlock Holmes, Father Brown, Raffles. She tutted. No Lady Molly or Miss Gladden. John Noble clearly didn't believe in female detectives. Peering more closely at the titles, she noticed one of the Sherlock Holmes volumes was not in line with the other books but gave the impression of having been replaced hastily. Curious, Maud bent and read the name of the story on the spine. *The Hound of the Baskervilles.* Was this the novel Beatrice had moved her crocheted work onto so hurriedly, to hide it from Maud's view?

The coincidences were mounting up. And Maud didn't like coincidences.

'*Psst*! Maud!' Daisy whispered loudly up the stairs. 'I can see Beatrice walking up the lane.'

Maud didn't need to be told twice. She had no intention of jumping out of the window. The only other avenue of escape was down the staircase and out through the rear of the cottage.

'Quick! Open the back door, Daisy!'

Maud shut the bedroom door behind her and flew down the stairs. Daisy stood at the bottom, her eyes wide. She pulled Maud through the kitchen and out the back door to the sound of Beatrice singing 'Lord of All Hopefulness' as the front door latch lifted.

'Out with seconds to spare,' Maud gasped, flattening herself again the stone wall of the house.

'Aye, that was a bit too close for my liking,' whispered Daisy.

They crept round the side of the house. As soon as they heard the clank of the water pipes, signalling Beatrice filling the kettle at the kitchen sink, they hurried into the lane and, breathing freely again, made their way back to Clara's house.

'Did you find anything, Maud?' Daisy asked.

'I saw cat hairs on John Noble's bed,' Maud announced.

'Never!' Daisy gasped. She thought for a moment. 'Do you

think the laird's cat might have somehow got into their house
and given him a fricht? How far does a cat go when it's on the
prowl?'

'Perhaps it hadn't got there under its own power. What if
Beatrice borrowed the cat? Maggie told us it had disappeared
recently. Is it too big a stretch to imagine Beatrice placing it on
her sleeping husband's chest?'

Daisy wrinkled her brow. 'Probably.'

'I found a copy of *The Hound of the Baskervilles* on John
Noble's bookshelf. It looked as if it had been replaced in a
hurry. I think Beatrice had been reading it, and it was the book
she covered with her crocheted work when we first went to her
cottage.'

Daisy drew in a breath and let it out noisily. 'That would
make sense, but we'd best keep an open mind and not do the
thing you're aye telling me *not* to do.'

'What is that?'

'Fitting the crime to what you *think* you've found.'

'I would agree with you if the cat hair was all I found. But
there were also envelopes the same as those sent to us
containing the clues, and books on gardening.'

'They're maybe nae as damning. After all, other people
might have those. But the cat hairs and that dog bogle story...'

'What about you, Daisy? Did you find anything of interest?'
Maud asked.

'Nae remains of blue cheese wrapped in a cloot, if that's
what you were thinking. But I did spot in the sitting room a wee
photo of Beatrice and her husband on their wedding day. I can
see what Clara meant about him being a bonnie fellow. Beatrice
was nae bad-looking either then. She's lost a muckle amount of
weight since that picture was taken.'

An interesting point, thought Maud. Mrs Wilson, the
laird's housekeeper, had described Emily as a sonsie lass – a
cheerful and plump young woman. Emily, Jane and Ivy all

could be described as having ample figures, and so had Beatrice once. But no longer. The painting on the wall of John Noble's bedroom depicted a curvaceous Venus. Clearly John Noble had a predilection for buxom females. Maud wondered what had caused his wife to lose such a large amount of weight.

Maud's brain was still in a turmoil of excitement the follow morning. There were so many clues that seemed to point to Beatrice being the killer. Daisy accepted that, but she also stuck to her opinion that the laird was their main suspect.

'But what have we got pointing to him?' Maud asked, once they were alone in Daisy's bedroom after breakfast.

'He kent John Noble well, so he was likely to ken about the man's fear of cats, and he said he found Emily Black in the loch, but he could easily have been the one to shove her in, and... but you ken all this, Maud.' Daisy took a biscuit from the glass jar on her nightstand and bit into it. 'Ginger. One of my favourites.'

'We've just finished breakfast,' Maud pointed out.

Daisy nodded absentmindedly.

Maud sighed and continued her argument. 'There doesn't seem any sense in it. I can't picture the laird as X.'

'Why?' Daisy exclaimed, crumbs flying. 'Because he comes from a good family?'

The two friends stared at each other.

'Of course not, Daisy,' Maud said softly. 'You know I would never think that.'

'No, Maud. I ken you wouldn't, I'm sorry. I think the complications of this case are getting to me.' Daisy took another bite.

'I'm going out for a walk,' Maud announced. 'It will help to clear my head.'

'You and your ideas about fresh air and exercise.' Daisy

hurriedly finished the biscuit. 'I can come with you, if you like,' she added with a complete lack of enthusiasm.

'I appreciate your kind offer, Daisy, but I will go alone. In fact, I will take the bicycle for a spin.'

Maud felt rather pleased that she had picked up the expression. When she returned to Edinburgh, she would buy a bicycle and a pair of divided skirts the better to ride the machine. For Daisy, too, if her assistant could overcome her dislike of what she termed too much exercise.

After finding Clara, informing her what she was about to do and drawing on her coat, hat and gloves, Maud collected the bicycle from the steading and set off.

It was a pleasant ride requiring only gentle pedalling and minimal braking. As she travelled along the lane, enjoying the sensation of the cool air on her warm cheeks, she admired the majestic snowy Ben Nevis. Part of her longed to climb it and, with her fitness regime of ballet and Indian club exercise, she was sure she could manage at least some of it. How far would she and Daisy have to climb to confront X?

The more she thought about it, the more Maud was certain the person they sought was Beatrice. She examined each clue carefully in her mind.

The three dead women were all plump. Beatrice's wedding photograph showed her as equally plump. In his bedroom hung a painting of a plump Venus. It was fair to say that John Noble liked plump women. Beatrice was now exceptionally thin. Something had caused her to lose weight. The housekeeper Mrs Wilson had told them John Noble was a charmer. Had he been having affairs with the three women: Emily, Jane and Ivy? In which case, had Beatrice killed her cheating husband and then decided to get rid of the women involved?

Considering the case of John Noble, Maggie the cook mentioned the castle's cat had gone missing recently and there were cat hairs of the same colour on John Noble's bed. There was also the matter of the recently read – presumably by Beatrice – copy of *The Hound of the Baskervilles*.

Maud was now in her stride, both in terms of sifting the evidence and on her bicycle ride. She considered the case of the three women. Had Beatrice's husband told her, perhaps even thrown it in her face, that he met Emily Black every Sunday by the side of Loch Linnhe? That theory would rely on Emily, knowing her lover was dead, returning to the same spot. That was feasible, Maud decided. A last visit to the place where she had been happy in his arms and where she could mourn the passing of all the promises he would never be able to keep. Beatrice could have gone there, confronted the girl and pushed her in the water. Had the older woman heard something of Jane Rankin's gossip that Emily was carrying John Noble's baby? Would that affect a woman's mind enough to turn her to *murder*? Maud didn't know.

As to Jane Rankin, that was a little more difficult to work out. Jane's loader on the shoot had disappeared. Beatrice's figure was slight, so she could have disguised herself as a man – after all, she and Daisy had done exactly that – and acted as the loader. But how did she manage to inveigle herself into such a role?

And now Ivy Fraser. Beatrice had an interest in gardening, but how much did she actually know about fungi? She enjoyed crocheting, but could she really have used a crochet hook to push pieces of the deadly mushroom into Ivy's cheese? There was also the question of where she had found the destroying angel. Maggie had told them it didn't grow round here.

And where on earth did Joseph Watson fit in? Why had Beatrice, if she were indeed X, killed the forestry worker? Maud could imagine how it might have happened. Having successfully disguised herself as a man before, Beatrice might have done so again to be present at the laird's excavation work and she could have stood further back in the trees to toss a stick of dynamite at Joseph. The man himself had not been part of the work, had been standing alone, and so would have been easy to target. But why had *he* been a victim? Had he discovered that Beatrice was the murderer, and had she acted to silence him?

As to the final victim: who was it to be? X had made it clear in the clue that the death on Ben Nevis was to be the last murder.

Once again, Maud felt herself accumulating more questions than answers.

Maud found she was approaching the back driveway to Linnhe Castle. In a few minutes, she decided, she would turn and cycle back to Clara's. The lane here went downhill and she had travelled several hundred yards when she noticed the brakes weren't working as they should. She pressed harder. The bicycle gathered speed. Ahead, an enormous rhododendron was fast approaching. Maud let out a cry of alarm and pumped the brakes furiously. She couldn't stop; she was going to crash. A terrifying blur of green rushed past her. Clinging to the handlebars, she fought against the swerving machine and hit a bump.

She shrieked with terror as the whole world keeled over. The bicycle reared up into the air, the sky dizzy above her. The greenery of the rhododendron parted and for a long second she seemed to hang suspended. Then she plunged, the bicycle sailing off one way and she the other, as the shrubbery swallowed her up.

Maud landed hard, her skirts tangled in the gnarled branches. She gasped and waited as the green universe came slowly to a standstill.

She clumsily brushed the leaves out of her eyes and ears in time to hear footsteps running up the lane. Then a twig snapped. She heard a rough exclamation. A man's arms were about her waist and holding her tightly before she could say or do anything.

A voice murmured in her ear, 'I have you safe.'

Lord Urquhart.

Maud was furious. Where had he come from? And how did he manage to be around when she was at her most incompetent? Yet now was not the time to be angry, said a voice in her head. Lord Urquhart was a kind and helpful man.

'Are you hurt, Miss McIntyre?' He half turned, to do what she never discovered, because a sudden shout of 'Miss McIntyre!' could be heard. And suddenly his weight pressed against her. She fell back onto the earth. Her heart leaped into a gallop. What was he doing?

For a moment she lay under him, crushed against his chest. He lifted his head and gazed down at her. She felt his breath on her skin and heard it, soft and rather fast.

She looked up at him, then seeing his grin put her hands against his chest and gave a hard shove. 'Get off, you great oaf. Someone is coming!'

The sound of the voice calling again came through the bushes. Lord Urquhart rose hastily and helped Maud to her feet. She glared at him. He smiled at her. Goodness, she realised, she had told him to get off because there was someone coming. What would she have done if there hadn't been that interruption?

Maud took a few calming breaths. She would not think about it. She set about disentangling herself from him and the twigs, and emerged from the rhododendrons.

Beatrice Noble stood there.

'Miss McIntyre!' she exclaimed, her face puce.

Maud retrieved her hat from the ground and attempted to tidy her disarrayed hair and coat. 'Mrs Noble,' she returned with as much dignity as she could muster.

'Jezebel!'

Maud flinched as if she had been struck. Jezebel might have been a brazen hussy and worse, but she'd had her good side. She'd been an outspoken woman in a time when women had

little status or few rights, and had faced her death every inch a
queen.

Maud straightened her shoulders. 'Mrs No—'

'You were cavorting in the bushes with Lord Urquhart,'
Beatrice said. 'Do not deny it.'

'You are mistaken.' Whatever she may have been doing,
Maud had not been *cavorting* with him.

'I saw you enter the bushes. I saw Lord Urquhart enter soon
after. The shrubbery was twitching.' Beatrice's face was purple
and only inches from Maud's own. 'I am not mistaken.'

'If you saw me enter the bushes, you will have observed that
I *crashed* into them,' Maud pointed out.

Beatrice opened her mouth. She closed it again, drawing her
mouth into a thin line.

Lord Urquhart emerged from the shrubbery, brushing down
his Norfolk jacket. 'Ah, good afternoon, Mrs Noble.' He smiled
politely. 'Can I escort one or both of you ladies anywhere?'

Maud declined his offer and crossed to where her bicycle
lay on the ground. She picked it up.

'What caused your accident?' Lord Urquhart was behind
her again. He crouched down to examine the workings of the
machine.

Maud drew her eyes away from his taut thigh muscles
which were straining the stitching of his trousers. He looked up.
'The rear brake rod has been sawn through.'

Maud's brows drew together. 'What do you mean?'

'I mean, Miss McIntyre,' he said, standing again and looking
down at her, 'that this was no accident. It was done
deliberately.'

TWENTY-THREE

'The brake rod was probably cut with a small hacksaw and would have taken only minutes to do,' Lord Urquhart said. 'You are very lucky it was not the front brake, as that would have been considerably more dangerous.'

'I don't understand.' Maud said. 'Why did it not happen when I first applied the brakes on my ride this morning?'

'The brakes would weaken each time they were used until finally the rod snapped. Which is what has happened here.'

Maud gazed at the bicycle. Someone had tried to kill her, or at the very least ensure she had an accident. She had been fortunate indeed to have landed in rhododendrons and not in front of a motor car.

'Let me borrow Charles's motor and take you back to the Ross's house,' Lord Urquhart was saying, concern evident in his voice and on his face.

'That is kind of you, but I will take the shortcut through the woods.' Maud glanced at Beatrice, who was frowning. 'Good day to you both.' She took the machine from Lord Urquhart and walked away.

Maud's thoughts were whirling, much as her bicycle wheels

had been a short while ago. Someone wanted her dead, but whom? And what had brought Beatrice to that exact same spot at that time?

She needed to talk to Daisy, and she needed a strong cup of tea, although not necessarily in that order.

'You look like you've been through a hedge backwards,' Daisy exclaimed, when Maud entered the sitting room on her return.

'You're not far off the mark, Daisy. I went through it forward. Or rather landed *in* it,' Maud told her. 'I've had something of an adventure.'

'Michty me, what happened?' Daisy took in Maud's bedraggled hair and disarrayed clothing.

'Nothing to worry about. At least nothing I couldn't deal with.' Maud's eye fell on the tea things. 'Ah, good. I am not too late for tea.'

'It's still hot, I'll get a cup for you.' Daisy darted out of the room.

Maud tossed her hat onto the sofa and sunk into an armchair. Within a minute or two, Daisy returned with a clean cup and saucer.

'I had a wee bit of a stushie with Netta as to who was going to bring the cup. I put up a good fight and won.' Daisy grinned as she set the porcelain on the side table by Maud and poured out the tea.

'Thank you, Daisy.' Maud tipped a little milk from the jug into her cup.

Daisy took her seat again. 'Did you have an accident?'

'It was most definitely not an accident,' Maud said. 'The brakes on my bicycle had been tampered with. One of the rods had been cut through.'

Daisy gasped, wide-eyed. 'Who would do such a thing?'

'It must have been X.' Maud took a sip of the very welcome

tea. 'Which means he wants to stop us investigating any further.'

'So we've almost got him!'

'Then why did he, or she, send us the last clue?'

Daisy frowned for a moment. Her brow cleared. 'He must have posted it before he learned we'd foiled his poisoning plan.'

Maud took another sip, the hot comforting liquid seeping through her body. 'That makes sense.'

'Who kent that you would be going for a bicycle ride this morning?' Daisy went on.

'No one could have known, as I decided to do so shortly after breakfast.'

'I wonder when X cut the brake rod?'

'According to Lord Urquhart—'

'Och, he was there, was he?'

'It wouldn't have taken a moment to cut through the rod,' Maud continued. 'The bicycle hasn't been out of the steading since I last used it when we visited Beatrice at home, Ivy at the tea shop and Maggie and Mrs Wilson at the castle. That was on Tuesday. The brakes could have been tampered with at any time during the last six days.'

'Aye, but isna it more likely that X did it after Ivy revealed the cheese failure on Saturday afternoon?'

Maud was inclined to agree with Daisy. It was the most logical explanation. 'I was lucky to have a soft landing in the bushes just outside the castle grounds.'

'That's where you met his lordship, is it? In the bushes?' Daisy smirked.

She didn't realise how right she was, Maud thought, willing herself not to flush. 'Beatrice Noble was also there.'

'In the bushes? It must have been awfa crowded in there.'

'No, Daisy, I did not meet Beatrice in the bushes, but in the lane.'

Daisy sobered again. 'What was she up to?'

'I don't know, but I assume she was merely out for a walk.' Maud decided against telling Daisy of Beatrice's tirade; it was too embarrassing to recount.

'Cutting the brake rod seems a hit-and-miss method of trying to kill you, Maud.'

'I have to hope that X wasn't attempting my murder, but simply sending me a warning.'

'But how would X know which bicycle you would be riding?'

They looked at one another, then scrambled from their seats and ran out to the barn. It was as they had feared. The rear brake rod on the other bicycle had also been sawn through.

Through their efforts to find the murderer, they had put both Clara and Susan at risk.

Maud was still thinking of this the following evening as they prepared to attend choir practice. It was bitingly cold outside, with the threat of sleet in the air. Alasdair gave them a lift to the hall in his Ford car, promising to return at the end of the hour.

Four days until the competition final, Maud thought darkly. Yesterday afternoon she and Daisy had attended Joseph Watson's funeral. Tomorrow was to be the death of the next, the last, victim.

Beatrice's fixed smile was in place as all the singers gathered in the wooden building, chatting about the cold and reluctant to shed their outer garments. Beatrice had arrived early as usual and got the stove going, but it was barely sufficient to heat the room.

'*Feasgar math*,' she called, clapping her hands for attention. 'The sooner we start singing, the warmer we shall become.'

The choir members slowly began to shed their coats and stand in their usual positions.

'This is our last opportunity to sing together before the

competition final on Saturday,' Beatrice continued, 'so this evening we will rehearse all four of our competition songs. I'm sure our little choir is perfect by now.'

Perfect in what way? Maud thought. Perfect in their performance, she would hope. But perfect, too, in Beatrice's mind, if she were indeed X, in that the undesirable members had departed?

They sang their voice warm-up exercises and moved on to their set pieces. The choir did sound rather good, Maud had to admit. Perhaps they might win. She glanced across to the sopranos and Daisy flashed her a grin, the same thought appearing to cross her mind.

'Excellent,' Beatrice said, looking round the hall when the four songs had been sung to her satisfaction. 'As a special treat, I'm going to teach you a new piece...'

There were one or two groans and a number of surprised looks.

'It's very short and quite simple, I assure you,' Beatrice went on. 'I would like us to sing this in memory of my husband.' A tear came to her eye.

Instantly the mutterings were hushed and they all waited.

'Thank you,' she murmured. 'It is a traditional song, from the Gaelic, called "The Guardian Angel" and reputed to be the last words of St Columba. We will learn only the last verse.'

In a beautiful, clear soprano, Beatrice sang.

> *I am tired and I a stranger,*
> *Lead thou me to the land of angels;*
> *For me it is time to go home*
> *To the grace of God, to the peace of heaven.*

There was silence when she had finished. The choir members were visibly emotional at such a heart-rending performance and no doubt thinking of those who were no longer with

them. Maud saw Daisy rub at her eyes, and in the bass section
Lord Urquhart gave a manly cough. Had she misjudged Beatrice, after all, Maud wondered, or was the woman deliberately
arousing pity? If the latter, to what end? The only reason she
could think of was to deflect Maud's suspicion, but that seemed
too elaborate an exercise.

At the end of the evening, everyone left the village hall a
little in awe of the sublimity of the words and tune. Even Daisy
had nothing amusing to say, Maud noticed with a wry inward
smile of her own. The threatened sleet had not appeared, much
to her relief, but a light rain was falling; she had not brought an
umbrella and she was grateful for Alasdair's Ford to take them
home. It waited in the rain, raindrops glistening on the metal.
Lord Urquhart had the laird's motor car and was shepherding
in as many of the choir ladies as it could reasonably fit. Maud
sent him a quick smile before Alasdair pulled away.

She gazed out of the window of the Ford as hedges flashed
past, illuminated only by the motor car's headlights and falling
back into darkness behind them. What tomorrow would bring,
Maud couldn't be certain.

Following X's pattern of killings, the final victim would be
scheduled to an afternoon death... and the singer would be an
alto. Which meant Anne Ritchie or one of the three Moffat
sisters, none of whom had a connection with the laird. Further-
more, Anne was slender and therefore presumably not to John
Noble's taste, and the Moffats were elderly and not at all likely
to be at the base, much less even part way up, Ben Nevis
tomorrow afternoon.

There was only one other possible victim.

Maud herself.

When she woke the next morning, Maud was relieved to find
the rain had stopped and the sleet had held off.

As she entered the dining room, she saw Clara still seated, finishing her breakfast cup of tea. Wagging her tail, Ellie rose from under the table and scampered towards Maud.

'Ellie, behave,' Clara warned the dog. 'Alasdair couldn't take her to the office today,' she told Maud, 'as he's had to go to Inverness for a meeting. Susan offered to take her to school.' Clara smiled. 'Can you imagine Miss Brown trying to keep the class's attention while this silly old dog plays the fool?'

'I'm sorry, Ellie,' Maud said, as she slid into her seat at the table, 'but you can't come with us today, either, as Daisy and I also have work to do.'

'Ellie, you heard Maud,' said Clara. 'Away you go.'

Ellie plodded a couple of steps towards the door, then looked back to see if Clara had changed her mind.

'Away you go,' Clara said more firmly, and the dog continued slowly towards the door.

'What is this work you have to do today?' Clara asked, her tone carefully light, as she poured tea for Maud.

Out of the corner of her eye, Maud saw Ellie turn at the door to slink back under the table and she tried not to smile.

'We are working on the last clue, Clara,' she said.

Clara raised an eyebrow. 'The *last* clue? You ken that, do you?'

'Yes, the note said so.'

Clara took a sip of her tea. 'Well, that's a relief, if the writer can be believed. So, what does this last clue involve?'

Maud rose and went to the sideboard to help herself to a plate of fried bacon and eggs. Keeping her back turned, she said, 'Ben Nevis.'

There was a clatter of teacup on saucer and Maud whirled round.

'You're never going to climb that mountain!' Clara's cup lay on its side in a saucer of tea.

Maud hastened over and righted the cup. 'Let me ask Netta to bring you clean china.'

'Never mind about that!' Clara waved Maud's hand away.

Maud resumed her seat and spoke calmly. 'I'm hoping that we won't have to climb it, but will be able to apprehend the culprit at the base of Ben Nevis.'

'Culprit?' Clara cried. 'You make it sounds as though the fellow has been a naughty boy and stolen an apple. He's a murderer!'

The door opened and in walked Daisy. 'I see that you've told Clara we've solved the last clue.' She made her way to the sideboard. 'It's all right for Maud with her exercises, but I'm going to need building up for the climb.'

Clara let out a muffled squeak.

'Daisy,' Maud said in a warning voice, 'I told Clara only because I thought it sensible that someone should know where we are, should anything...'

'Go wrong,' finished Clara.

'Well, yes. I didn't want to worry you unnecessarily.'

'Och, I'm nae worrying *unnecessarily*. My worry is entirely *necessary*. Look at what happened to Susan's bicycle on Monday!'

'I can only apologise again for the damage—' Maud began.

'We dinna care about the damage to the *machine*, Maud. It's what might have happened to *you*.'

Daisy sat down at the table with her loaded plate and reached down to fondle the dog's ears. 'We'll be careful, Clara. Maud always is, and I follow her lead.'

Maud decided it would be wise not to contradict the last part of Daisy's sentence. 'We do have to see this case through to the end,' she told Clara. 'The person responsible for the killings must be brought to justice.'

'Aye, I can see that...'

'It's just that you dinna want to think your husband might be paying for us to be murdered,' Daisy added cheerfully.

'Daisy! That really is too much. Your poor cousin has lost all her colour.'

Daisy looked at Clara. 'As grey as porridge, right enough. Sorry, Clara. We really will be careful, I promise.'

'Do you have an Ordnance Survey map of the area?' Maud asked Clara. 'It would be a great help.'

'If you must go, it's best that you're as prepared as possible. There's one in Alasdair's study. I'll get it for you.' Clara rose and hurried from the room.

Maud and Daisy ate their breakfast in silence. Daisy surreptitiously fed Ellie a piece of bacon under the table. Clara returned within minutes. 'Here you are.'

'Thank you,' said Maud. 'As soon as we have finished our meal, we will examine it.'

No doubt deciding she could do nothing to persuade the pair to stay at home all day, Clara said, 'I'm going to find something to keep me busy until you are both safely back here.' She left the room again.

Maud and Daisy hastily finished their breakfast and made space on the table. On the white linen tablecloth, Maud unfolded the map and opened it to the section showing Fort William and the mountain.

'If we walk along here' – Maud traced the path from the town – 'it will bring us to the base of Ben Nevis.'

'How long do you think that will take?'

Maud unfolded the map further to see the scale. 'It appears to be a short walk, less than a mile, I estimate.'

'What then?' Daisy looked at her.

'Then we shall see if we have to climb or not.'

'And then?'

'When we catch X in her attempt to... finish what she has

started, I will extract a confession from her, and you will be the witness.'

'I'm nae sure I like the sound of that.'

'You will hide and be in no danger.'

'Nae, but *you* will be.'

Maud was silent for a moment. She was about to place them both in danger. 'I should inform the police, and you should stay safely here at your cousin's house.'

'Haivers!' Daisy snorted. 'We've been friends for a gey long time, Maud. If you think I'd abandon you, you're wrong.'

'Daisy, I think that the last victim is to be me...'

Daisy didn't look surprised. 'I ken. That is, I thought it might be.'

'That means X will devote all her energies to inflicting her revenge on me.'

'Her?' Daisy seemed to notice the pronoun for the first time. 'You're sure it's Beatrice?'

'I am.'

Daisy thought for a moment. 'I think you're right. Can we nae arrest her this morning, then none of us need to go to Ben Nevis?' She didn't sound hopeful.

'You know that we can only make a citizen's arrest, which requires us to witness a crime or be the victim.'

'And *then*,' said Daisy, perking up, 'we can use reasonable force—'

'Only if the person resists,' Maud cautioned.

'Aye, but she's bound to.'

'And the arrested person must be handed to the police as soon as possible.'

'Aye, aye, I ken.'

'Perhaps you should stay at Clara's,' Maud said, eyeing Daisy, 'and I will ask the constable to come with me.'

Daisy's small chin jutted out. 'I'm sticking with you.'

Maud tried once more. 'Beatrice's *raison d'être* has gone. She has nothing to lose any longer.'

'I'm going with you,' Daisy said firmly.

Maud accepted her decision with relief. She had more faith in her friend than in Constable Beggs.

'Thank you, Daisy. Now, in case we have to do some climbing,' Maud went on, 'we need to be warmly dressed and stoutly shod.'

'And we should take that map.' Daisy nodded at it open on the table.

'A compass, too, if Alasdair has such a thing.'

'I'll ask Clara.'

'We should rest this morning,' Maud said, 'so we're ready for whatever happens this afternoon.'

After luncheon, they took the Glen Nevis road out of town. After a walk of some fifteen minutes, they reached the woods on the right-hand side of the road and turned into it.

'The base of Ben Nevis,' Maud said.

She and Daisy looked around them. There was no one in sight, which was not surprising given the scent of snow in the air and the cold that threatened to make her forehead ache.

'What time is it?' Daisy asked.

Maud eased back her coat sleeve to consult her wristwatch. 'It's three o'clock. We are too early for the killer's usual time to strike.'

'I ken that's my fault, Maud.'

'It's no one's fault,' Maud hastened to reassure her friend. 'We were both on edge.'

'I just hope we dinna end up on another type of edge,' Daisy muttered darkly.

The thought had crossed Maud's mind too, but she forced it away. 'I confess I don't think Beatrice expects us to meet down here. We should start walking.' She knew it was too late in the day, with its fading light, to begin such a climb, but they had to bring this case to a conclusion.

Daisy gave a little groan, but said, 'I'm ready when you are.'

'Just think,' Maud went on, to distract them as they followed the level track, 'of the motor car that Mr Alexander drove to the top of Ben Nevis. We're not going that far,' she said with a smile, seeing Daisy's face, 'but it is quite something to imagine the little Ford bumping its way up here.'

'Lucky little Ford, is what I say.'

Maud laughed. 'That, Daisy, is why the clue referred to the option of taking a car to the top.'

After a while, they crossed the River Nevis and the track began a steep ascent. They saved their breath to climb. Some four hundred yards up, the ground levelled and Daisy let out a sigh of relief. Then the track turned sharply to the right and they were climbing steeply again. It was rocky underfoot, their boots occasionally slipping on the damp stones. Maud sent Daisy a glance that said *take care*.

'When the motor car reached the summit,' Maud went on as if their conversation had not been interrupted, 'the Ford company arranged for a special train to bring journalists from London to Fort William. The Fleet Street men were persuaded to climb the mountain.'

'So if they can, so can *we*, you mean?' Daisy sucked in another breath.

Maud smiled. 'When the journalists examined the little Ford, they found it had made the climb without a single scratch.'

'Aye, but what about the downward journey?'

'We'll take it carefully.'

They startled a small flock of ptarmigan. The birds rose from the ground, white in their winter colours and making a harsh grating sound.

The stones under their feet were becoming icy. *Mind your step and where you go,* Maud mentally recited the last two lines of the rhyme, *beware the scree and rocks below.* The higher they climbed, the colder it grew. The clouds were grey and low in the sky, and Maud was sure it would snow. Their woollen tam-o'-shanter caps with cheerful bobbles on top would keep their heads dry only for so long.

'Look, Maud, a mountain hare!' Daisy pointed excitedly.

They paused to admire the creature, like the ptarmigan in its white winter coat. Long ears alert, it raised its head from nibbling at a tussock of grass poking through a patch of snow and bounded away.

The mountain hare apparently forgotten, Daisy grumbled as she trudged along behind Maud on the narrow path.

'What a wonderful view over Loch Linnhe.' Maud indicated the water far in the distance, with snow-covered mountains beyond.

'I dinna care if I never hear of Loch Linnhe again,' Daisy muttered. 'My legs ache.'

'It's only two and a half miles from the bottom of Ben Nevis to the halfway point,' Maud said, 'and I don't believe Beatrice intends us to climb any higher.'

'Two and a half miles? That's nae *so* bad.'

Maud didn't mention that the route took a zigzag path, so it would seem a lot further. On the other hand, a straight climb would be very steep indeed.

They continued their ascent, until ahead of them Maud spotted a waterfall. 'That must be the Red Burn, the halfway point,' she said, remembering the map they had consulted that morning and which now nestled in the pocket of her coat.

'Thank the Lord. I need a wee rest,' said Daisy.

Maud glanced at her wristwatch. It was a few minutes to four o'clock. It would be dark up here by now, if it weren't for the whiteness of the snow.

They followed the path up to the burn and stood there, catching their breath. The clear water ran down from boulders and over stones. Maud took some comfort from the fact that the temperature hadn't been sufficiently cold for long enough to freeze the waterfall. The narrow, snow-covered mountain track curved round a bend, a sheer wall of rock on one side and on the other the ground falling away steeply...

Sherlock Holmes at the Reichenbach Falls, Maud thought, her mouth suddenly dry. It was one thing to know they were walking into danger; quite another to actually be in it.

'Maud,' whispered Daisy.

Maud turned and looked into the pinched face of a figure stepping round the bend in the path.

It was Beatrice Noble.

TWENTY-FOUR

'You don't look surprised to see me. Did you work out who I was?' Beatrice asked, stepping forward.

'We did,' said Maud, clearing her throat.

'Clara was right, you're quite the detectives. I'm beginning to think I was foolish to give you any help.'

'There is still much we don't know.'

With a gloved hand, Beatrice cleared the snow off a boulder and sat down. 'Such as?'

'Such as why you killed members of your own choir,' said Daisy.

Beatrice exhaled, her breath visible in the cold air. Even in the fading light, Maud could see the strain in her face, the skin pulled tight against her cheekbones. Her coat, Maud noticed for the first time, hung off her thin body.

'My husband was having affairs with those Jezebels. He liked plump women; I used to be buxom once, you know.' Beatrice's voice was tired. 'He said I was too scrawny for his taste. He told me all this and threw it in my face. Then that strumpet Emily... He said she was carrying his child. Even if it weren't true, it would have been sooner or later.'

Maud felt a pang of sympathy for both women. 'But why kill Joseph?'

'He hit the wrong note once too often.' Beatrice gave a harsh laugh. 'How could we win the final with him in it?'

The pang of sympathy Maud felt disappeared. The woman was mad, she realised.

'Couldna you just have asked him to leave the choir?' Daisy asked.

'Then we would have too few members to be able to take part.'

'But you were bumping them off anyway.'

'Things have a way of working themselves out. You, Miss Cameron, and Miss McIntyre here, came along, and then Lord Urquhart. And I could sing any part myself.'

'Even bass?' asked Daisy.

'Perhaps not that, but I can manage a pretty decent tenor.'

'Especially in "Loch Lomond",' Maud said, remembering the voice of the ghost that night in the hall.

Beatrice smiled. 'That was a rather good performance all round, don't you think?'

'How did you make the window tirl?' demanded Daisy. 'And the burning red eyes?'

Beatrice's laugh was genuine. 'I had you fooled, didn't I, Daisy Cameron? I attached a length of string to the window handle; the frame was loose anyway, so it was not difficult to make it rattle and there were shadows in the hall. It worked well, I thought.'

'And the glowing eyes?' Maud asked.

'A lantern covered with red paper, a piece of black material over it with circular holes cut out.' She spoke so casually.

'I suppose you did it to frighten us off?' Maud said.

Beatrice nodded.

'And the cutting of the brake rod on my bicycle?'

'That, Miss McIntyre,' Beatrice said, looking straight at her, 'was done to kill you. You were so wrapped up in your thoughts that you failed to notice my following you at a distance. I wished to ensure you had an accident. But then Lord Urquhart appeared.' She grimaced. 'You foiled my plan to get rid of the hussy Ivy Fraser and for that I wanted revenge. I still do.'

Maud knew they were running out of time and she must ask her other questions quickly. 'Did you put the laird's cat on your husband's chest to induce his heart attack?'

'Of course I did!' Beatrice sounded happy again. 'He was taking his afternoon sleep, the curtains drawn, snoring his ridiculous head off. It wasn't difficult to persuade the animal to come to me,' she added, 'not when I offered it a piece of doctored chicken.'

'You *drugged* the cat?' Daisy sounded more offended by that than by the murder of four people.

'Naturally. Have you ever tried to carry a cat in a bag?'

'I canna say I have.'

'Then I bundled it into the hessian sack and took it home.' Beatrice seemed to be enjoying confessing. 'I crept into John's bedroom with the cat.' She closed her eyes as she relived the moment. 'I put the thing on his chest. He must have felt its weight or perhaps the animal clawing at the bedspread because he woke with a start. He saw the creature's eyes staring at him, glowing in the darkened room.' Beatrice opened her eyes and laughed. 'It gave me such joy to see him gasp, attempt to push the cat off and then fall back on the pillow.'

She fixed her eyes on Maud. 'You can ask me one more question and then we must complete this business.'

Stay calm, Maud told herself. Choose a question, and then be prepared...

'One question each,' put in Daisy.

Beatrice turned to gaze at her. She sighed. 'Very well. You realise you must die too, of course.'

Daisy took a step forward. 'Where did you get the mushroom you put in Ivy's cheese with your crochet hook?'

'Step back, Miss Cameron,' Beatrice said sharply.

Daisy cast a glance at Maud, then did as Beatrice had instructed.

'So you worked out the crochet hook, did you? You can have a pat on the back for that. Where did I get the *Amanita virosa*, the destroying angel? Arisaig. I knew that it grows well there from my previous visits to my sister. I was fortunate to find a small clump just in time...'

'Aye, very fortunate,' muttered Daisy.

Beatrice ignored her and continued. 'Just in time, as it was rather late in the season. Being near the coast, Arisaig is slightly warmer than Fort William. The mushroom has to be used fresh, you know, so I picked a small one on Thursday and brought it back with me in time for Ivy's birthday on Friday. And talking of temperature, it is getting rather cold, so I'd appreciate your last question as soon as possible, Miss McIntyre.'

Maud's mind raced. There were still questions to be asked, and somehow they also had to effect Beatrice's arrest. 'Jane's vanished loader at the shoot,' she said. 'I assume that was you.'

'It was.' Beatrice rose from the boulder. 'Now, that was your last question.'

'That was a comment, not a question. My question is this: how did you convince Jane to allow you to act as her loader?'

'Oh, that wasn't difficult at all.' She waved a hand in dismissal. 'I told the foolish woman it was to be a bit of a jape. I knew what the work involved as I used to do it for my father when I was younger. I persuaded Jane that I should dress as a man and we could show the laird and the other men that two women could beat the male shooting teams.'

Beatrice stepped closer to Maud and Daisy. 'Let me answer one final question for you both. Why did John and I marry? There was love – at first. I'd never been beautiful, but I was buxom. Then I lost a baby, and another... and, well, I lost weight and eventually I became as you see me now.'

The pain and bitterness was evident in Beatrice's eyes.

'As to why I stayed, what might I have done if I'd left him? I would have had no money, no status...'

'You could have got a job,' suggested Daisy.

'A job? I dinna think so.' Beatrice mocked Daisy's speech.

Beatrice pushed a hand into her coat pocket and pulled out a knife. She pointed it at Maud, then Daisy, and back again. 'Who would like to go first?'

As she spoke, the first few flakes of snow came drifting soundlessly out of the leaden sky.

'Look,' said Daisy, 'it's snowing.'

Automatically, Beatrice glanced up.

Daisy, small but fierce, lunged towards Beatrice. Through the whirling snowflakes, Maud saw the two women grapple. Beatrice shouted a curse. Then there was a gasp. It all happened in an instant.

'Daisy!' Maud leaped forward, her boot catching on a stone. She heard a frantic shout.

'Maud! Run! Get away!'

But Maud could do nothing. She was powerless to stop herself from hurtling down the slope.

TWENTY-FIVE

Maud landed on her knees in deep snow. She could just about make out the ledge from where she had fallen, but could not see what was below her through the swirling white flakes. The cold wet snow was already soaking through her skirts. Too afraid to move quickly and risk plunging down the side of the mountain, Maud shifted carefully into a crouching position.

It was only then that she noticed the complete silence. The sounds of the struggle had ceased. Even the waterfall ran muted in her ears. She strained her eyes to see above her.

Then she heard someone breathing loudly.

There was one soft step, followed by another. A clump of snow dropped off the ledge above and again there was silence. Something told her the person above wasn't Daisy.

The breathing had stopped. Maud's heart thudded. Where was Beatrice? Was she getting closer? Waiting for her at the top of the ledge?

And where was Daisy? Oh God, had Beatrice killed her? A cold nausea washed over her.

She fought to quell her rising panic. Close your eyes and listen, she told herself. Beatrice was still above, she was sure of it. Yes, she was. Maud could hear the woman's breathing, shallow and rapid.

'Where are you, Miss McIntyre? I know you must be near-by,' came Beatrice's taunting voice. 'You thought you and your little friend were so very clever, didn't you? That was why I sent you the clues. Oh, I admit you got on better solving them than I had expected, which is why I mentioned you to Mr Austin. That was to give you another case to slow you down. Well, never mind, I almost achieved everything I set out to do.' She paused and Maud found herself shaking, before Beatrice began again. 'Why didn't I find employment, your pert red-haired assistant asks? Well, we can't all be lady detectives.' Beatrice laughed.

Her voice was fluctuating in volume, so Maud felt certain she was looking around. She prayed that her downward slide in the snow had already been obliterated by fresh snowflakes. She must stay quiet and not alert Beatrice to where she hid.

'And so,' went on Beatrice, 'I intended to end with Ivy, but you interfered with my plans, so you must take her place. Of course, John will wonder who you are when you arrive in his heavenly choir, but he will have to make do with you as his second alto.'

Maud could not stay where she was and freeze to death. And Daisy needed help. Cautiously, she put out a gloved hand and felt for a hold above her in the rock. She could not have fallen more than ten feet. She was young and fit. If those two women could climb Salisbury Crags, then she could certainly manage ten feet.

Putting one tentative boot in a gap in the rock, Maud pulled herself up, her heart beating fast. Refusing to give in to the impulse to glance down, she climbed slowly.

She reached the edge and peered over. The sky was muted, but the snow gave off its strange blue glow. There was the boulder where Beatrice had sat, but of Daisy there was no sign.

Her heart turned to lead. Had Beatrice thrown her friend's body over the side of the mountain? Had she, Maud, brought about the death of her dear friend?

No, that could not have happened, and she would not allow it to be so. Wherever Daisy was, she was still alive. The thought gave Maud a boost of energy.

She scrambled up onto the path and climbed to her feet. Through the flurry of snowflakes, soft as feathers, a rock clattered down beside her. She looked up at the ridge – standing on a high pinnacle was Beatrice, her coat flapping in the breeze, the knife in her hand.

'Are you coming down, Mrs Noble, or am I to come up?' Maud called, her hands on her hips, her strong voice reverberating off the rock.

'I have no intention of allowing you to remove my liberty.'

'It is not my action that will bring about your incarceration and the hangman's noose, but your own.'

Beatrice tutted. 'This situation has become impossible.'

'Have you any suggestion to make?'

'You could take your own life,' she said.

'*That* is impossible.'

Beatrice sighed. 'I am quite sure that a woman of your intelligence will see that there can be only one outcome to this affair. It has been a pleasure to see the way in which you and your assistant have solved the clues and found the places...'

Not all of them in time, Maud thought with shame.

'Not all of them in time,' Beatrice went on as if she had read Maud's thoughts, 'but it almost grieves me to have to perform this deed.'

'I am ready,' Maud said. 'Danger is part of my trade.'

'This is not danger, it is inevitable.' Beatrice shook her head sadly. 'It seems a pity, but what can I do? Otherwise my husband will be an alto short in his celestial choir.' She laughed, a look of triumph on her face.

'Nae so fast,' came Daisy's voice.

A great wrench of relief tore at Maud's throat. 'Daisy!' She couldn't see her friend. 'Oh, do be careful! Beatrice is up on the rock.'

Maud saw in Beatrice's face a white blaze of anger. Then, through the falling snow, Daisy shot forward and launched herself at Beatrice, smashing her fist into the other woman's face.

A cloud of snow billowed up. Beatrice was sliding slowly but surely towards the edge of the pinnacle. The knife falling from her hand to disappear into the snow, she slid over the edge, crying out as she landed on the rocky path below. Maud ran to where she lay. Stretched on the ground, Beatrice let out a groan, her nose smeared with blood and breathing heavily.

Before Maud could stop her, Beatrice rolled over the ledge that Maud had just climbed.

'No!' Maud shouted. She threw herself flat onto the snow, catching hold of the woman's hands just in time.

'Hang on, Beatrice,' she cried. 'I will help you get back up.'

Beatrice gave a breathless laugh. 'Oh no. I'm going to be leader of the new celestial choir and make my husband's life hell. See how he likes it for all eternity.' Slowly she eased one hand from Maud's gloved grasp.

Beatrice peeled Maud's fingers from around her other hand, smiling all the time. Her pale, bloodied face was the last thing Maud saw as the woman plunged into the white abyss.

Maud got to her feet and was still shaking when Daisy joined her.

'The daftie threw herself over the edge,' said Daisy.

'I think she went over the edge, metaphorically speaking, some time ago.'

'Maud, are you crying?' Daisy put a hand on her arm.

'It's just the snowflakes wetting my face.' Maud dashed

them away with a wet glove. 'Oh, Daisy, I thought she had killed you.'

'Haivers! It'd take more than her to get rid of me.'

Maud gave a shaky smile. 'But are you all right? I didn't know where you were or what had happened to you...'

'I let the besom think I was deid. She was too busy looking for you to bother about me. I lay low, waiting for the right moment. It's all a matter of timing, you ken?' Daisy adjusted her wet tam-o'-shanter, which was collapsing about her ears, and smiled.

Maud wanted to laugh with relief at the ridiculous picture Daisy presented, but time was against them. 'We must go. The fresh snow will make the track easier underfoot than ice, but it will be completely dark soon and we won't be able to find our way off the mountain.' Maud looked at her wristwatch. The glass was cracked and the hands bent. 'It must have broken when I fell,' she heard herself say.

Maud woke on Thursday morning to a soft bluish light through the curtains. She rose and drew them back. Snow had fallen in Fort William during the night and now the world was white.

'Do you think we'll get snowed in?' Daisy was asking anxiously, when Maud joined the rest of the family at the breakfast table.

'It happens,' said Alasdair, 'but the snow isn't thick enough for that.'

Clara could barely wait for her husband to finish speaking. 'Maud, Captain Farquharson has asked us to the castle for tea this afternoon,' she said excitedly. 'He wants to ken all about your investigation.'

'I've said what happened yesterday.' Daisy indicated those round the table, her eyes shining with pride.

Maud smiled at Clara, Alasdair and Susan's eager faces. 'Did you also tell the laird?'

'I'm afraid I did that,' put in Alasdair. 'I took the liberty of letting him know last night that you had both solved the case. He said he'd send out a couple of stable boys at the crack of dawn to help in the constabulary's search for the body.'

'Did you tell him whose it was?' Maud reached for the teapot.

'No, I didn't, although the police might, with him being the laird. That's why he wants us all up at the castle. He wants everyone to know who has been killing off his friends and his servants.'

'I'm going to be a detective when I'm an adult,' Susan said in a firm voice.

Maud poured herself a cup of tea. 'That's a laudable ambition, Susan. Perhaps you'll be the first female detective working *for* the police in Scotland.' It had to happen one day, after all.

'Instead of *despite* them,' put in Daisy.

'Now then, Susan, off you get to school,' Clara told her.

Susan ate the last of her porridge and glanced out of the window. 'There's a lot of snae out there...'

'*Snow*,' said her father.

'That's what I said, faither.' She turned to her mother. 'Do I have to go? I want to come to the laird's tea party with you all.'

'It's nae a tea party,' said Clara. 'It's only for those involved in the investigation.'

'But you're going?'

'Your faither is naturally invited and I'm going as I'm his wife.' She picked up her teacup.

'And I'm his daughter!'

'You heard what your mother said, lass,' Alasdair said sternly. 'Off you go to school. You'll be late as it is.'

Susan sighed. She rose and kissed her parents goodbye. 'Can I kiss you too, Maud?' she asked shyly.

Maud smiled and offered her cheek. Susan kissed her and then Daisy. 'I want to hear all about it when you get back, mind.' She grinned, and she looked so much like her mother and Daisy that Maud couldn't help but laugh.

'I promise,' she said.

Their breath forming clouds in the cold air, the four walked up the avenue to the castle. Alasdair was correct – the snow wasn't deep, but it lay as beautiful and clean as freshly laundered white eiderdowns across the fields. Other feet had already walked on the avenue, indicating they would not be the first of the laird's guests to arrive. A powdering of hoar frost sparkled on the trees in the sinking sun. And then Linnhe Castle with its tower and battlements came into view, a sight fit to grace a Christmas card.

'You know, Daisy,' Maud said softly, 'I feel a bit of a fraud. Beatrice Noble was the only one whose name appeared regularly on our lists and with credibility. The clues were all there. Not just the major ones, but also minor ones such as Beatrice singing those lines so lustily in church: *Dispel the long night's lingering gloom.* I felt sympathy for her, thinking she was trying to be brave, and all the time she was relishing how well her plan was working.'

'And there was her favourite saying. *If I am spared.* I thought she meant if she didna fall victim to the killer.'

'I wondered that myself, but we were told that she always used that expression at the end of choir practice.'

'But she meant she would carry on unless the Lord stopped her.'

'There was that song too,' continued Maud, 'the one she introduced at the last session, about being tired and wanting to go home. She had not expected to get away with all the deaths, after all.'

'Or even wanted to, any more.'

'You think she was regretting it all at the end?'

'She threw herself over that ledge, didn't she?'

'She did,' Maud said with a sigh. 'I wish we could have put the clues together in time to save Jane and Joseph.'

'So do I.' Daisy slipped her arm through Maud's. 'But we did save Ivy – and you. The laird's name popped up often too, and if anyone is to blame, it's me. I was so sure it was him.'

'You are not to blame,' Maud squeezed her friend's hand.

'And neither are you,' Daisy squeezed back. 'We're braw detectives.'

Maud smiled. 'We still have a lot to learn, but we are getting there.'

They strode on, the spring in their step a little bouncier as together they approached the huge door of the castle.

'*Feasgar math*, Crichton,' Maud said, as the butler opened it and stood back for them to enter.

The pannelled hall was warm and cheerful today, with a fire roaring in the large fireplace. There was no sign of Tessie and Bessie, the laird's black Labradors; Maud wondered if they had been placed in a different part of the castle in honour of the occasion. On cue, excited barking from a distant room could be heard in the hall.

Maud raised an eyebrow at Crichton.

'In the kitchen, madam,' he murmured in reply, before adopting his formal voice. 'May I say what a pleasure it is to see you again, Miss McIntyre. You and Miss Cameron have proved that ladies' brains can be at least as good as gentlemen's.' He bowed politely to Daisy.

Daisy inclined her head just so, the way she had seen Maud do when receiving a well-meant compliment.

'*Tapadh leibh*,' Maud said hastily, pleased to be able to thank Crichton in Gaelic, but infinitely more pleased to stop Daisy from giving the butler a piece of her mind.

'This way please, ladies and gentleman,' he said. 'The captain is expecting you in the drawing room.'

Waiting maids took their hats and coats, before they followed the butler up the spiral staircase, along stone passages and past doors, until they reached a larger wooden door. The butler turned the handle and led them through.

The drawing room was magnificent. Already a large room, two very tall gilt-frame mirrors hung on walls facing each other to give the impression of an immense space. Huge windows, facing east, west and south, added to the illusion. The curtains were embroidered with a design of birds and trees; a tapestry depicting two deer, their antlers locked in combat, hung on one wall and on the floor lay rich oriental rugs. A mahogany grand piano stood at one side of the room, where family portraits looked down imperiously. Logs crackled and burned in the hearth of the enormous black marble fireplace. The flames from the fire and the candlelight from the four-branched silver candelabra reflected brightly in the mirrors.

Arranged loosely around the fire were sofas and upholstered chairs. From these a small sea of faces turned towards Maud and Daisy as they entered, the atmosphere humming with expectancy. Maud just had time to note all the remaining members of the choir were there, before the laird, wearing an impeccably pleated red kilt, rose from his wing-backed chair to welcome them and indicate the seats they should take. Maud and Daisy had been allocated all to themselves a floral sofa facing the fire. Clara and Alasdair were seated to the left of the laird, Lord Urquhart in a dark suit and white silk cravat on his right.

All the choir were dressed in their finery. The ladies wore freshly pressed skirts, colourful blouses in cotton or chiffon and their best hats; the men looked ill-at-ease in their suits and ties, and at being seated in the laird's drawing room. Nervous relief covered their faces, although the three Moffat sisters, as usual dressed in black, looked as if they were about to cry.

Maud and Daisy always took care not to travel without suitable attire. Daisy looked charming in a red flowery top with sleeves to the elbow, a red skirt and small gold-coloured earrings. Maud wore a lilac silk dress with a V-neck at the front and back and a high belt of the same fabric. Round her neck was an amethyst and pearl cluster drop pendant and she wore earrings to match.

Everyone seemed to be waiting for Maud to speak. She tugged her long white gloves further up her arms and began.

TWENTY-SIX

'It is good of you to invite us all here this afternoon, Captain Farquharson,' said Maud.

'My pleasure,' he said. '*Noblesse oblige* and all that.'

'Eh?' Daisy murmured to Maud.

'Privilege entails responsibility,' Maud whispered back.

'Right.' Daisy nodded.

'It was good of you to come, Miss... er...'

'*McIntyre*. My assistant, Miss Cameron, and I,' Maud went on, 'would like to explain how we found the murderer...'

Walter Stevenson interrupted her in his bullish tone. 'Amateur detectives are only any good in crime novels.'

'You dinna ken anything about our work.' Daisy glared at him, spoiling the effect of her ladylike costume and jewellery.

His square, stolid face turned a pale red to match his whiskers. 'You must have had a man to help you.'

'That's all you ken.'

'Mr Stevenson, please,' said Lord Urquhart, 'let the ladies speak. What they have to say will surely be of great interest.' He smiled at Maud.

'Thank you, my lord,' she responded politely. She looked

around at the choir members, their faces alert as Maud got down to business.

'We must start our story with the two dead women, Emily Black and Jane Rankin, and the killer's intended third female victim, Ivy Fraser.'

A muttering and shifting greeted this news, with glances sent towards Ivy, who immediately gazed down at her hands in her lap. She had kept her word, thought Maud, and not told a soul about the poisoned cheese.

'What did they all have in common, we asked ourselves,' Maud said, silently adding *eventually*. 'Comeliness,' she went on. 'All three ladies were cheerful, attractive, with nicely rounded figures. As indeed Mrs Fraser still is.'

Ivy looked up, blushed and squared her shoulders, the better to display her bosom.

'These ladies' attributes are at the heart of the case, through no fault of their own,' Maud added.

Daisy picked up the story. 'The killer's first victim was John Noble.'

The murmurings in the assembly began again.

'Aye, Mr Noble,' Daisy said in a loud voice. She paused and they quietened down. 'He liked sonsie women and that brought about his downfall.'

'Which led to the deaths of poor Emily and Jane,' Maud said.

Now those gathered in the drawing room looked around them, perhaps noticing for the first time that Beatrice Noble was missing.

'The killer had to ken John Noble was feart of cats and—'

'And that narrowed down our lists of suspects.'

Daisy flashed Maud an excited look and carried on. 'The suspect got hold of a moggy and put it on the sleeping mannie's chest. We worked out that he must have woken and saw it, which gave him a heart attack.'

'When he was found dead in his own bed, there was no reason for the doctor to suspect foul play.'

'Apart from me and Maud, that is. And finding cat hairs on his eiderdown confirmed our suspicion.'

'That and a recently read copy of *The Hound of the Baskervilles* by Sir Conan Doyle.' Maud was keen to give credit where it was due.

'I said they'd had a man to help them,' muttered Walter Stevenson.

Goodness, the man was a bore, Maud thought. She couldn't prevent herself from glancing across the room at Lord Urquhart and saw that he, the only man they might have asked for help should the need have arisen, lounged in a deep armchair, his eyes closed. Maud tutted.

'If we can return to Emily,' she went on. 'It was known amongst the castle servants that she was seeing a young man. The adjective *young* had been used in good faith and Emily did nothing to contradict this, doubtless to keep attention away from her lover, who was in fact a much older man.

'Next, we come to Jane. It was clear that she had been shot at close range and the most likely suspect was her loader. When we attempted to track this person down, we discovered they had disappeared.'

Oh dear, thought Maud, she was using the third-person pronoun. But to say *she* would be to reveal the name too soon.

'Now Joseph,' put in Daisy. 'You might be wondering what he had to do with a man who was feart of cats and had a fancy for three plump women. So did we, to start with. He wasna part of the work on the laird's pond excavation and yet the killer kent he'd be there. He was blown to smithereens.'

'Daisy...' murmured Maud, seeing the faces around them turn pale despite the heat from the fire in the hearth.

'Blown to pieces,' Daisy amended.

'I made sure Mr Watson was behind the safety line,' put in the laird in a worried voice.

'Aye, your lordship, and he was. But the killer still managed to hide and fling an explosive at him and blow him to—'

Maud wondered if she should say they had initially suspected the laird. No, that would not be a good idea. Before Daisy could come clean and confess to this part of their investigation, Maud went on hastily.

'And that leads us on to Ivy. She was sent a birthday present of a blue-veined cheese. An appropriate gift, you might think, for a lady who manages a tea shop and enjoys food. But...' Maud paused and gazed round at the attentive faces. 'The killer had an interest in horticulture and the cheese had been poisoned.'

'Oh, Ivy, my dear,' said Helen Wilson, seated beside her and taking her hand. 'What a dreadful experience for you.'

'How was it poisoned?' asked Maggie in a small voice.

'A few tiny pieces of a fungus known as—'

'*Amanita virosa*. The destroying angel,' finished Maggie.

A collective gasp filled the room and the assembly turned as one to stare at her. She went bright red.

'It wasna Maggie who did it,' said Daisy.

'I came across Maud and Daisy by the side of the loch one day and we talked about deadly fungi for a wee while,' Maggie explained.

'A strange topic for conversation,' put in Anne Ritchie, the slender young alto who worked as a housemaid in town.

'We were investigating a particular clue,' Maud told her, 'and Maggie's information was very helpful. In fact, it made our job easier as it turned out.'

Maggie face was still red, but now she looked pleased.

'And lastly,' said Maud, 'yesterday the murderer tried to kill Miss Cameron and me on Ben Nevis.'

This information was finally too much for the gathering, and they all began to talk at once.

'Ladies and gentlemen, please,' called the laird. 'If we remain quiet, we will hear the name of the person who has been murdering members of your beloved choir.'

There was immediate silence. The mantel clock chimed the half-hour.

'Goodness me,' said the laird, 'it's time for tea.' He rose to press the bell for Crichton.

'Charles.' Lord Urquhart put out a restraining hand. 'I think we should hear the name of the murderer first.'

'Oh yes, of course.' The laird sank back in his chair. 'Please do go on, Miss... er.'

'McIntyre,' said Maud, repressing a sigh. How difficult could it be to remember her name? She turned to Daisy, 'Would you like to reveal the name of the killer?'

Daisy nodded and gazed round at them all, savouring the moment. 'I'm sorry to tell you it's your choir mistress, Beatrice Noble.'

The group now erupted. Maud heard exclamations of disbelief, other voices asking where the woman was, had she been arrested, and others simply repeating 'Beatrice?'

Maud clapped her hands to get back their attention. 'John Noble was...' she hesitated. She could not say 'having an affair' because Ivy Fraser was still married and she lived and worked in the community. 'Enamoured with these three women.'

It was also not Maud's place to repeat Beatrice's sad story about the loss of her babies. 'Beatrice was a woman scorned and she took her revenge by killing first her husband and then moving on to the three women. The methods she chose were ingenuous. Her husband's death could be seen as natural causes and the other deaths as accidents...'

'And they were, but nae by *us*,' put in Daisy.

'Yes, thank you, Daisy.' Maud shot her a quick smile. 'All the other deaths were regarded as accidents, but ask yourselves how probable was that?'

'So, why did she kill poor Joseph?' called out Anne Ritchie.

'Because he kept hitting the wrong notes,' said Daisy.

'Seems a wee bit harsh,' Anne replied.

'When you've killed once, or three times in the case of Beatrice, it's perhaps easy to do so again for the slightest of infringements. One might as well be hanged for a sheep as a lamb, as the saying goes.'

'Well, well,' said the laird, getting to his feet and stroking his neat grey moustache. 'Who would have thought it? And now my lads are out helping to look for Beatrice Noble's body.'

'Indeed.' Maud looked round at the gathering. 'I'm afraid there was a tussle on Ben Nevis, Beatrice slipped over the edge and that was the last I saw of her.' She sank back, the memory of Beatrice's thin face disappearing into the snowflakes.

'You're obviously in need of a nice cup of tea,' said the laird, 'and a slice or two of Maggie's excellent buttered fruit loaf.'

Maud and Daisy exchanged glances. There was no chance of calling the group back to order.

'If you have any questions,' yelled Daisy above the general hubbub, 'just come and ask us. We'll be here for a wee while.'

'Really, Daisy, you cannot say that,' Maud admonished.

Lord Urquhart was making his way over to them. 'I have a question.'

'I have one for you first,' said Daisy.

He inclined his head. 'Yes, Miss Cameron?'

'Why was Jane Rankin buried in the laird's family cemetery?'

Oh well done, Daisy, thought Maud. She had completely forgotten about that anomaly.

Lord Urquhart flushed slightly. 'It's a delicate matter.'

'But I'm nae a delicate person, so you can tell me.' Daisy grinned. 'And remember that the M. McIntyre Agency's motto is discretion.'

'Funny. I had thought it was *No Case Too Big or Too Small?*'
He smiled.

'Aye, it's that too.'

He lowered his voice. 'As to your question, Miss Cameron, there is some talk about Mrs Rankin having been born on the wrong side of the blanket.'

Daisy gawped. 'Do you mean she's the laird's—'

'No, it cannot be that, Daisy,' Maud was quick to add, keeping her voice low, 'as Jane Rankin's age must be not so very far below the captain's.'

'I don't know the exact connection,' said Lord Urquhart, 'but suffice it to say Charles was content to agree to Mrs Rankin's wish to be buried there.'

Daisy seemed satisfied with the answer.

'And now my question,' he went on.

'Go ahead,' Maud said warily.

'How did Mrs Noble obtain the explosive she used to kill Mr Watson?'

'We canna be sure,' Daisy replied, 'but the laird had a supply ready to blow a muckle hole in his garden, so she must have got it from him somehow.'

'I was afraid you would say that.'

'Why?' asked Maud. 'Do you know something?'

'Charles was rather proud of his building works, and apparently Mrs Noble expressed a wish to see everything before work started, including his small stock of dynamite. She must have stolen a stick then.'

'That clears up that mystery,' Maud said. 'You do realise the police sergeant will have to be told about this?'

Another person claimed Daisy's attention and she moved off a little way to answer them.

'Yes, as unfortunate as that may be, I see your point,' continued Lord Urquhart. 'It's not that Charles forgets things, it's just that he can't remember them.'

'I see.'

'Like not remembering your name, for instance, Miss McIntyre.'

'Oh, you noticed, did you?' she said. 'I thought you had gone to sleep.'

'No, I was merely thinking.'

'Good heavens. That thought never occurred to me.'

'I admit it is unusual,' he said with a grin. There was a pause as they looked at each other. 'Another very impressive investigation, Miss McIntyre, if I may say so.'

'You may.'

'What now?' he asked.

'In terms of...?'

'The competition final, of course. What else did you think I meant?'

'I could not say. As to the final, I doubt the choir will be able to take part.'

'Oh, why is that?'

'Because the Fort William choir is now sadly depleted, not to mention without its choir mistress.' Maud glanced over to where Daisy stood, chatting animatedly to Thomas, the good-looking younger McDougall brother. 'Poor Daisy. She so wanted to meet the King.'

'Perhaps she will yet,' murmured Lord Urquhart with a smile.

Maud and Daisy were amongst the last to leave the castle, some hours later.

'Goodnight, Miss McIntyre. Goodnight, Miss Cameron,' said the laird, as he waved them off on his doorstep.

Goodness, thought Maud, he had remembered her name at last.

'Goodnight,' called Lord Urquhart, stepping forward from

beside the laird. In the glow from the lamps in the hall, he appeared to be studying her face. 'We will meet again soon.'

Maud knew it was wrong of her, because her work intrigued and stimulated her, and she did not want to be like other women, but she hoped he was right, that they would meet again soon.

Bright moonlight shone on the snowy landscape. It was bitterly cold, but it failed to dampen their spirits. Maud found herself thinking of Christmas time and Hogmanay at her father's house, with warm brandy punch and a roaring fire in the grate with her brothers and their wives and children talking and laughing.

'Tomorrow we'll return south,' Maud said.

'Aye, and with another case solved.' Daisy smiled.

'It's a shame about the choir no longer being able to take part in the finals,' observed Maud, clearing a peephole in the misty train window through which to survey the snow-clad country-side, which glittered in the sharp white light. 'But not a surprise in the circumstances.'

'Aye.' Daisy stared out of the cleared window.

The glens and mountains were dazzling in their untrodden whiteness. Maud peered through the glass, watching the wild landscape as it rolled by. The fresh snow of the previous night lay under the crisp, blue-skied December morning, lending a silvery sheen to the burns and lochs.

Part of her was sad to be saying goodbye to Fort William. She would miss the Ross family, the choir, the friends they had made. But at the same time, she was ready to leave.

'But we'll see the choir again tomorrow at Holyrood Palace.' Daisy grinned. 'And meet the King.'

After all that had happened, they were going to have dinner with His Majesty. It seemed that King George had sent a telegram to Linnhe Castle last night, requesting the pleasure of the company of the Fort William choir at the celebratory meal for the winners. Had Lord Urquhart arranged this? Maud suspected he had, and she was pleased for Daisy's sake, although she also found her heart beating a little faster at the thought he might be there tomorrow evening.

'It was very kind of the King to invite us all,' Maud said.

Daisy frowned. 'I've just had a thought. I havena got a gown to wear.'

'I will buy you one.' Maud smiled. Before Daisy could protest, she added, 'I couldn't run the agency without you, Daisy.'

'Thanks, Maud. We've had some braw times, havena we?'

'And they are not over yet, my friend!'

Daisy let out a satisfied sigh. 'How much longer until we're back in Edinburgh?'

Maud glanced at her wristwatch and saw the broken dial. She would need to get it mended on their return to the city.

'Not long,' she told Daisy. 'And surely there will be a new case waiting for us there.' That prospect was exciting. A new case, a new chapter.

But Maud could see that Daisy wasn't yet thinking about a new chapter. She was too preoccupied with thoughts of the King.

The following evening, a carriage containing Maud and Daisy drove down the Royal Mile and approached the huge wrought-iron gates leading to the Palace of Holyroodhouse.

'The King's official residence in Edinburgh,' said Daisy, the pitch of her voice rising. She gazed out of the window, hardly able to sit still.

Their carriage came to a halt at the sentry box. A soldier stepped forward, wearing a doublet, kilt and spats with black buttons, and on his head a Glengarry bonnet decorated with a rosette cockade and a black feather. Their invitations checked, they drove on. Baskets of fire lined the avenue. The sound of bagpipes floated on the chilled night air.

Their carriage pulled into the forecourt. Lamps were lighted in the palace windows, the warm glow shining out. Smoke rose from chimneys, straight up into the still air. One of the rooms on the first floor must be the grand dining room, thought Maud, a flutter of nerves in her stomach.

The palace was certainly a sight to behold. A classical building in sandstone with matching circular towers at each end, the vast roof covered with a dusting of snow. And if there could be any doubt as to the resident's title, above the door was a carved Royal Arms of Scotland.

A kilted piper stood to the side of the entrance to welcome them. More carriages were arriving, with excited faces peering out.

'Are you ready, Daisy?' asked Maud, preparing to gather her fur wrap about her shoulders with one hand and with the other to raise daintily the skirts of her silver-grey silk crêpe gown.

Daisy's raspberry organdie skirts rustled as she readied herself to move towards the carriage door. 'As ready as I'll ever be,' she said, eyes burning bright in her flushed face.'

Maud recognised what was happening. Despite all her bravery in any situation of extreme danger, Daisy Cameron was nervous.

'As Sherlock Holmes says in *A Case of Identity*,' Maud said, in the hope of putting Daisy at ease, 'it has long been an axiom of mine that the little things are infinitely the most important.'

'I dinna ken what axiom means,' replied Daisy. 'I dinna ken what anything you just said means.'

'What I mean, Daisy,' said Maud, taking her friend's hands in her own, 'is you should think of this evening as nothing more than dinner with a group of friends.'

'Dinner with a group of friends,' repeated Daisy, as if Maud were a hypnotist and she the subject. She took in a deep breath. 'It's nothing more than a posh dinner with a wee group of friends.'

'That's right, that's all it is. Now, come on.'

Maud was helped from the carriage first. Daisy followed, taking the proffered hand of the footman. She stepped onto the gravel without tripping over. 'It's nothing more than a posh dinner with friends.'

'That's right, just keep that thought in your head and everything will be fine.'

'And the King.' Daisy stared at the giant columns framing the entrance.

'And the King,' Maud said softly. 'Be proud, Daisy. That's another case solved, my friend. We work well together, don't you think?'

'Aye.'

'Nothing clears up a case so much as discussing it with another person.'

Daisy grinned. 'Did Sherlock Holmes say that?'

Maud slipped her arm through Daisy's. 'Aye, he did,' she said with a smile, escorting her through the magnificent front door.

A LETTER FROM LYDIA

Thank you so much for reading *Mystery in the Highlands,* the third in the Maud McIntyre private detective series. I enjoyed writing it and I hope you found it enjoyable to read.

If you would like to keep up-to-date with my latest releases, please sign up at the following link. Your email address will never be shared and you can unsubscribe at any time.

www.bookouture.com/lydia-travers

I have discovered that when you create a fictional character or two, and take them through a series of books, they assume in some way a life of their own. I find that I am not just writing about Maud and Daisy; I've become their close friend and where I go, they go too. No doubt we will have other adventures together.

If you liked *Mystery in the Highlands,* and I really hope you did, I would be very grateful if you could leave a short review. I'd love to hear what you think, and reviews also help other readers discover my books.

Thank you for reading.

Love,

Lydia x

KEEP IN TOUCH WITH LYDIA

www.bookouture.com/lydia-travers

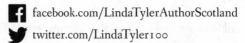 facebook.com/LindaTylerAuthorScotland
twitter.com/LindaTyler100
instagram.com/lindatylerauthorScotland

ACKNOWLEDGEMENTS

No book is ever written without the help of a number of people. Huge thanks go first, as ever, to my wonderful writing buddy Julie Perkins for all her advice and suggestions; I honestly cannot thank her enough. I am also deeply grateful to Joan Cameron for her enthusiastic involvement in Maud's adventures from the beginning.

Special thanks are also due to Sheila Gray for the delightful rhymes in this novel!

I am grateful to the following additional friends for their help: Jon Tyler, former Procurator Fiscal Depute Laura Sharp, Vicki Singleton, Rachel Stewart and Frances Jaffray.

I am indebted to Chris Robinson and Vanessa Martin at the West Highland Museum, and Anne Nicholson at Fort William Library.

Special thanks go to my singing friend Anne Ritchie, who asked that Maud and Daisy investigate a series of murders in a choir.

I must also thank the team at Bookouture.

Mushrooms and other fungi of Great Britain & Europe by Roger Phillips was invaluable. Other influences on my writing have been *The Adventures of Maud West, Lady Detective* by Susannah Stapleton, the work of comic genius PG Wodehouse and, of course, the various detective stories beloved by Maud.

Thank you, too, to my readers.

Some liberties have been taken with the workings of the

Scottish criminal justice system in 1911 and with the winter climb of Ben Nevis. The haunting by the hanging-tree ghost is a 'true' story, although the tree wasn't cut down until the new library was built in the 1970s. Any mistakes are my own.